The race to find a kidnapped baby leads the newly formed secret agency Colorado Confidential to a fire in a hospital records room. Now agent Shawn Jameson will match wits with an arsonist while trying not to fall for a beautiful doctor whose secrets he's sworn to expose...

"Did I hurt you?" Shawn demanded.

Kelley's dazed eyes searched her body as if determining that everything was intact. Shawn followed her gaze, feeling warmth ignite inside. She looked damn good to him. "I... No, I'm all right. But... Thank you for following me—for keeping me from being hit. The driver must have seen us. Why didn't he stop to make sure we're all right?"

"Yeah, why?" But Shawn knew the answer. "Come on. I'm taking you to my place."

"No, I'm fine. I can drive. I need to get home."

"You don't need to get home. Not now."

"But—"

"Don't you get it? Someone just tried to run you over, Dr. Stanton. Intentionally. And since he didn't succeed, he might just try again."

Dear Harlequin Intrigue Reader,

We wind up a great summer with a *bang* this month! Linda O. Johnston continues the hugely popular COLORADO CONFIDENTIAL series with *Special Agent Nanny*. Don't forget to look for the Harlequin special-release anthology next month featuring *USA TODAY* bestselling author Jasmine Cresswell, our very own Amanda Stevens and Harlequin Historicals author Debra Lee Brown. And not to worry, the series continues with two more Harlequin Intrigue titles in November and December.

Joyce Sullivan concludes her companion series THE COLLINGWOOD HEIRS with *Operation Bassinet*. Find out how this family solves a fiendish plot and finds happiness in one fell swoop. Rounding out the month are two exciting stories. Rising star Delores Fossen takes a unique perspective on the classic secret-baby plot in *Confiscated Conception*, and a very sexy *Cowboy PI* is determined to get to the bottom of one woman's mystery in an all-Western story by Jean Barrett.

Finally, in case you haven't heard, next month Harlequin Intrigue is increasing its publishing schedule to include two more fantastic romantic suspense books. That's *six* titles per month! More variety, more of your favorite authors and of course, more excitement.

It's a thrilling time for us, and we want to thank all of our loyal readers for remaining true to Harlequin Intrigue. And if you are just learning about our brand of breathtaking romantic suspense, fasten your seat belts for an edge-of-your-seat reading experience. Welcome aboard!

Sincerely,

Denise O'Sullivan
Senior Editor, Harlequin Intrigue

SPECIAL AGENT NANNY

LINDA O. JOHNSTON

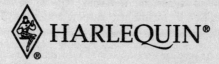

HARLEQUIN®

TORONTO • NEW YORK • LONDON
AMSTERDAM • PARIS • SYDNEY • HAMBURG
STOCKHOLM • ATHENS • TOKYO • MILAN • MADRID
PRAGUE • WARSAW • BUDAPEST • AUCKLAND

Special thanks and acknowledgment are given to Linda O. Johnston
for her contribution to the COLORADO CONFIDENTIAL series.

Dedication:

To the other Colorado Confidential authors,
as well as the authors of all the other Confidential series.
I appreciate being in such good company. And, of course, to Fred.

Acknowledgments:

Thanks to Denise O'Sullivan, Melissa Endlich and Allison Lyons for allowing me
to participate in Colorado Confidential. It's been fun!
Also, thanks to Dr. Donald Zangwill and
Dr. Kenneth Zangwill for their medical information.
Any mistakes or misdiagnoses are the result of
my poetic license, and not their medical licenses.

ISBN 0-373-22725-6

SPECIAL AGENT NANNY

ABOUT THE AUTHOR

Linda O. Johnston's first published fiction appeared in *Ellery Queen's Mystery Magazine* and won the Robert L. Fish Memorial Award for "Best First Mystery Short Story of the Year." Now, several published short stories and novels later, Linda is recognized for her outstanding work in the romance genre.

A practicing attorney, Linda juggles her busy schedule between mornings of writing briefs, contracts and other legalese, and afternoons of creating memorable tales of the paranormal, time travel, mystery, contemporary and romantic suspense. Armed with an undergraduate degree in journalism with an advertising emphasis from Pennsylvania State University, Linda began her versatile writing career running a small newspaper, then working in advertising and public relations, later obtaining her J.D. degree from Duquesne University School of Law in Pittsburgh.

Linda belongs to Sisters in Crime and is actively involved with Romance Writers of America, participating in the Los Angeles, Orange County and Western Pennsylvania chapters. She lives near Universal Studios, Hollywood, with her husband, two sons and two cavalier King Charles spaniels.

Books by Linda O. Johnston

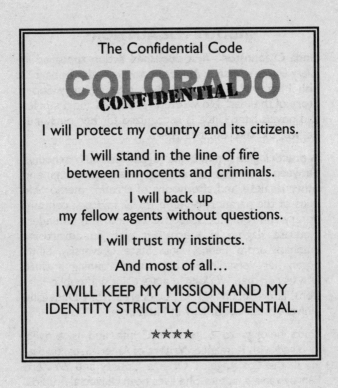

The Confidential Code

COLORADO CONFIDENTIAL

I will protect my country and its citizens.

I will stand in the line of fire
between innocents and criminals.

I will back up
my fellow agents without questions.

I will trust my instincts.

And most of all…

I WILL KEEP MY MISSION AND MY
IDENTITY STRICTLY CONFIDENTIAL.

★★★★

CAST OF CHARACTERS

Shawn Jameson—An undercover investigator, he never thought much about kids until he had to play nanny to interrogate a beautiful suspected arsonist.

Dr. Kelley Stanton—The lovely doctor spends a lot of time combating rumors against her...as well as fighting her attraction to the man investigating her.

Jenny Stanton—Were the three-year-old's tantrums after the fire the result of agitation...or something more sinister?

Dr. Randall Stanton—Is Kelley's ex-husband the source of the rumors against her...and are his allegations designed to cast suspicion away from himself?

Cheryl Marten—Randall's latest conquest, who has an agenda of her own.

Louis Paxler—The administrator would do anything to minimize the hospital's liability.

Juan Cortes—The janitor knows everything that goes on around the hospital...including who set the fire.

CAST OF CHARACTERS

Shawn Jameson—An undercover investigator, he never thought much about kids until he had to play nanny to interrogate a beautiful suspected arsonist.

Dr. Kelley Stanton—The lovely doctor spends a lot of time combating rumors against her...as well as fighting her attraction to the man investigating her.

Jenny Stanton—Were the three-year-old's tantrums after the fire the result of agitation...or something more sinister?

Dr. Randall Stanton—Is Kelley's ex-husband the source of the rumors against her...and are his allegations designed to cast suspicion away from himself?

Cheryl Marten—Randall's latest conquest, who has an agenda of her own.

Louis Paxler—The administrator would do anything to minimize the hospital's liability.

Juan Cortes—The janitor knows everything that goes on around the hospital...including who set the fire.

Prologue

Six weeks ago

Dr. Kelley Stanton rounded the corner in the hospital corridor, massaging the ache in one temple with her free hand. At least she was out of her lab coat and in light street clothes appropriate to Denver's August weather. Too bad she couldn't shed the paperwork pending as follow-up to the day's patients as easily. She inhaled deeply as a sigh formed in her chest. Except—

Smoke! She smelled smoke!

"Oh, no," she whispered, automatically pulling her purse off her shoulder and grabbing for her cell phone. *Don't panic. It might be nothing.*

She looked around. The corridor was long. Peach-colored walls. Lots of closed doors and hanging signs to direct patients. It was empty now. She was the only one there.

This wasn't the hall to the parking lot exit. By habit, she had gone the wrong way, toward the administrative wing of Gilpin Hospital. Toward the area where her three-year-old daughter, Jenny, went to day care.

Thank heavens it was late. Her ex-husband, Randall, also a doctor, would already have picked up Jenny. And the admin wing held offices, not patients.

Still—

She sped forward. Surely someone had simply over-cooked microwave popcorn in a staff lunchroom. Or it was something equally innocuous. There couldn't be a fire in Gilpin Hospital.

The heels of her low, comfortable pumps clicked briskly on the shiny linoleum floor. The rapidity of her pulse matched her pace.

She turned right, toward the increasing smell. An ominous gray cloud billowed at the end of the short hall.

In the direction of KidClub.

"Fire!" she shouted.

At least no one should be around. It was seven o'clock at night. The child-care center closed at six-thirty. Most admin staff were already gone by then.

Quickly she dialed 9-1-1 and gave the particulars. The operator promised to send firefighters immediately.

"Fire!" she shouted again. "Is anyone here?"

No reply. Good. Maybe everyone else had left.

But she couldn't be certain.

Kelley glanced up at the walls, looking for a building fire alarm. The whole hospital should be alerted. The evacuation plan might need to be implemented.

She had to get out, too. But first she needed to make sure no one was in danger.

There was a fire alarm outside the child-care facility. She would go down the hall that far and pull the alarm. She had to make sure no one remained inside. No child. *Jenny.*

KidClub was three quarters of the way down this relatively short hallway. Its door was closed but not locked. The lights were still on.

The smell of the surrounding smoke gagged her.

She ran inside, checked the three large playrooms. The kitchen. The bathroom.

Thankfully, no one was there.

She hustled back to the corridor. A crackling roar filled the air from down the hall. The smoke was thicker. She coughed as she broke the glass and set off the alarm. The cacophonous pulsing blare surrounded her.

Where was the fire? In the large records storage room at the end? No one would be there, but all that paper would provide a huge source of fuel.

She coughed again. Her eyes stung, teared. She had to get out. "Is anyone here?" she called again to be sure.

And heard something.

Was it her imagination? The sound had been so tiny compared with the alarm and the thundering from the end of the hall, punctuated now by an occasional crash.

She had to check.

It wasn't easy to see with her eyes smarting. A hand on the wall, she inched along. "Who's there?" she called.

And heard the noise again. Like a child's whimper.

"Please, God, no," Kelley murmured, moving faster.

Another short hall veered from the main corridor. Kelley tried to peer down it, then heard a small voice. "Mommy!"

"Jenny? Oh Lord, Jenny?" Kelley shoved at the air, as if to erase the smoke. Below, on the floor, she got a glimpse of bright yellow.

Jenny had worn her bright yellow jumper that morning.

Kelley knelt. Her tiny, blond-haired daughter was crouched on the floor. At least there the smoke was not as thick, but Jenny coughed as Kelley lifted her into her arms and hugged her tight. The tears running down her face now were not entirely due to the fire.

Where the hell was Randall? How could he have left their daughter alone?

No matter now. There would be plenty of time to censure him, once Jenny and she were safe.

Coughing as she reentered the main corridor, her precious cargo snugged safely against her, Kelley glanced right. The only area on fire seemed to be the records room. She'd seen no one flee after she'd cried out and set off the alarm. Hopefully, no one else was here.

The siren still shrieking, Kelley hurried away from the smoke to the outside where people gathered in excitement and concern.

Her daughter and she would be fine, though they'd both have to be checked for smoke inhalation.

But thank heavens the only damage appeared to be to paperwork. Things. Hospital records.

The fire was certainly unfortunate.

But at least there should be no major consequences.

Chapter One

The Present

''You want me to *what?*'' Shawn Jameson shoved his chair back from the table, stood and stared at Colleen Wellesley. ''You can't be serious.''

His boss crossed her arms without rising. About forty-five years old, with irritation narrowing her blue-green eyes, she appeared *very* serious. And that did not make Shawn happy at all. ''You've got your orders,'' she said quietly. ''Your cover will be as a caregiver in the child-care center at Gilpin Hospital.'' She was dressed like a rancher in a plaid flannel shirt and jeans. But that did not keep her from looking authoritative.

Shawn heard muffled laughter. He turned to glare at Fiona Clark, another Colorado Confidential operative, who had joined Colleen and him in the secret, basement meeting room of the Royal Flush Ranch. By the time he was able to turn a fierce gaze on her, the blond former FBI agent had pasted a sympathetic expression on her face. But there was mirth in her brown eyes.

Fiona, like Shawn, was dressed similarly to Colleen for hard work on the ranch—but that was not all they were here for. In keeping with his cover, Shawn wore a leather vest over a comfortable blue work shirt that was tucked into well-worn, faded jeans. He'd bought his boots in Texas when, while in training, he'd visited the Smoking Barrel Ranch, the cover for the original Confidential agency.

Shawn turned back toward Colleen. What could he do? These were his first orders directly from her, though she'd been his employer for a while. He had joined the staff of Investigations, Confidential and Undercover, a private investigation agency known as ICU, a couple of years ago. At first, he'd been aware that there was a secretive boss, known only as C. Wellesley, in the background calling the shots. He had only recently learned she was a woman, and even more recently met her. Here. On the ranch. When she had recruited him into Colorado Confidential, a very new, very special covert arm of the Colorado Department of Public Safety. He'd undergone training here for the past few months. It was definitely time to go to work.

But this…?

"What the hell—er, heck—do I know about tending a bunch of kids?" He ran his fingers through his short, dark blond hair in frustration. "You hear that? I don't even know how the hell to watch my language."

"You'll learn," Colleen said mildly. "Either that, or the kids'll bring home some interesting new vocabulary."

"Damn." This wasn't getting Shawn anywhere. He thought fast, taking his seat at the table once more. "Look, Colleen," he said in a cool and logical tone. "You have someone here who can undoubtedly do a better job with this than me—Fifi."

A growl issued from behind him. Fiona hated that nickname, but she had earned his use of it now by laughing at him.

"The fact that Fiona is female doesn't mean she'd do better with this cover than you, Shawn," Colleen said mildly. "And this assignment requires someone with your particular expertise—arson investigation. You do know something about that, don't you?"

She knew full well he did. He had devoted his life to fighting fires—and to bringing down the people who set them. With good reason. Damned good reason.

"Yeah," he agreed softly. "I know something about that."

"There's more to the situation than the fire that destroyed the records department of Gilpin Hospital six weeks ago," Colleen continued. "Wiley Longbottom thinks that the fire could be connected to the flu epidemic that ran through Silver Rapids a few months back." Longbottom was the director of the Colorado Department of Public Safety. Colleen reported to him. "He believes there's a chance the flu was caused by the same type of microbe found in the blood samples Michael took from the sheep at the Half Spur Ranch."

Michael Wellesley, Colleen's brother, had just returned from an undercover assignment at that sheep ranch, which was partially owned by powerful Colorado senator Franklin Gettys. Not a man you wanted to accuse of anything without indisputable proof. He'd also brought back an unanticipated reward, his new love, Nicola Carson. She'd been the target of an assassin, and was staying at the Royal Flush under Michael's personal protection.

Colleen continued in a deceptively mild voice, "And if so, we definitely need more information. When we got the test results from the Center for Disease Control, the blood samples showed antibodies for Q fever."

"That's a disease carried by livestock anyway, isn't it?" Fiona asked.

"Yes, but Wiley thinks the Silver Rapids flu epidemic might not have been flu after all. It may have been an outbreak of Q fever. And while Q fever is often found in livestock, a human epidemic of that proportion is... suspicious. And the whole mess could have some bearing on the Langworthy kidnapping.''

"How?'' Shawn demanded, stunned by Colleen's implication that the flu could have a human source. If so, no doubt someone had a vested interest in covering it up.

"The missing baby's mother, Holly Langworthy, was one of the people infected. At the time, she was still pregnant with little Schyler. We have to look into the fire and the flu, in case the baby's disappearance is somehow related.''

Ah, Shawn thought. That was the crux of it. Colorado Confidential's first major case wasn't just high priority. It was *the* priority. Schyler, the infant grandson of one of Colorado's most influential citizens, Samuel Langworthy, had been kidnapped. So far, regular law enforcement agencies with jurisdiction, even the FBI, were stymied. The Department of Public Safety had turned to the newly constituted covert agency, the country's fourth Confidential organization, for help.

It was a case they couldn't afford to blow. A baby's life was at stake. More lives might hang in the balance.

"There's a doctor on staff at the hospital, Dr. Kelley Stanton,'' Colleen continued. She slowly drummed one finger on the table as if using the rhythm to remind her of the facts. Her hands were blunt nailed and work roughened. She owned this ranch, which, Shawn knew, had been in her family for generations.

"Dr. Stanton is a suspect in the arson,'' Colleen went on. "She was involved with treating the flu patients, including two elderly people who died. You'll have access to her by working at the child-care center, since she has a three-year-old daughter who goes there. Rumors around the hospital suggest she set the fire to hide her negligence in treating those patients.''

"A pretty nasty allegation,'' Shawn noted.

"That would be ugly enough,'' Colleen agreed. "But if Wiley's right and there's some relation to the kidnapping, this Dr. Stanton could be more than a quack who wants to hide some mistakes. She could be helping to cover up an act of bioterrorism as well as the kidnapping. And Wiley isn't wrong very often. So…?'' She looked directly into Shawn's eyes and paused.

Colleen was waiting for his assent. "Yeah,'' he said. He knew he would regret it. He also knew he had no choice.

"Good.'' Colleen rose. "I'll get things set up. You'll start in three days.''

A SHORT WHILE LATER, Shawn left the others behind and stealthily oozed his way from behind the huge, movable wine rack that hid the door to the secret basement room. He had to think about this new assignment. Prepare himself for it mentally.

He headed upstairs, into the plush room that had once been the bar. One of Colleen's ancestors had once run the Royal Flush as a saloon and bordello. The room maintained the flamboyant ambiance, complete with sexy red velvet curtains. It still housed the original long bar of dark pine, which had obviously been well polished over the many intervening years. The faint, pungent-sweet scent of fine wood preservative hung in the air. The ranch's caretakers, Raven and Melody Castillo, took great care of the place.

Too bad the room wasn't still used as a bar. Shawn could have used a drink. A good, stiff one.

Behind the bar was a portrait of a woman, who seemed out of place in the sumptuous and suggestive room— Eudora Wellesley, he'd been told. Colleen's ancestress.

There was nothing flamboyant or even particularly attractive in her appearance. In fact, she was dressed primly, in dark clothes, and there was a set to her mouth as if the lady was shocked by the things that had gone on in this room. And yet, the artist had painted a sparkle into her alert gray eyes.

Grumbling to himself, Shawn headed outside. He wasn't the imaginative sort. This new twist to his career as an arson investigator turned covert agent was giving him fits.

As he stepped through the front door onto the porch, he nearly ran into Dexter Jones, the foreman. His other boss, for his cover at the Royal Flush as ranch hand.

"You seen Ms. Wellesley?" Dex asked. The foreman was in his early fifties. He kept his hair, obviously once dark but now sprinkled with silver, no-nonsense short. He seemed a no-nonsense guy, dedicated to making sure the ranch ran smoothly.

As smart and wily as tough-acting Dex seemed, the foreman supposedly had no idea of what went on in the basement. But Shawn sensed the man's strong suspicion that more went on at the Royal Flush than just ranching.

As part of his Colorado Confidential cover, Shawn had to act as if he'd no clue what Dex was talking about when the older man blew off steam by guessing what his lady boss was really up to.

"I saw Ms. Wellesley a while ago," Shawn told him. "I came in to ask whether she was going to ride Dora today, and if so when she wanted me to have her saddled." Dora was Colleen's horse, a mare she'd named after the illustrious lady whose picture hung over the bar. The bay and white paint was a lot prettier, in Shawn's estimation, than her namesake.

"And she said—?"

"She'd let me know. I think she's back in her room on

the phone. Or maybe she's getting changed. In any event, she said she didn't want to be disturbed for the next hour.''

"Right," Dex muttered, and turned on his heel without entering the house.

If Shawn wasn't mistaken, the gruff foreman had a thing for his employer. That wasn't any of Shawn's business.

But his new assignment certainly was.

Shawn walked down the porch steps and to the side of the main house. He inhaled crisp, clean air tinged with the scent of the nearby horse enclosure. To his left was the winding road to the ranch, and beyond it the meandering South Platte River. To his right were rolling green acres of ranchland, surrounded by the massive, tree-covered slopes of the Rocky Mountains. Some of the ranch's red Hereford cattle grazed in the distance.

Heaven.

But he wouldn't be here much longer. In three days, he'd be back in Denver. Investigating Dr. Kelley Stanton. The main focus of his assignment.

Colleen would provide further details first, the results of the initial investigation into the woman and her background as well as information about the hospital fire.

A fire in a hospital, damn it. He felt his teeth grind.

Sure, the fire had been confined to a records room, but who knew what damage it could have done? People could have been killed.

What would drive a woman with a young child to set a fire? Shawn would sure as hell find out.

"OKAY, SWEETHEART. We're here." Not that Kelley had any doubt that Jenny knew full well that they'd arrived at the Gilpin Hospital KidClub day-care center. As soon as they went through the door into the main playroom, the blond three-year-old, clad today in a flowered T-shirt and

matching red slacks, stopped prancing at her mother's side
and stood still, thumb in her mouth. With her other hand,
she clutched Kelley's midcalf-length black skirt. Tears
filled her brown eyes.

Before the fire, Jenny had been eager to come here to
play. She had always dashed into the midst of the kids who
started their day in this charming room adorned with bright
rainbows on the walls. Mostly, the little ones congregated
at one of the child-size tables, coloring until it was time
for the caregivers to begin planned activities.

But since the fire, her daughter had demonstrated every
symptom of separation anxiety—tears, protests and tantrums.

It broke Kelley's heart every morning. She'd spent days
at home with Jenny after the fire, and had taken her to a
kind counselor. But Kelley couldn't stay off work indefi-
nitely. When Jenny had started to recover emotionally, Kelley had returned to her demanding medical practice. Luck-
ily her office was in the adjoining building, and she spent
a lot of time seeing patients in the hospital itself. She
dropped by often to look in on Jenny, staying far in the
background so that her daughter, busy playing, wouldn't
notice her.

Once Jenny got used to being there each day, she seemed
to thrive once more, with all the other children to play with
and the excellent staff who watched over the kids while
teaching them things commensurate with their ages and
abilities.

But those first minutes when she dropped Jenny off…

"Good morning." At the gruff, masculine voice, Kelley
raised her gaze from her daughter—until she stared into
eyes as blue as a cloudless winter sky. They looked about
as cold, too. But the man behind them was one of the most
gorgeous hunks Kelley had ever seen.

She felt her face flush at the direction her thoughts had veered. But that didn't deter her mind from noting the breadth of shoulders beneath an off-white shirt and leather vest, the slim cut of faded brown jeans, the sturdiness of a set jawline and the short hair that was a cross between dirty gold and golden brown. And the cowboy boots.

"Good morning," she returned, knowing her tone was quizzical. Was he the father of one of the half dozen kids settled at places along the tables? Kelley forced herself not to look at his hands to see if he wore a wedding ring. That wasn't her business. Besides, a man who looked like him had to be taken. Either that or he had a bevy of beautiful women at his beck and call.

Not that Kelley cared. She wasn't interested in any man, great-looking or not. In her experience, not one was worth a fraction of the aggravation he caused.

"And who is this?" The man looked down at Jenny, who clutched at Kelley's clothes all the tighter. The smile on the man's face looked sour, as if he had sucked on a lime.

"This is Jenny Stanton," Kelley said, her tone cheerful for her daughter's benefit. "Are you the daddy of one of the kids?"

"No, I'm the new caregiver."

What? Kelley stared. He certainly didn't look like the other child-care providers, who were mostly college-age men and women who studied teaching and needed to earn money in their spare time. A few were career preschool teachers. But this man…?

He knelt in front of Jenny. "My name is Shawn," he told her. Then he rose. "Shawn Jameson. And you're Mrs. Stanton?"

No. Kelley nearly shuddered. She definitely wasn't *Mrs.* Stanton. That implied she was Randall Stanton's wife.

She hadn't been his wife for two years now. And that was fine with her.

It was her turn to force a smile onto her lips. "I'm Dr. Kelley Stanton," she told the man. "I'm one of the doctors on staff here."

Was it her imagination, or did Shawn Jameson's straight, thick brows dip just a little before he resumed his uncomfortable smile? "Very nice to meet you, *Dr.* Stanton." He stressed the word "doctor," but it did not sound like an apology. She hadn't expected one, but neither had she expected to be subtly insulted.

Didn't he like doctors? If so, he shouldn't be working in a hospital, even with children. Especially with these children, since many were doctors' kids. But maybe she'd imagined his inflection.

"Good to meet you, too," she clipped out, then knelt, gently extracting her skirt from Jenny's hand. "Okay, sweetheart. Time for me to go, but I'll be back for you soon."

"No, Mommy," Jenny said in her sweet little girl's voice. "I don't want you to go."

Kelley inhaled, knowing the scene that was to come. Hating it, for she always felt as if she were hurting Jenny. "I have to, honey, but—"

"But we're going to have a great time here today, Jenny."

Kelley looked up in gratitude as Shawn Jameson took Jenny's hand and tried to gently lead her away.

Jenny began to cry.

Shawn's blue eyes widened. Surely that wasn't fear Kelley saw in them? He glanced at her as if for help, but she mouthed, "Thanks," and backed away.

Jenny began to cry even louder.

"Would you like a piece of doughnut?" Shawn asked,

gesturing toward a box on the tall reception desk. "Or some fruit?" As usual, the treats had been left there that morning.

Kelley swallowed her objection to his bribing her child with sweets. It didn't help anyway. Jenny did not calm down.

"Then let's go color with your friends." Shawn tugged on Jenny's hand. The child was no match for the brawny man and followed him, but her sobs didn't stop. He led her to an empty seat at the closest table and urged her into a chair. "Here are some nice crayons and a pad of paper," Shawn said. "Would you like to draw something?"

"No," Jenny wailed, pushing her chair back from the table.

"Well...would you like a cup of juice, Jenny?"

Kelley continued to watch from the doorway, wondering if she should go rescue her child. Or the man. He seemed to be growing panicked. None of the other caregivers were in the room. They were probably with kids in the facility's other rooms. Or maybe in the kitchen, working on the day's snacks.

In any event, this did not look good.

"I don't want juice," Jenny screamed. "I want my mommy!"

She looked at Kelley. So did Shawn. Kelley took a deep, uneven breath but did not move. If things didn't improve in a minute, though, she would have to step in.

If she did, if she had to complain about this man, he could lose his job. That might be a good thing, but on his first day? Didn't he deserve a chance?

Besides, Kelley had enough enemies these days. She didn't need another if she could avoid it.

But why didn't he seem to know what to do with the child? Worse, why did he appear so rattled? Surely he had worked with kids before. Otherwise he wouldn't have been hired.

"Mommy!" Jenny shrieked again, rising from her chair. She looked as if she was about to run toward Kelley, who wondered if she should just leave. Maybe things would calm down when she was gone.

Maybe they wouldn't.

The other children watched the exchange, eyes huge. The lower lips of a couple began to quiver, as if they might cry in sympathy for Jenny. Or for their own absent parents.

Obviously Shawn noticed, for he looked around nervously.

"Hey," he said, grabbing a pad of paper and some crayons from the table. He looked desperate. What was he going to do? "Do you have any pets at home, Jenny?"

No, Kelley wanted to tell him. *Don't remind her.* Jenny wanted a puppy or a kitten. Having a pet was even a recommended therapy to help Jenny recover from the trauma of the fire. But the timing wasn't right.

If Kelley were a stay-at-home mom, the way Randall had wanted her to be, she would be able to take care of a pet. But that wasn't reality. It wasn't what Kelley wanted, either for herself or her daughter. She wanted Jenny to have a strong role model.

Not the kind of role model Kelley herself had had.

"I don't have no pets," Jenny told Shawn, shaking her head sadly. But at least she was no longer crying.

"Would you like one?"

It was time for Kelley to intervene. The man couldn't be allowed to distract her daughter by making her feel bad about other things.

As Jenny nodded in response to his question, Shawn said, "Well, then, you shall have one."

That was it. Kelley began crossing the room toward

them, but Shawn Jameson must have noticed, for he held up one large hand. Kelley paused, but only for a minute. If he didn't stop—

And then she got it. Kneeling on the floor beside the pint-size table, Jameson used the crayons to sketch on the pad. In a moment, the outline of a fuzzy spaniel puppy took shape, one with big, sad eyes and a lolling tongue. And that with only a few strokes on the paper.

It was an adorable caricature.

"Here you are, Jenny," Shawn said. "This is your new puppy. And—" he made a few more strokes on the page. A child appeared beside the dog—a child with Jenny's straight, blond hair and soulful chocolate-brown eyes. She wore a crown, like a princess.

"For me?" Jenny asked in obvious delight. Her tears had dried, replaced by a big, amazed grin.

"For you," Shawn replied. "But you'll have to think of a name for the dog."

"Okay," Jenny replied, her small brows knit as she gave the matter a lot of thought.

Before she came up with a name, the other kids were crowding around, looking at her drawing. Demanding, "Me, too, Shawn. Please. Me next," all in a chorus that earned from Shawn Jameson a foolish, pleased grin.

Kelley turned toward the door. No matter what the man's qualifications, he had obvious talent in one direction. And the kids loved it.

Maybe he would work out after all.

SHAWN WATCHED AS Dr. Kelley Stanton left KidClub.

"Okay, Teddy," he told the nearest child and began to sketch a kitty-cat, as requested.

Amazing. He had all but forgotten his old ability to draw caricatures. Thank heavens it had come back to him when he'd really needed it. As he'd once really needed it to survive.

"I'll call my puppy Gilly," Jenny told him solemnly as he continued to sketch on the pad. "For Gilpin. That's this hospital."

"And a damn—er, darned good name that is," he told her. He knew the hospital had been named for William Gilpin, the first governor of Colorado Territory back in the mid-1800s. A nearby county bore his name, too.

Jenny was a cute kid. Looked like her mother. Shawn had silently evaluated Dr. Kelley Stanton with the eyes of an artist.

And an arson investigator.

She was certainly a woman whose appearance was arresting. And he might have to be the one to ensure she was *arrested.*

Her auburn hair glinted, as if someone had painted flames through the shimmering brown. Her face was heart shaped, her expression even more solemn than her daughter's. As if she had forgotten how to smile.

And no wonder, if she set fires for a hobby.

Even if she was innocent of that, she might have treated the flu patients from Silver Rapids improperly, as the current rumors unearthed by Colleen indicated.

Two people had died from that flu outbreak, right here at Gilpin Hospital. Two of Dr. Kelley Stanton's patients.

Did she know anything about that flu? Its origin? Whether it was actually an outbreak of Q fever, antibodies for which had been found in the blood of sheep on a ranch that had already been investigated by Colorado Confidential?

Finding out might help rescue a child even younger than her own sweet daughter. A child who had been kidnapped, whose mother had caught the flu and whose kidnapping could in some way be related to that very strange epidemic in Silver Rapids.

The lovely Dr. Stanton just might be in the middle of the whole thing.

Lovely? Hell, she was extraordinary-looking. Shawn had an urge not only to draw her caricature, but to paint her.

Nude.

He laughed ruefully aloud.

"What's so funny, Shawn?" Jenny asked.

"I just thought of a joke." Yeah. Very funny. He had a very sudden, very real urge to make love to this kid's mother. A possible arsonist, of all people.

There was nothing he hated more than someone who set fires.

Someone like that had damn near ruined his life.

He turned to little Teddy, who sat at the table beside him.

"Here you are. Here's your kitty and you, together."

"Thanks!"

Shawn couldn't help but feel a burst of pleasure at the honest wonder and gratitude in the little boy's fervent exclamation.

"Me next," chorused the other kids.

Shawn started on his next work of art. Maybe he'd found his way to manage this assignment after all.

He'd begun to make friends with little Jenny Stanton.

Now all he had to do was get to know her mother well enough to start asking questions. A lot of them.

And the fact this woman made his fingers itch to touch her... Hell, he'd just have to get over it.

Chapter Two

Despite the bustle of people hurrying by, Kelley walked slowly down the hall as she left KidClub, wondering whether she should go back. Check on Jenny.

Make sure Shawn Jameson remained in control of all those rambunctious young rascals in his charge.

Not that she had any interest in seeing the handsome caricature-drawing cowboy again. But she fretted about her daughter and Jenny's transition back into day care, today and every day.

No, things would be fine. She had to stop worrying so much.

As if she could. About Jenny or anything else in her life lately.

Resolutely, she picked up her pace.

The scent of fresh paint still hung in the air. The repaired walls were a lighter shade this time, though still a pale peach. After the fire, they'd been smoke-stained and dark, and the place had smelled awful. Most of the signs and fixtures had had to be replaced, too.

She turned the corner at the end of the hall and nearly ran into a cart full of cleaning supplies.

"Hello, Dr. Stanton."

"Good morning, Juan," she said to the tall, thin man

beside the cart. Juan Cortes was one of Gilpin Hospital's janitors, a pleasant man in his thirties who always wore a toothy smile beneath his neat, dark mustache. He had a faint Spanish accent. Relatively new at the hospital, he apparently loved kids. Each morning, before most people arrived, he came by KidClub with sliced fruit plus a box of doughnuts, each carefully dissected into several pieces to appease parents' concerns about too many sweets.

"I saw the treats you left on the desk," Kelley told him. "Thank you. Again."

"You're welcome again," Juan said. His grin sobered. "How is Jenny?"

Like the rest of the staff, Juan knew Jenny had been in the child-care center when the fire broke out.

Inside KidClub. That was what Kelley told everyone, to protect her daughter. The fire had at first been called accidental, but the official cause was later ruled arson. So far no one had been arrested. Kelley had no reason to think Jenny had seen what happened, but just in case…

"She's doing better," she told Juan, "but it'll take time before she can put it all behind her."

"Of course. Well, I made sure I got her favorite today, a twisty glazed doughnut. She can have the whole thing if she wants, not just a piece of it."

"That's sweet of you, Juan." Kelley hesitated. She suspected that providing doughnuts and fruit every day might create a dent in the janitor's salary. "How about if Jenny and I bring the treats tomorrow morning?"

"Well…" Juan didn't look keen on the idea.

Kelley did not want to make him feel bad, though she had been meaning to make this offer for a while. "Another day, then," she said quickly. "You know I always teach her to take turns. If you tell me what kind your favorite doughnut is, we'll be sure to bring you one. Okay?"

"Maybe next week sometime," he said without enthusiasm. But he added, "My favorite is chocolate with peanuts."

"Good. We'll work out when soon." She should probably also find out what kind of treats Shawn Jameson preferred, she thought as she continued down the hall.

The way he looked, his preference in treats probably had nothing to do with sweet rolls.

She shook her head. Why was the new child-care attendant so much on her mind this morning?

She turned the corner to the main hallway and glimpsed the back of Dr. Madelyne Younger. The short, platinum-blond cap of hair over the signature purple lab jacket was a giveaway.

Kelley's own lab coats were light in color. Conservative. Unlike Madelyne's.

"Hey, Madelyne, wait up," Kelley called, but not too loudly.

Though this was the administration wing, it was still part of a hospital.

Her voice had apparently been loud enough. Madelyne, an internist who specialized in infectious diseases as did Kelley, turned to face her. She didn't have the same compunction about raising her voice, which boomed down the hall. "Hey, kiddo, how ya' doing this morning?"

"Not bad." Kelley, smiling, caught up with the older woman.

"Not good, either, I'd say." Madelyne's narrow face screwed into a frown as she studied Kelley. Lines radiated from the edges of her barely made-up eyes. She gestured for Kelley to join her at the hall's periphery to let the crowd of hospital staff and visitors pass by. "What's wrong, kiddo?"

Kelley moved to the wall and shrugged one shoulder. "Nothing new. It's just hard to leave Jenny these days."

"I figured. Are things around here improving?"

Kelley didn't want to think about that but replied with a sigh. "Not really. All the innuendoes appear to be taking on a life of their own and sneaking into every corner of this place."

"Remember they're only that—innuendoes. I was there. I didn't see you do a damned thing wrong. That influenza epidemic was a beast and a half, and those two older patients who died—well, they simply arrived too late to be helped. Got it?"

"Got it," Kelley affirmed, unable to stop herself from grinning back at her irrepressible friend. But she'd noticed the way Madelyne had phrased her reply. She hadn't *seen* Kelley do anything wrong.

That didn't mean she would swear that Kelley hadn't *done* anything wrong.

"Anyway, there's nothing—oh, puffballs. There's the chief innuendo manufacturer now. Just remember the source, kiddo."

Kelley sighed. Madelyne was glaring over her shoulder, and Kelley chose not to turn to see who she was looking at.

She already knew.

"Good morning, Kelley. Madelyne."

The stilted masculine voice that had once been the stuff of her daydreams was now one of her worst nightmares.

Slowly, Kelley turned and found herself looking up into the face of Dr. Randall Stanton, cardiologist extraordinaire. Star of Gilpin Hospital's surgical staff.

And her blasted ex-husband.

Randall wore a lab jacket with as much finesse as most gentlemen wore tuxedos. He wasn't a particularly tall man,

but Kelley, at five foot three, had to look up at him—a fact
that suited him just fine. Silver-haired, silver-tongued Randall thrived on adulation the way sports stars did. Though
the hallway was broad here, he seemed to take up its entire
width with his presence. And of course he wasn't by himself.

"Good morning, Randall," Kelley said with forced ci-
vility, adding through gritted teeth, "You, too, Cheryl."
Even more than Kelley disliked her ex, she loathed the
woman by his side.

"Yeah. Hiya." Madelyne sounded even less enthusiastic
than Kelley.

Kelley's ex seldom traveled alone, even through hospital
halls. His most constant companion these days was his assistant, cardiac nurse Cheryl Marten.

Cheryl was a little taller than Kelley, but she, too, had
to look up at her boss. And lover, if Kelley was any judge.
Cheryl carried a clipboard—most likely Randall's.

Other than her height, Cheryl was not at all similar to
Kelley. The nurse was more voluptuous and flaunted it.
Though she wore an unprepossessing colorful smock over
her clean white slacks, its top buttons were undone, revealing a hint of substantial cleavage.

She was probably a year or two younger than Kelley,
which made her ten years younger than Randall. She radiated Randall's air of superiority. More than once an ir-
ritated Kelley had itched to remind the woman that she was
a nurse, while Kelley was a doctor. But Kelley always
swallowed the urge. There was enough animosity between
them without giving in to the woman's obvious baiting.
And Kelley knew that, with the esteemed Randall on her
side, Cheryl would prevail in any catfight. Even with what
she'd done.

Especially since Kelley's formerly rising star at Gilpin Hospital had lost its luster.

"How is our daughter this morning?" Randall asked, pointedly ignoring Madelyne.

As if you care. Though they shared joint custody, Kelley had primary physical custody, which suited her fine. Randall was supposed to have visitation on certain nights and weekends, but often claimed to be too busy to take sweet little Jenny.

Kelley always made excuses for him, more to soothe Jenny than to protect Randall.

She had done enough of the latter when they were married.

Despite everything, Randall had not admitted to the slightest bit of responsibility for Jenny's being left behind the night of the fire. Even though it had been his night to care for their daughter, even though his assistant had been the one to sign the child out, he blamed Kelley.

"Jenny's fine," Kelley said. "I'll bet she'd love for you to ask her yourself. Do you plan to take her tomorrow night?"

Randall didn't answer until he had glanced at Cheryl, whose smile looked forced to Kelley, but no matter. Apparently it had been the permission Randall needed.

More likely, he had just made sure a baby-sitter was available.

"Of course," his voice boomed. "I can't wait."

I'll bet. "Great," Kelley forced herself to say.

"Umm—and your caseload these days? Can you handle it?"

"My caseload is growing, Randall." An exaggeration, but she wasn't going to tell him that. "And my patients are doing fine. Thank you for asking." *You nasty, vindictive jerk.*

She hadn't even been the one who'd demanded the divorce. She'd simply not knuckled under to his insistence that she change her lifestyle to suit Randall and his image.

"See you later, Kelley," Randall said. "Madelyne." He nodded toward the other doctor and headed down the hall, Cheryl trailing in his wake.

"Son of a boring snitch," Madelyne hissed in an undertone after them, making Kelley laugh despite all the malaise turning ugly cartwheels inside her. "Ignore him, kiddo." She paused for only a second before continuing, "But there's someone no red-blooded American woman can ignore. If I could whistle, I'd do it right about now. Who the heck is *he?*"

Kelley inhaled sharply. She knew just who Madelyne was talking about but didn't let on. Instead, she turned to look in the direction her friend was facing. "Oh," she said as she spotted Shawn Jameson coming down the hall toward them. "He's the new child-care attendant at Kid-Club."

"Well, damn. If I'd known that, I'd have had myself a kid or two to leave with him." As Shawn reached them, Madelyne looked at Kelley expectantly.

What could she do but introduce them? "Hi, Shawn. This is my colleague, Dr. Madelyne Younger. Madelyne, this man is a genius with crayons. He staved off an entire room of fussy children this morning by drawing them into submission. Including Jenny."

"No kidding?" Madelyne said. Kelley was almost embarrassed by the frank way her colleague looked Shawn up and down.

He appeared both amused and uncomfortable. Kelley considered rescuing him, but he did it himself.

"It's very nice to meet you, Dr. Younger, but—"

"Madelyne," she corrected swiftly.

"Madelyne," he said. "But I'm off to a meeting. I'll see you around, I'm sure. And I'll be at KidClub later when you pick Jenny up, Dr. Stanton." The look he turned on her with his cool blue eyes seemed to impart a message that Kelley could not decipher.

She wasn't certain she wanted to.

In fact, she suspected, with the way things were going around here, that even from the new guy on the block, a great-looking man who couldn't possibly blame her for anything, the message would not be one she wanted to hear.

"SO YOU'VE STARTED working at KidClub?"

Shawn, sitting casually in the small but luxuriously appointed hospital administrator's office, nodded at Louis Paxler.

The hospital administrator, fiftyish, had a sweep of hair several shades darker than his thin brown brows. It looked real but not natural, probably dyed rather than a hairpiece. He wore a dark suit, and the red tie fastened over his white shirt appeared to lift up the extra flesh beneath his chin.

"I got there early this morning." Shawn leaned back in the tall leather chair facing Paxler's mahogany desk. "Marge showed me around." Marge Ralston, head of KidClub, had no sooner arrived than there was a minor emergency in the kitchen. She had hurriedly left Shawn in charge of greeting the children. The way his credentials had been presented to her, she'd obviously had no concern about dumping that small responsibility on him.

If only she'd known...

Louis Paxler knew the truth—a version of it. He watched Shawn as if trying to analyze him from beneath his gold-rimmed glasses. "Does she suspect who you are?"

"If so, she didn't let on."

"Fine. So...who did you meet there?"

Shawn hid his amusement at the administrator's thinly veiled question. He knew who Paxler meant. He decided to play him for a minute. "Well, there were about a dozen kids. Can't tell you their names offhand, but I'll learn them. And—"

"Any of their parents?"

"A couple." Enough of this game, Shawn told himself. Stringing the administrator along wouldn't get him answers he needed. "One was Dr. Kelley Stanton." The lovely, sexy Dr. Kelley Stanton....

"Ah, yes, Dr. Stanton." Paxler's tone was decidedly chilly. "I'm not sure how much you know, Mr. Jameson, but—"

"Call me Shawn. And I was told you relayed your suspicions about Dr. Stanton and her involvement with the blaze to the fire department's Fire Investigation Bureau. Right?"

Paxler nodded, grim satisfaction narrowing his mouth. "Of course, they first thought it was an accident, but then decided it could be arson. They didn't find enough evidence to accuse anyone, though."

"And you thought it might be Dr. Stanton? Why don't you fill me in?"

"Of course, Mr.—er, Shawn. Except...the hospital will still collect on its insurance claim, won't it?"

"As long as you cooperate," Shawn assured him. "But if an arsonist is found, the insurance company may be able to recoup the damages." Which was probably correct, although Shawn wouldn't have anything to do with that decision. But Paxler had been told only that Shawn was an investigator for Investigations, Confidential and Undercover, a private agency whose nickname seemed appropriate for an inquiry at a hospital. ICU was supposedly looking into the fire for the insurance carrier. The administrator had been told nothing about Colorado Confidential—or that the flu epidemic was the subject of deeper inquiry.

At first Paxler had resisted, but then had agreed to co-operate, particularly after getting an official call telling him that the more helpful he was, the faster the hospital's claim—already delayed—was likely to be processed.

Colleen had contacts in a lot of useful places.

"Okay, then," Paxler said. "About five months ago, the hospital was besieged by cases of flu transported from Silver Rapids, a town just north of here. It's too small to have a major hospital of its own, so the people who were most ill were brought here for treatment. Two died. Older folk who had a harder time fighting off the illness. But..."

"But what?" Shawn prompted.

Paxler stood, pushing aside his desk chair, which appeared too modern to fit with the rest of the ornate furnishings. Shawn glanced around and wondered where the three doors at the room's perimeter led to.

The administrator walked to a window, peered out as if looking for an answer on the Denver street below, then turned back. His gut made his belt protrude, but he otherwise did not appear heavy. "Look, Shawn. Though I expressed my concerns to the authorities, I didn't intend to. Not exactly. I mean, if what I fear is correct, the hospital could have liability here. But if I am right... Well, it just can't happen again. In my position, I simply can't allow it."

"And your fear is...?"

"That Dr. Kelley Stanton was negligent in her treatment of those patients. Now, look." He raised his hands as if trying to halt Shawn, though Shawn hadn't moved. "I can't prove anything, but the couple who died, their course of treatment—well, I think the most telling thing is the fire in the records office."

"It's why you can't prove Dr. Stanton was negligent?"
Shawn knew the background. But after having met Kelley
Stanton, even briefly, he couldn't believe she was less than
an excellent doctor. Yet he had nothing to base that feeling
on other than a first impression that had left him wanting
to get to know her better. Much better. And not entirely
because she was a suspect.

Which meant he had to pay attention to what Paxler said,
to steer his irrelevant, unscientific impressions back on
track.

Paxler nodded. "I'd begun to make inquiries. Randall…
Are you aware Dr. Kelley Stanton was previously married
to one of our most esteemed physicians, Dr. Randall Stanton?"

Shawn nodded. He hadn't met the man yet but he already
despised him—the *esteemed* Dr. Stanton.

What man in his right mind would have let Kelley Stanton go?

Stay objective, Jameson.

"Of course there's bound to be some animosity," Paxler
continued, "and I certainly don't know the reasons for their
marital difficulties, but since their divorce Randall has
hinted that it was at least partly due to his concern over
Kelley's…er, her lack of abilities. At first I chalked that up
to hard feelings. I had no reason—then—to doubt Kelley's
skill. But after the deaths I couldn't ignore Randall's inti-
mations. I had just begun to conduct an inquiry when the
fire occurred."

"And Dr. Kelley Stanton was aware of the investigation?"

"Of course. I questioned her and began to put together
a panel of her peers to look into the situation. I personally
don't have the medical expertise to determine whether the
treatment she prescribed was substandard."

"Would the medical records have supplied the answers?" They might also have contained other answers Shawn needed.

"Possibly." Paxler resumed his seat and rubbed his eyes beneath his glasses. "Now we'll have to rely on Kelley's recollection of what she prescribed, plus the memories of the attending nurses. Those can get colored by time—and by personal relationships, since Kelley has friends here who might protect her."

"I see." And Shawn could see that someone who seemed as warm a mother and as friendly a person as Kelley Stanton could have a cheering section. But looks could be deceiving. And if Paxler was right, the warmth he thought he'd seen in Kelley could instead be a tendency toward playing with fire. Real fire.

Shawn's jaw tightened. "You're certain the pertinent records were destroyed?"

Paxler nodded. "When I took over as director five years ago, the place was an administrative nightmare. One problem was the lack of standards for patient records retention. I instituted a procedure. The charts for current patients were kept with those patients. Those of patients from more than a year ago were copied into computer files and stored. But information about patients discharged less than a year ago was kept in the records storage area. There was a procedure for signing them out. The sign-out sheets were kept in another room, and weren't touched by the fire. And no one had signed out the records for the Silver Rapids flu patients." He sighed. "I should have kept them myself under the circumstances, but I'd no reason to believe they wouldn't be safe there."

"Don't you think it would be overkill for Dr. Stanton to destroy all those records and endanger everyone in the hospital just to get rid of a few files that might implicate her?"

Shawn had seen arsonists set fires for less substantial reasons, just for the fun of seeing things burn. But often there was a better motive. Like covering up a truth. Or several truths…

"Of course, but what better way to hide who set the fire and why? And she was there that night. She was the one to call the fire department, pull the alarm for the hospital system. She even came running out with her daughter, screaming that Randall had left Jenny in KidClub." Paxler shook his head. "The poor child. I can't imagine a mother who would subject her own daughter to such danger, but it appears that's what happened."

That was one place that the story fell down, in Shawn's estimation. He had seen Kelley with her daughter that morning. Whatever else she had done, Shawn doubted she'd have put Jenny in danger that way.

But that might be his own first impression, coloring his judgment.

"There's no on else you can think of with motive to destroy the files?" he asked.

Paxler shrugged shoulders that appeared padded beneath his suit jacket. "I can't imagine who. And the fire department tells me now that the fire was definitely arson."

Shawn respected the Denver F.D.'s Fire Investigation Bureau. He'd once been among them.

But he would double check their conclusions.

It was possible that the fire had been an accident, as they'd initially thought. But if it had been arson, the indication seemed to be that Dr. Kelley Stanton was the one who'd played with matches.

Whatever the answer, whatever Kelley's involvement, Shawn would learn the truth.

Chapter Three

The day had felt abysmally long. Kelley couldn't wait to go home. But mostly she couldn't wait to see Jenny.

Smiling at the thought of her daughter, she picked up her pace down the nearly empty halls that connected the medical building with the hospital. Before the fire, she'd often stopped to see Jenny during her lunch break. Since the fire, she only did that when she could make sure Jenny wouldn't see her. Every time Kelley left her now, Jenny went through the agonies of separation. And there were days when Jenny threw tantrums, yelled at the other kids, even spilled their lunches on the floor.

The counselor they'd been seeing said it would take time for Jenny to get over her fears about the fire. She was too young to understand much except how scared she'd been. Talking about it would help. But Jenny didn't want to talk about it.

Today Kelley hadn't been able to get away at lunch to peek in on Jenny. Every time she'd left her office, someone had beeped her. At least her services were in demand.

As she turned the corner to the KidClub, she recalled that morning.

The new attendant, Shawn Jameson, might still be there. So what if Kelley thought him a hunk? Or that Madelyne

Younger did, too? He would probably catch the attention of every woman in the hospital. But all that counted was whether he connected well with the children.

She pushed open the door and walked in. Her grin broadened.

Marge Ralston was there, leading some kids in an endearing off-key rendition of "I'm A Little Teapot." Marge, in her early thirties like Kelley, loved children. A perky, curly-haired brunette, she wore paint-splashed smocks over her jeans, never caring if she got additional spots on them. She had studied to be a grade school teacher but had elected to work with little ones and was great with them.

Kelley waved at her. Then, not seeing her daughter, she mouthed, "Where's Jenny?"

Without missing a beat or a teapot gesture, Marge pointed toward the door to one of the other rooms. Kelley headed there.

And stopped in the doorway. Large, brawny Shawn Jameson sat at a tyke table surrounded by kids, looking like a giant at an elf's tea party. He appeared tense. His eyes darted from one child to another, as if he was unsure which would do something unexpected first.

Jenny sat beside him. She barely looked up when Kelley approached. On the table in front of her was a large paper on which she was sketching with crayons. Her drawing of uneven circles and lines was a credible rendering of a smiling pig.

"Jenny, that's wonderful!" Kelley exclaimed, leaning over her daughter's shoulder.

"Shawn teached me. He says he can teach me lots of an'mals."

"Me, too," said the little girl on Shawn's other side. Claire Fritz, Jenny's best friend, was the daughter of a woman who worked in the hospital pharmacy. Claire also had a colorful stick drawing in front of her, as did the other five children.

Kelley turned to thank Shawn and found herself looking straight into his blue eyes. They brightened a little as they found hers, as if the appearance of another adult put him more at ease. Her smile faltered as something seemed to spark between them, and she pulled herself upright so she was looking down on him. "This is wonderful, Shawn. Thank you."

He quickly pushed back his chair and rose, unfurling his long limbs. He was probably just short of six feet, Kelley guessed, for she was eight or nine inches shorter and felt dwarfed not only by his height but also by his brawny breadth. From his hurried yet easy grace, she had no doubt that what expanded his vest and shirt was muscle, not flab.

"You're welcome," his deep voice rumbled. "Can I speak to you about Jenny's behavior this morning?"

Kelley's gut clenched. "What happened?"

He shook his head quickly. "Nothing bad. I just want to talk about how she was when you left her. I'll get another attendant to keep an eye on the kids. Can we go get a cup of coffee in the cafeteria?"

Kelley blinked. Was he just looking for an excuse to get away from the kids? If so, why was he here?

Or was he hitting on her? That idea almost made her smile. Her miserable relationship with Randall, and their subsequent divorce, had taught her that what men thought of her was irrelevant. But to have one as handsome and as kind to kids as Shawn seem interested…? Well, that felt awfully good.

But inappropriate. He was on the hospital staff. She had enough problems these days. She didn't need another.

Besides, she'd probably misread his simple invitation. Despite his apparent unease, he must like kids or he

wouldn't have taken this job. He'd be concerned about any
child in his charge. He undoubtedly just wanted to discuss
her troubled daughter.

They had an appointment with Jenny's counselor that
evening. And Kelley knew all about the problem with
Jenny's behavior when Kelley left her at KidClub—all the
more reason to speak with Jenny's therapist.

"Maybe another time," she said. "Time to go, Jenny."

THAT NIGHT, SHAWN lost count of the sit-ups he did on the
worn gray carpet in the shabbily furnished apartment he'd
leased near the hospital for the duration of his assignment.

When he was exhausted, he dragged his aching body up
and forced it onto the tattered green sofa. The place smelled
of cleaning products, but they failed to mask that the previous tenant had been a heavy smoker.

Shawn unbuttoned his shirt, feeling slightly strange without the shoulder and ankle holsters he wore on his other
ICU assignments. Working with kids meant carrying no
firearms, which was okay. Likely, the only danger he might
face on this mission was the arsonist lighting up again.
Improbable, given the suspected motive. Hospital records
could only burn once.

He picked up the cool soft drink can he had left on the
end table. As he took a swig of cold, sweet cola, he wished
it was a beer.

"Well, damn," he said to the stark white walls. The
television news was on mute. He let the blessed quiet and
sense of solitude wash over him, a relief after being surrounded by screaming tots for what seemed forever. He
liked it quiet. He liked to be *alone*.

Oh, the day had gone well enough. Though he was still
sweating his cover—dealing with a bunch of rowdy pre-
schoolers—he'd found a method that at least calmed them.

Sort of. For a few minutes at a time, though unfortunately not all at once.

After learning to work with stubborn and skittish horses at the Royal Flush, and to use them for herding a few head of cattle at a time, he'd thought he had already gone beyond the call of duty to establish his cover.

Now this.

But damned if the kids didn't like to draw cartoons. The talent he had thought he'd tucked away forever had come to his rescue again. And the kids were so cute and earnest about it that they'd unexpectedly made him smile.

Other than his short conversation with Louis Paxler, he'd hardly accomplished anything that day to further his investigation. Of course, he had to establish himself and his cover. Only then could he gain people's confidence, get them to answer questions without suspecting why he was there.

But Shawn's strong suit was not patience.

And it bothered him more than he wanted to admit that Kelley had turned him down when he'd invited her for coffee.

He'd known rejection. Hell, it had been part of his life, but he'd gotten over it. Still, figuring out Dr. Kelley Stanton and her relationship to the flu and the fire was his mission. That meant he needed to spend time with the lovely physician. Not exactly a hardship—though her presence had already caused part of his anatomy to grow hard.

He laughed derisively at himself. Shaking his head, Shawn reached for the phone on the end table beside the couch. He had to report in.

But before he lifted the receiver, the phone rang.

"Jameson," he answered.

"You were supposed to call," said Colleen Wellesley without preamble.

"I was just about to." He put the soft drink can on the table and leaned forward, alert, ready to talk.

"Right. So how did it go? Did you learn anything?"

Shawn responded in a tone reminiscent of the kids' chanting. "I didn't blow my cover yet but didn't learn much, either. Except for where the potty is."

"Don't get smart."

"Who, me? I take it you're still at the ranch."

"Right, though I'll be at the Denver office later in the week. Tell me about your day."

He pictured his solemn, serious lady-boss pacing and holding a cordless phone to her cheek beneath the curve of her chin-length brown hair. She had to be in her bedroom or one of the secure rooms in the basement to be talking like this, for she wouldn't want the foreman, Dex, or the Castillos to overhear.

"Okay, C., it's like this," he said. "I talked with the administrator, Paxler, and got a rundown of who's who and what's what, at least in his opinion."

"So he's still cooperating? Good, but is he helpful?"

"Yeah, a little *too* helpful—like he's covering his butt and the hospital's insurance by pointing fingers where he can."

"Well, you'll have to sort out what's true and what's butt-protecting. Is that all?"

"No. I've met Dr. Kelley Stanton and established a rapport of sorts with her daughter, so—"

"Really?" Colleen sounded incredulous.

"Why did you create this cover if you thought I couldn't handle it?"

"Did I say that? I just expected it to take you longer to settle in. You'll have to tell me all about your experience one of these days."

"Right." He would definitely not tell her how rattled he

remained around a bunch of screaming munchkins. "Anyhow, now that I know the layout and have met some of the cast of characters, I've been working on a game plan. I should have more to report next time."

"Fine, but don't push so hard that you blow your cover. We need answers fast. *Real* fast. But we won't get them if we have to start over."

"Don't worry," he said firmly. "I'm in."

As USUAL, KELLEY hesitated the next morning at the entry to KidClub. Jenny was holding her hand tightly. Her thumb was in her mouth.

Inhaling deeply to steel herself for the scene to come, Kelley pushed open the door.

Shawn Jameson, tall and broad-shouldered, looking as confident as if he had always worked there, stood to the right of the entry. Maybe he just appeared confident because he was engrossed in conversation with Marge Ralston, who was obviously hanging on his every word.

A group of kids sat on floor mats in a far corner of the room. A TV on a stand had been wheeled in, and they were watching a public television children's show.

At Kelley's side, Jenny hesitated. Kelley felt her daughter's grip tighten.

Shawn turned away from Marge and looked straight at Kelley as if he had been expecting her.

Which of course he was, as he expected all the kids' parents. He wasn't anticipating seeing her in particular.

Still, the way his lips curved slowly into a lazy but welcoming smile made her insides melt. She shook her head to bring herself back to reality.

He said something else to Marge that Kelley couldn't hear. The facility's head caregiver continued to gaze at him as if in rapt attention. Then he broke away from Marge and approached Kelley and Jenny.

"Good morning, Shawn," Kelley said.

"Hi." He wore no vest today. Instead he had on a navy blue shirt that enhanced the deep color of his eyes. He still looked like a handsome cowboy in his jeans and boots. "How are you both?"

"Fine, Shawn," Jenny said softly.

"Good. Are we going to have fun today?"

"Can we draw an'mals?" Jenny's voice quivered, and Kelley braced herself for her daughter's next tearful farewell.

"Sure," Shawn said.

To Kelley's surprise, Jenny let go of her and held out her hand. After a slight hesitation Shawn took it and led her farther into the room. He met Kelley's eyes over the child's head.

No separation anxiety today? Kelley was so relieved that she felt her whole face brighten.

Shawn's return smile was smug but brief. He looked toward Jenny. "You can choose the animals you'd like to work on," he said. "And maybe one of these days your mama and I can talk about the animals, too." He raised a light brown brow at Kelley, then turned his back and led Jenny from the room.

Kelley watched with bemusement and delight.

"Wow!" Marge joined her, grinning after the man and child as they walked into the adjoining playroom. "He's something, isn't he? Even Jenny is responding to him."

"He's something, all right," Kelley agreed. "He...well, he doesn't strike me as the typical day-care worker. Do you know his background?"

"Sure," Marge replied. "He was in the military—army, I think. He got out after a couple of hitches and is now in college studying child psychology. He wants to work with kids, so he's here earning a little money and learning about children on a school internship.''

''I see,'' Kelley said, though she was puzzled. He didn't seem the type. But obviously she was wrong.

Maybe one day she would take him up on that offer to have coffee in the cafeteria—so they could discuss his drawing talent, and the way he worked with kids.

Now, though, it was time to leave the child-care center.

This morning seemed to be the start of a good day.

IT CONTINUED THAT WAY, too, for a while.

She ran into Juan Cortes, who gave her a hearty, ''Good morning.'' She'd noticed the usual treats in the KidClub, so she thanked the janitor but reiterated her offer to bring some soon.

Next, she passed hospital administrator Louis Paxler on his way to his office. He actually managed a civil greeting.

Then the day began to deteriorate. She saw her ex-husband at the nurse's station talking with Cheryl Marten. They both seemed engrossed in conversation, and Kelley attempted to slip by unseen.

No such luck. ''Good morning, Kelley,'' Randall said in his usual contemptuous, booming voice.

A couple of nurses seated behind the tall U-shaped desk looked up in interest. Damn. They had an audience.

''Good morning,'' Kelley said neutrally.

''Which patients are you seeing here today?'' Randall had turned to face her. As usual, he was dressed immaculately in a pristine white lab jacket, a stethoscope around his neck. His silvery hair was combed as perfectly as an actor on a set playing a doctor's might be.

None of your business. ''A couple of influenza cases and an infection.''

"Take care that they survive," he said in mock concern.

Kelley's chest constricted. She'd done all she could to help those poor influenza patients who'd died several months ago, yet she knew Randall was a major source of the rumors that she'd messed up.

She'd told herself over and over that he was wrong.

But if so, why did so many people listen to him?

"They'll be fine, thanks, Randall," she said coolly, not rising to his bait.

"I'm sure," he said.

Cheryl smirked over her shoulder. Kelley could have smacked her. She was the one who had left little Jenny alone the night of the fire, then had lied about it. Implicated Kelley.

"If something happens to them," Cheryl said, "I've got a friend in the fire department. I'll alert him that our records department is in jeopardy again."

Oh, Lord. Kelley had heard that more than once, too— that she'd set the records room on fire to destroy the charts that would reveal what she'd done wrong in her treatment of those patients.

There was just one little flaw to that reasoning…but she hadn't revealed it to anyone.

For one thing, it would have sounded defensive.

For another, she would be revealing something that she actually *had* done wrong.

Without saying another word, Kelley hurried down the hall toward her first patient's room.

And ignored the murmuring behind her.

THAT EVENING, AS HE prepared to leave KidClub for the day, Shawn was damned disappointed.

Of course he would be. He'd been trying to think of a

way to talk to his chief suspect, Dr. Kelley Stanton, alone, and she hadn't been the one to pick up her daughter.

He should have been pleased that he'd gotten the opportunity to meet her ex-husband.

The condescending ass. Randall Stanton hadn't been alone, either. Nurse Cheryl Marten had been with him.

"I'm going to leave now, Shawn." Marge Ralston's vivacious voice interrupted his thoughts.

He turned. "Are all the kids gone?"

She nodded, and her dark curls bounced round her pretty, animated face. "Yes, we're the last ones here." She looked cute, cleaned up without the usual kid-proof smock over her knit top. She hesitated, then said, "I'm going to grab a bite to eat on the way home. Care to join me?"

"Another time." He flashed her a friendly smile. She was a chatty woman, and he figured he had already gotten from her all she knew about the flu epidemic and the fire in the records room.

Which amounted to zilch.

"Okay." She looked disappointed. But though she would probably be good company, he knew better than to date someone when on assignment.

Unless she was part of the assignment. Like Kelley...

"You'll lock up when you leave?" she asked.

He nodded. "See you tomorrow."

He wasn't ready to leave the hospital yet. He needed more information, and not just reports generated by people officially on the investigation, no matter how competently they had handled it so far. He needed to get a feel for what had happened.

It was what he was good at.

Yet it had been awhile. He would have to prepare himself for what he would find. What he *wouldn't* find. And the way his own damned gut always twisted into knots at arson fire sites.

Once he was sure Marge was gone, he headed down the empty hall.

SINCE THE FIRE, Kelley hadn't trusted Randall to pick up Jenny when he said he would, though she called to remind him.

As a result, she found herself on her way to KidClub late that evening. Later than anyone should be there.

As late as it had been the night of the fire, when Jenny had been there alone....

"No," she whispered aloud. Her daughter wouldn't be there. Though Randall had manufactured an excuse for not having retrieved Jenny himself that night, surely not even he would be stupid enough to forget about her now. Or to send his beloved, lying assistant Cheryl to fetch his daughter.

In any event, Kelley would make certain no one was around.

That no one had left Jenny.

When Kelley reached the closed door of the child-care center, she tried it. It was locked. She stood still and listened, just in case. She heard nothing from inside. No whimpers from outside. No menacing crackles or crashes.

Except... There was a noise from the direction of the former records center.

Even after six weeks, the area was still cordoned off with yellow tape demanding that no one enter. Kelley had heard that, though experts on fire and water damage repair had made recommendations, reconstruction would not begin until the fire department and the insurance company gave the go-ahead. The walls, or what remained of them, were covered by plywood sheets. One sheet was now a door, kept locked at all times.

But Kelley had heard a sound from that area.

Could the arsonist have returned to the scene of the crime?

Not likely, but *someone* was there.

Carefully, she crept down the hall.

And stopped. Inhaled sharply. The door was ajar. Slowly, quietly, Kelley ducked under the yellow tape. Without opening the door further, she looked inside.

A man with a flashlight stood in the middle of the damaged but otherwise empty room. He didn't move. In a moment, when her eyes adjusted to the dimness, Kelley could make out who it was.

Shawn Jameson.

What was he doing here? The psych student hadn't even worked at Gilpin at the time of the fire. He couldn't be the arsonist. Could he?

She watched for a long moment. His shoulders were hunched, as if he was in pain. He remained very still.

She wanted to approach him.

He aimed his flashlight at the blackened floor. Knelt and touched it. Inhaled deeply, as if absorbing the now-faint odor of burned building materials and paper.

Though she felt immobilized, Kelley must have made a sound, for he abruptly stood and stared right at her.

She took the offensive and pulled the door open farther. "What are you doing here?"

"What are *you* doing here?" he countered. At first, she thought she glimpsed raw fury in his eyes. But it must have been a trick in the dimness, for his gaze was flat.

"I heard something and thought I'd better check it out," she said.

"Sorry," he said. "I heard about this fire in the news a

few weeks back. I was curious, so I figured I'd take a peek.''

His words were light, but Kelley sensed something behind them. Frustration? Anger? Pain?

Definitely lies.

''I don't suppose you'd like to get that cup of coffee now, would you?'' he asked.

To her surprise, she wanted to say yes. And yet—she felt a pang of unease. ''Maybe tomorrow,'' she replied noncommittally. When it would be daylight. Plenty of people around.

And she would have had time to prepare herself for a conversation with this very disconcerting man. There were some questions she definitely wanted him to answer.

''Tomorrow,'' he confirmed. ''See you then, Kelley. It's okay to call you Kelley, isn't it?''

She nodded automatically, then wished she hadn't. Being on a first name basis with Shawn eliminated a barrier between them. One she suspected she would miss.

He brushed past and left her standing there, alone in the burned out, empty room, lit only from the hallway behind her.

Tomorrow? She didn't really need those answers. She could always make up an excuse to put off their meeting. Put it off forever.

Yet she wondered, as she hustled out the door, if she would.

NIGHTTIME.

The arsonist stood alone, outside the administrative wing of Gilpin Hospital, and looked up at the stars.

It was better to look at them far from here, without the bright city lights of Denver interfering. There were a lot of fascinating things in the sky that couldn't be seen here.

But Denver was still home.

And on this side of the building, at this hour, there were few office lights to disturb the darkness.

The arsonist liked the night, even here. When ambulance sirens weren't shrieking to herald yet another serious case requiring emergency attention, the area around Gilpin Hospital was quiet, with only traffic sounds interrupting the stillness.

This was a time when things could be done in darkness.

Without being seen.

Like setting fires, when necessary.

Fires like the very successful one that had destroyed the Gilpin Hospital records center.

That task had been a pleasure as well as a duty. The arsonist had enjoyed watching the room burn, all the while anticipating the money to come for that job.

But several weeks later, the job wasn't over yet. Too many loose ends.

Like Dr. Kelley Stanton.

There were things she knew. Things she didn't realize she knew...yet.

But she had to be neutralized, in case she recognized them.

If discrediting her was effective, so much the better. It was certainly the least messy way.

If not...well, there were many kinds of accidents that could occur around a hospital.

The arsonist would keep an eye on her. Listen to her, and to what was being said about her.

Report it, when asked.

And, when ordered, the arsonist would act quickly. Efficiently.

Effectively.

Again.

Chapter Four

Shawn had a major need to kick someone's butt. Preferably his own.

Of course he'd had to visit the scene of the Gilpin fire, and as quickly as possible. He'd done the right thing, waited until it was late and everyone had left—or so he'd thought.

But he'd still nearly blown his cover.

Shawn Jameson, child-care worker, had no business being in that burned-out room. And of all the damned bad luck, his number one suspect, the lovely Dr. Kelley Stanton, had been the one to catch him there.

Since he hadn't planned his examination of the site, hadn't been in there long, he hadn't even gotten much useful information, just initial impressions and the room's layout.

Not something he wanted to admit to Colleen that night.

One way or another, though, he would talk to his lady boss. Like last night, she'd probably call if she didn't hear from him soon enough.

He pulled his blue SUV out of the hospital parking lot, spinning his wheels like a demon driver. Out of cussedness, he drove around the block. Past the hospital's admin wing.

Past the place where he'd nearly blown his damned assignment.

He spotted someone standing on the sidewalk below the area where the fire had been, but he couldn't make out, in the dimness, whether the person was male or female. Whoever it was hurried away, as if wanting not to be seen.

Damned imaginative fool, Shawn chastised himself. More likely, the person was just being smart, getting out of the way of the loco driver. He took a deep breath, pushed the button to open the window beside him, and slowed down.

Denver was far from a sleepy city. There were popular restaurants in the downtown area, people strolling sidewalks along the Sixteenth Street Mall, enjoying this cosmopolitan western town.

Shawn had enjoyed it, too, when he'd first gotten here and joined the Denver Fire Department as a firefighter. Later, he'd moved into the Fire Investigation Bureau.

"That's what you do, smart guy," he told himself aloud as he turned a busy, well-lit corner. "You investigate fires."

But for the first few minutes in the Gilpin Hospital records room, he'd felt like a scared kid again. He'd stood there. Remembering.

He wasn't sure whether Kelley had seen him then, all his damnable emotions on display. He prayed now that he'd been alone at that moment. He'd needed to be alone.

But she'd at least seen him start to scrutinize the residue of that scorched room, and that wasn't much better. It wasn't something children's caregivers did. And the impression he made on Kelley was all-important.

On impulse, he pulled into the nearly empty parking lot of a minimall. He pulled out the cell phone stashed in the glove compartment and called Colleen.

"I made some progress today," he told her, watching a kid walk by eating a hot dog from the nearby convenience store.

It was the truth. Just not all of it.

"I started my examination of the arson site. I continued my inquiries. And I got our number one suspect to agree to talk to me tomorrow." That was something he looked forward to. A lot.

"Good job," Colleen said. "I'll be interested in your next report."

Me, too, Shawn thought. He was determined it would be a lot better than this one.

THE NEXT MORNING, Kelley visited Jenny after Randall left her at KidClub. Fortunately, Jenny, though teary-eyed, didn't create a scene when she left.

Unfortunately, Shawn Jameson bulldozed her into setting a time and place for their impending meeting.

If she hadn't had her mind on that discomfiting situation, she might not have felt so blindsided by what happened later that morning. But when she walked into the room of the third patient on her rounds, she was taken aback to see Dr. Madelyne Younger beside her patient's bed. The other bed in the room was empty, so there was no mistaking who Madelyne was there to see.

"Good morning," Kelley said, but her eyes asked her friend and colleague if anything was wrong.

"Hi, Dr. Stanton," Madelyne said cheerfully. "Just came in to see how Tom's doing today."

The patient, Tom Layton, had been admitted for emergency treatment of an aneurysm a week earlier. His surgeon had been Randall.

Occasionally, despite all the care taken at the hospital, surgical patients like Tom developed infections. That was one of Kelley's specialties—caring for the infrequent post-surgical infection cases. She had put Tom on a regimen of antibiotics that seemed to be working.

"And how are you doing?" Kelley smiled at him.

Tom Layton was a middle-aged man who had indulged too much in his passion for eating and had apparently believed that joining a gym satisfied his need to exercise, whether or not he ever went there. His small brown eyes were morose, but Kelley thought that might be the way he always looked. "Better, but—" He looked toward Madelyne as if for assistance.

Kelley's heart sank. She knew what was going on. "You've requested a second opinion from Dr. Younger," she said. "An excellent idea."

It had happened more often than usual in the past weeks…since the fire. She had no idea how the rumors circulating the hospital made their way to patients' ears, but she could guess.

Yet why would Randall stoop that low? It could bite him in his own wallet. If her reputation disintegrated because of allegations that she had not treated patients properly, her medical practice would disintegrate, too. Then Randall would have to pay more in child support to make sure their daughter was properly provided for.

"Tom's family has asked me to take over his care." Madelyne's voice was uncharacteristically modulated, and the distress in her eyes told Kelley that she felt embarrassed.

But the reality was that Kelley had been replaced. Again.

"Well, then," she said too cheerfully, making a note on the chart on her clipboard. "I wish you all the best, Mr. Layton. And if there are any questions I can answer for Dr. Younger or you, I'll be glad to." She turned and left the room.

Of course Louis Paxler would be right there, by the nearest nurse's station. "Dr. Stanton, may I see you for a minute?" he called.

"Sure," she replied. "After I powder my nose." As if she ever refreshed her makeup while on rounds. Today, she wished she carried an under-eye concealer with her, to hide the redness. But that would not dispel the threatening tears.

She hadn't felt so upset the first couple of times this had happened. But now…

It took her a few minutes to calm herself. When she finally left the rest room, Paxler was gone. "He said to call later and set up an appointment," a duty nurse told Kelley. "He wants to talk to you."

"Thanks," she said. She could guess what the administrator wanted to talk about.

She could conveniently forget to call. Or get too busy. Or— She glanced up at the clock on the wall. It was almost eleven. Darn! That was when she had agreed to meet Shawn for coffee.

She'd figured, when she gave in to his insistence, that she could deal with coffee one time. Make it quick.

Maybe even learn what he had really been doing in the burned-out records room last night.

But now she felt too upset to talk to anyone.

Particularly Shawn. Not that it mattered, but she didn't want to appear disheveled and weepy to him.

With a sigh, she headed toward the cafeteria.

Not to have coffee with Shawn, but to tell him she was too busy.

SHAWN DIDN'T BUY IT. Or maybe it was simply that he was so damned disappointed.

Hell, it didn't matter if she didn't want his company. He

had a job to do. He kept his voice neutral. "Another time, then."

They stood just inside the doorway to the cafeteria, where he had been waiting. She had arrived a minute late, her usual clipboard under one arm—only to tell him she hadn't time for coffee with him.

"Sure." She seemed relieved when he acted so understanding. "Another time."

To hear her over the roar of voices in the crowded eating area, he had moved close to her. Close enough that he could inhale her clean female fragrance.

Stop getting distracted, Jameson, he commanded himself.

He focused instead on the way she looked. Beautiful, as usual, of course. But there was something else, as well.

"Is anything wrong, Kelley?"

Her expressive brown eyes held a stricken look, as if someone had dealt her a blow. One the lovely doctor seemed determined to be brave about, but she was clearly having a tough time.

He wanted to know what was bothering her.

"Sorry if I seem preoccupied," she replied with a small shrug of one slender shoulder, "but I'm concerned about a case." Her smile looked forced. "Doctors worry about patients, like you worry about the kids in your care." Her soft auburn brows rose as if she expected him to confirm his professional concerns.

"You've got that right." Actually, he did worry about the kids—and whether what he did would cause them to kill each other. Or him. So far, so good. No one in his charge had suffered an injury worse than a scraped knee.

Kelley stood stiffly beside him in her tailored white lab jacket. A dark skirt peeked out at the bottom. Who'd have thought that a starchy hospital uniform would hint at ripe curves beneath it? Her low heels made the top of her head reach nearly to his mouth. He could have leaned forward and kissed the top of her auburn tresses, if he'd wanted to. But what he wanted was to keep his mind on business, not on how much this lady doctor turned him on.

This lady doctor who might have set a fire to cover her butt—or someone else's.

"This afternoon, then," he said too gruffly, then added, to pump incentive into her agreement, "We need to discuss Jenny."

"She's all right today, isn't she?" Kelley demanded quickly. Shawn felt an uncharacteristic pang of guilt gouge through him as the obvious pain in Kelley's expression deepened. He hadn't intended to add to her worries.

He just wanted to find out what they were.

"Better than ever," he assured her, hoping he was right. The kid was definitely cute. Loved to draw "an'mals." And he'd found he enjoyed drawing her every kind of "an'mal" she could think of. Even some she'd never heard of. But he hadn't the slightest idea of what was normal for a three-year-old.

"I—er, for my internship, I've been told to get to know the parents of the kids in my charge. Discuss their children's strengths and weaknesses, what I can do to help their learning process, that kind of thing." Whew! He'd been reaching for that. But wasn't it the sort of claptrap that real child-care workers said?

"Of course." Kelley glanced down at her clipboard, flipped through the pages. "I'm not really sure of my schedule, but maybe I can drop by KidClub between two and two-thirty. I'll have a better idea then if I can fit in a chat."

"Fine."

She gave him a small smile that her eyes failed to mirror,

then turned and headed away, leaving him totally unsatisfied with how their meeting had gone. He'd have to do better.

Well, he had some free time now, since he'd arranged for enough to have coffee with her. He sure as hell couldn't go snooping in the burned-out records room at this hour. The next best thing to talking with his chief suspect would be to watch her. Closely.

A surge of something he did not want to recognize shot through him. Sexual heat. A fire almost as inappropriate as arson.

Sure, he would watch the extraordinary Dr. Stanton. Learn all he could about her.

Use it against her, if appropriate.

Against her... That had a nice ring to it. He laughed aloud at his own folly, then winked when he met the eye of a sweet-looking nurse who stood near him. She smiled, but he did not follow up on the flirtation.

He had work to do.

SHAWN PICKED OUT SOME snacks to carry as he wandered the halls. If Kelley spotted him, he'd say he'd been sent back to the cafeteria for the food and took the long way back to KidClub.

Of course, it took so long to pay for the stuff that he wasn't sure he could find her. Fortunately, he spotted her talking to a janitor in a crowded hall near the elevator on the main floor. Her back was to him. Drawing closer, he used the opportunity to study her.

The janitor, whose name badge said he was Juan Cortes, was studying her, too. His smile was wide, his look adoring. If Shawn was any judge of such things—and he was— the guy had a crush on her.

Shawn suddenly had an urge to slug the man.

"Friday," Kelley was saying. "That will be our new day to bring morning treats to KidClub, okay, Juan? Jenny will be thrilled. I'll let her help peel the fruit. Better yet, she can be the one to dip the slices in lemon juice to keep them fresh."

"You really don't need to bother, Dr. Stanton."

"It's no bother," Kelley said.

The janitor pushed his cart away just as an elevator bell dinged, and Kelley turned—toward Shawn.

He forced a grin and lifted the bag. "Emergency afternoon rations for KidClub."

He did not get on an elevator immediately but waited until she entered a car. He watched the display above its door after it closed. The car stopped on several floors. One would lead to the hall to the administrative wing. Others would take her to patients' rooms.

Stupid idea, Jameson, he told himself. Surreptitious surveillance on a suspect didn't work well in hospital corridors. Interrogation was more promising.

Maybe.

He would have to convince Kelley this afternoon that she did have time to meet with him.

In the meantime, he'd continue his investigation in other ways.

ON HER WAY TO Louis Paxler's office, Kelley felt as if each footstep was one pace closer to doom.

She hadn't forgotten that the hospital administrator had commanded her to call for an appointment, but she'd planned to put it off as long as possible.

But he had left a message at her office that she was to see him immediately. Without consulting her, he had even insisted that the receptionist she shared with three other doctors reschedule a couple of patients.

She was not looking forward to this. She looked down at the pager on her pocket. *Beep, damn you.* But it remained silent.

When she reached Paxler's office, she was ushered in immediately by his receptionist, a no-nonsense older woman named Hilda. Paxler was not alone.

"Ah, Dr. Stanton," he said in a booming, cheerful voice. His suit jacket was buttoned.

Kelley took a deep breath. This meeting must be important.

"Please, have a seat." He gestured expansively toward one of the two chairs facing his vast oak desk.

The other was occupied by a gray-haired woman with a square jaw, dangling gold earrings, and a scowl aimed at Kelley. Kelley couldn't place her, but the woman looked familiar.

"Do you remember Mrs. Borand?" Paxler asked.

Borand. Oh, yes—the wife of a former patient. Kelley had treated Ben Borand for an infection after his extensive cardiac bypass surgery. The poor man had nearly died, but fortunately the treatment she prescribed had ultimately been effective. He had been effusive in his thanks when finally released to go home.

"Of course I remember Mrs. Borand," Kelley said with a smile. "How are you? And how is Ben doing?"

"He's well now, thank you." The woman's voice was curt, and she quickly turned from Kelley to face Louis.

The administrator's mouth still smiled, but his thin brows, beneath wire-rimmed glasses, were knit fretfully. He ran fingers through the edge of his dark brown hair and let the palm of his hand cup his loose jowls for an instant. The gesture showed a nervousness uncharacteristic of the man.

And that made Kelley nervous.

"Dr. Stanton, Mrs. Borand is here as a courtesy," Paxler

said. "She and her husband are planning to sue Gilpin Hospital for negligence in his treatment here."

Kelley felt the blood drain from her face. She knew now why she had been summoned.

Once again, she was about to be blamed for incompetence.

It's not true, she wanted to cry out. But how could she know for certain until she heard the claim and reviewed the files?

She recalled Cheryl Marten's nasty words from that morning regarding files. *If something happens to them, I've got a friend in the fire department. I'll alert him that our records department is in jeopardy again.*

"If Ben had received adequate treatment—" Etta Borand interrupted Kelley's thoughts with a voice that grated at her nerves like a shrill car alarm "—that terrible infection would have been dealt with quickly, and he'd have been out of here quicker and suffered a lot less pain."

Kelley hoped her expression reflected peace, sympathy—and a detachment she did not feel.

"Do you have anything to say, Dr. Stanton?" Louis Paxler demanded. He wasn't smiling now. In fact, his thick lower lip trembled as if he were outraged.

With dignity, Kelley stood and faced them both. "I am sorry Mr. Borand endured discomfort. Despite our efforts, infection does set in from time to time. Fortunately, he responded to the treatment. I do not know any reason to claim fault in how his case was handled."

With a nod in the general direction of both of them, Kelley left the room.

Only when she had found her way into the rest room and ascertained that she was alone did she lock herself in a stall and collapse against the wall. Shaking so hard she could barely stand, she began to cry.

Chapter Five

Shawn had been at Gilpin Hospital long enough to suspect the origin of at least some of the allegations against the beautiful Dr. Kelley Stanton. Maybe all of them, true or not.

He strode quickly through the bustling, pastel-painted halls toward the high-rise medical office building connected to the hospital, boot heels clomping on the polished linoleum floor.

His mind wrapped around his questions for Dr. Randall Stanton. Sure, Kelley's ex-husband probably had an ax to grind. Maybe a tool chest full of axes that, given an opportunity, he'd gladly wield against his former wife. Figuratively, of course.

But while Shawn considered that clichés often had a basis in reality, another came to mind. One that was Shawn's very own motto: Where there was smoke, there was fire.

Sure, Randall might have been looking for reasons to discredit the ex-wife against whom resentments may have simmered for years. But that didn't mean the reasons did not exist.

While Shawn was at it, he would learn if Randall had any idea what was bothering his ex today. He was determined to learn what had sucked the blood from Kelley's too-pale complexion and thrust a haunted look into those gorgeous brown eyes.

He almost growled in frustration when the receptionist at Randall's medical office informed him that the doctor was in surgery for the rest of the morning.

He felt a crocodile smile emerge, though, when, back in the hall, he nearly ran into nurse Cheryl Marten. Shawn had been at KidClub last night when Cheryl had come in to pick up Jenny. She'd made it clear she was the esteemed Dr. Randall Stanton's agent, with authority to sign his daughter out. Before Shawn had given up the kid to her, though, Randall had joined them.

That had all occurred before Kelley had caught Shawn in the destroyed file room.

"Ms. Marten," he said now, "glad you're here. I was hoping to speak to Dr. Stanton about Jenny, but he isn't available. I know you're close to both of them."

She glanced up from beneath lashes too long and thick to be real. He didn't notice her move, yet it seemed suddenly as if her bustline was displayed more prominently at the open neck of her colorful nurse's smock. "Of course Randall is very dear to me," she said. Then, obviously as an afterthought, she added, "His daughter, too."

Shawn felt only contempt that this woman could profess closeness to one man while flirting with another. But he needed to talk to her. She was undoubtedly the second-best source of information about Kelley, after Randall.

According to the information Shawn had received from Colleen, there was an ongoing dispute regarding the night of the Gilpin Hospital fire. Cheryl Marten had signed Jenny out from KidClub. No one questioned that. But there was plenty of uncertainty about what happened next. Had Cheryl left the three-year-old there alone? Or had Kelley dropped the ball and neglected to pick up her daughter...until after she had set the fire?

Shawn stopped himself from shaking his head. No matter what he might believe about Dr. Stanton, Kelley endangering her child was the least credible possibility.

"Is something wrong with Jenny?" Cheryl asked, bringing Shawn's thoughts back to her.

"No, but I'd like you to answer some questions. You know I'm here on a college internship? I'm studying child psychology and want to learn as much about each child as possible. Do you have time to join me for a cup of coffee?" He looked into her pale blue eyes and grinned, though flirting with this woman scraped at every nerve in his body.

"Well..." She glanced at the oversize watch on her wrist, then back at Shawn. "Sure." Her feline smile revealed small but perfect teeth.

He followed her sashay through the office tower and into the crowded hospital halls. In a few minutes, they were seated at a table in the cafeteria—right where Shawn had hoped to interrogate Kelley that morning. He sighed as he took a sip of the coffee into which he had poured only enough cream to keep it from being starkly brown.

Cheryl had chosen a big, foamy cappuccino. After taking a drink, she smiled at him. "What would you like to know?"

She didn't refer to Jenny. Was she hoping he would ask something about *her?* Her ample measurements? Her phone number?

He had been a private detective for a few years before ICU had formed its covert Colorado Confidential arm. Long before that, as a child whose sole defense, besides drawing caricatures, was to hide emotions, he'd learned not to react to anything—getting kicked out of his latest foster home, whatever. Not revealing his real thoughts was a piece of cake.

He aimed one of his most disarming smiles at her. "I'm new here, Ms. Marten, so though I've seen you pick Jenny up, I don't know if you ever drop her off at KidClub in the morning."

"Call me Cheryl," she said, her grin even more come-hither.

Shawn responded by drawing a little closer across the table. But not too close.

"Sometimes after Jenny has spent the night with her father," she continued, "he asks me to drop her off."

"Then you know she isn't always...well, happy to be left." He didn't mention that Jenny had improved considerably in the couple of days since he had started showing her how to draw "an'mals." A small sense of pride shot through him, but he squelched it. No sense becoming too confident just because the child had been distracted for a day or two. Who knew how she'd be in the future?

Besides, this was just a segue into a more important discussion.

"Yes," Cheryl said, "I know she's sometimes a little br—er, she's a little reluctant."

At the hard look on Cheryl's face, Shawn filled in the word she'd censored. Brat. He swallowed his impulse to tell the woman off. Jenny might have difficult moments, but the cute kid was hardly a brat. And she had been through an ordeal.

Had maybe even seen her mother set a fire....

Of course, having met Kelley, he found that hard to believe.

Hard, but not impossible.

"I gathered that Jenny has had a difficult time for such a young child," he said. "Her parents are divorced..." He allowed his voice to trail off, waiting for Cheryl to pick up the line and run with it.

Her fingers were tipped with long red nails that contrasted with her white coffee mug. She clenched the cup so hard that her hands paled nearly to match it. "Yes," she said coolly. "They are. Randall has been so patient with that bitch—I'm sorry." She caught Shawn's gaze, then looked down as if she rued what she'd said. Her tone as she continued, though, suggested otherwise. "The thing is, she's still in his life, whether he likes it or not. She's Jenny's mom, even if she's a horrible one, and—"

Here was his opening! "I heard something about her abandoning Jenny at KidClub the night of the fire…?" He shook his head as if totally disgusted at the idea. Which he was. But he suspected that the disgust should be aimed at the woman sitting before him.

She ran her fingers through her short blond hair. "That's right. And she had the nerve to say *I* was the one who left Jenny." Rage turned her pale blue eyes into hard, sparkling nuggets.

"Really?"

"She still hasn't admitted that she and I spoke earlier that evening. I told her I would sign Jenny out but that she had to pick her up, since Randall and I had plans."

"Mmm-hmm," Shawn agreed noncommittally. "I heard that. And there are also rumors that she set the fire in the records room."

"I wouldn't put it past her," Cheryl spat.

But that was another innuendo, not an eyewitness account. It wasn't something Shawn could accept as a statement of fact. "To hide something?" he asked.

"She killed some patients, did you hear that?" Cheryl had started to breathe audibly. Her spite was getting the better of her. But she apparently realized she might be going too far. "Er—of course, the flu patients who died here just might not have reached the hospital on time. They were pretty sick. And it's not really clear why some got worse. But there are other patients, even now…" She tapered off.

"Really?" he prompted. "Are there patients now that Dr. Stanton might be…well, not treating as she should?"

"I shouldn't tell you, but just today a family threw her off a case. Called in another doctor to treat a man for a postop infection since they didn't trust Dr. Stanton's judgment."

Ah! That might explain why Kelley seemed so upset. On the other hand, doctors probably got taken off cases a lot. Her reaction could still have other causes.

Could be that wasn't all she was dealing with that day.

"Anyway, enough about her. Tell me about you," Cheryl said in a near purr. She leaned over the table almost enough to rest her cleavage upon it.

I'm an undercover government agent, he thought, *and I'll throw that pretty little butt you like to flaunt in prison for child endangerment, if I find you left Jenny alone when the fire was set. And if you set it—well, your butt'll be toast.*

But he said with a glance at his watch and an apologetic grin, "Sorry, but I have to get back to KidClub. We'll have to leave that to another day." *Like, when I figure out the right questions to get you to spill your guts.*

"Any time," said nurse Cheryl Marten with an I-want-to-kiss-you smile in return.

KELLEY SAT ALONE in her compact office. Her metal desk was cluttered with charts to be updated and files to be reviewed. Her next patient wasn't due for another half hour.

If that patient didn't fire her, too. Or the other half dozen patients she was to see that day.

I am a good doctor, she reassured herself as she reached

for the phone to listen to messages. They were all from other doctors, nurses and pharmaceutical companies.

None were from other patients leveling claims of incompetence against her.

And none was the return phone call she had been awaiting for weeks now, in response to her own multiple messages.

If she was really a good doctor, would she be in this kind of a mess? Why did everything seem to be going wrong?

She stood and walked to the window, where she stared out without registering the view of the street.

She had been removed from one case today. Another patient was suing her for incompetence.

"Damn." She returned to her squeaking chair and glanced around the room. It was cramped and in need of renovation, like her examination room. The offices of a doctor with no seniority, though she had been on staff for several years. She'd planned to leave when she and Randall had split, but she hadn't had time to look for something else.

And lately, she hadn't dared to make waves for fear of finding herself on staff at no hospital at all.

She hadn't tried to locate the files on Ben Borand's case yet. Undoubtedly, if they hadn't been destroyed in the fire, they were in Louis Paxler's office. Or in the hospital's attorney's office being reviewed for the lawsuit that would be served on them any minute, if Etta Borand was to be believed.

And Kelley had little doubt that the angry, vindictive woman was serious.

Had Kelley done something wrong that had extended Mr. Borand's treatment, his pain?

''No,'' she whispered aloud. She had become a doctor to help people, not hurt them.

But that hadn't stopped two patients from dying, all those weeks ago, during the influenza epidemic in which the ill had been rushed here from Silver Rapids.

Was there something more she should have done? Something she *shouldn't?*

Grimly, she approached the four-drawer file cabinet in the corner of her office. She reached into the top drawer and into a folder labeled ''Myles,'' her maiden name. At the bottom was a single key. She pulled it out and returned to her desk.

After unlocking the bottom right-hand drawer, she pulled out the file folders that might, somehow, hold the secret to her future.

The files regarding the Silver Rapids patients, including the two who had died.

Files that should have perished in the fire, but hadn't.

Kelley had skimmed through them in the intervening weeks, hoping to find something obvious to explain everything.

Instead, they had generated only more questions—very puzzling questions she hadn't yet had time to resolve, assuming that resolution was even possible.

Now, maybe it was time to study them.

She looked at the name on the first. Peg Ahlers. One of the two elderly patients who had died.

Kelley remembered the wizened, silver-haired woman as weak yet cheerful. Until the end. Her symptoms had been similar to the others'—nasty, debilitating influenzalike symptoms that came upon her suddenly—high fever, cough, runny nose and muscle aches.

When Mrs. Ahlers had come in, Kelley had been swamped with treating Silver Rapids patients who had already been admitted. She'd tested Mrs. Ahlers the same way, with nasal swabs sent to the lab to check for viruses. A virus similar to influenza type A was found in all samples.

But Kelley hadn't waited for test results to start treatment. She had prescribed a common antibiotic. It wouldn't help in the event of viral infections, which was what she had suspected. Still, it was standard treatment and could prevent further infection in a patient whose resistance was lowered. When the virus was discovered, as she'd anticipated, Kelley had prescribed an antiviral medication, as well.

She'd been most concerned about a patient who was pregnant—Holly, a member of the esteemed Langworthy family, though it was her pregnancy, not her ancestry, that mattered to Kelley. But Holly had improved more quickly than Mrs. Ahlers, who, like most others, had gotten worse. The severity of their chills and their terrible headaches hadn't seemed normal for influenza. Nor had their gastrointestinal symptoms. On a hunch based on the symptoms, Kelley had had blood drawn for IFA tests or indirect immunoflourescence assays. The IFA tests would show antibodies for a number of harmful microbes that might cause such symptoms. She'd been surprised when nothing unusual had shown up. Still, she had changed the medications, even increased the dosages within acceptable limits.

Most of the patients had begun to improve. Not Mrs. Ahlers, or the elderly gentleman who had also developed pneumonia and died.

Was there something she had overlooked? She sat very still and began to read Mrs. Ahlers's file—every word.

Until—"Mommy!"

Her door was flung open. Jenny rushed in, arms outstretched in her pink blouse over rose-colored jeans.

Behind her was Shawn Jameson. His shirt was beige, his jeans rugged blue and he wore his usual vest and cowboy boots. His lazy half grin suggested he was pleased to have given Kelley a delightful surprise—her daughter's presence.

And his. For Kelley couldn't help the rush of pleasure that pulsed through her at the sight of the handsome child-care attendant whose presence filled her tiny office.

"Hi, Jenny." She gave her daughter a hug. "Hi, Shawn."

As his gaze swept over her, she felt a rush of heat that had nothing to do with the closeness in her office. She glanced down, wondering if she imagined the interest in his gaze. Surely there was nothing sexy about her dark skirt and white blouse. When she looked up again, Shawn's eyes were not on her, but on the paperwork on her desk.

Papers that were no longer supposed to exist.

Oh, Lord. Trying to appear nonchalant, she swept the pages into the folder, then returned the folder to her desk drawer, which she locked.

"So who wants to go to the cafeteria for orange juice?" she asked brightly, hoping she had time before her next patient arrived.

"Me," Jenny piped up.

"Me, too," Shawn said, but there was a strange look on his face.

Kelley told herself she had mistaken the look as she left the room behind Shawn, her daughter's hand in hers.

Why would a child-care worker care about hospital files?

SHAWN SIPPED HIS JUICE slowly, as if it were a screwdriver laced with vodka. And watched, across the table in the crowded, noisy cafeteria, lovely, auburn-haired Kelley Stanton in animated conversation with her daughter.

Too animated. As if she realized that if she stopped talking, he might start asking questions.

"And if you'd like," she was saying loudly enough to be heard over the throngs of people grabbing afternoon snacks, "we can rent a movie this weekend."

"Okay, Mommy. A cartoon one. One with lots of an'mals in it, okay?" The little girl sat on the edge of her seat. She was dressed in a frilly pink outfit that day. She looked damn cute, with that big smile on her face.

"Fine, sweetheart," Kelley said. "Did you have enough juice?"

"Yes. And we can invite Shawn to our house to watch the an'mals, too, okay?" Jenny's face turned toward him, beaming.

Kelley's face turned toward him, too, but her smile held considerably less delight.

Big surprise. But it bothered the heck out of him.

Of course she wouldn't extend the invitation. To her, he was a lowly day-care worker.

Damn it all, the woman turned him on. Heat suffused through him as he surreptitiously looked at the slender curves outlined by her white blouse, her creamy, though pale, complexion.

She was keeping secrets. That reminder cooled his ardor more quickly than chugging his ice-filled glass of juice.

He had come to her office with Jenny because he'd figured she wouldn't throw him out with her daughter there. He had been right. He'd come with planned questions, designed to keep him looking naively curious. But within them were a few zingers that could lead to answers he needed on fires and flu bugs.

She hadn't thrown him out, but she'd made it clear she wanted him gone. Fast.

He had barely gotten a glimpse of the papers on her desk before she'd locked them in a drawer.

One he would definitely get into. Soon.

"Right, Shawn?" she asked.

Damn. He hadn't been paying attention. "Sorry." He made himself appear abashed. "I was concentrating on my orange juice. What did you say?"

"I said that Shawn is much too busy on weekends, when he's not working, to have time to see a movie with us." She looked at him levelly though her soft brown eyes seemed to contain a plea.

"What does he do, Mommy?" Jenny piped before he could respond. "Does he draw an'mals then?"

"Sometimes," he told the child. "Sometimes I watch them. I especially like cartoons that have animals in them, don't you?"

"Me, too," Jenny said.

"Well, then," Shawn said. "I heard there's an animated movie in theaters this week that stars a talking pig. Maybe all three of us can go see it."

"Yeaaay," Jenny said, standing up and clapping.

"What do you say, Mommy?" Shawn asked, looking at Kelley.

He saw the trapped expression he'd anticipated pass quickly over her face. It was replaced by irritation, then...resignation?

She did not give a direct reply. "We'll see, honey." As she gave Jenny a hug, she glared at Shawn as if daring him to say something else.

He only smiled.

"So, Shawn," she said, as if to change the subject. "Where do you go to school?"

"The University of Colorado." Shawn extracted this part

of his cover story from memory. "I'm majoring in child psychology."

"I've a friend in the psych department and know some other profs there. Who's your favorite?"

"My advisor is Dr. Wells. He's a pretty cool guy. But my favorite is Professor Anderson. Her theories on child development make a lot of sense." If Kelley asked what they were, he'd have an answer, though if she tried to dig too deep he'd have to change the subject.

Good thing Colleen was thorough in preparing her agents for assignments. And if anyone contacted Professors Wells or Anderson, they would support his story.

Of course, Shawn wasn't especially pleased that Kelley had turned the tables and was now interrogating *him*.

She was the one with things to hide.

Of course, so was he....

What could he ask, here and now, with Jenny present?

"So Kelley," he began, "I heard through the hospital grapevine that—"

"Oh, sorry," she said, reaching down to pluck her pager from her pocket. "It's vibrating me a reminder of a patient appointment. I have just enough time to walk Jenny back."

How convenient, Shawn thought. And how bogus.

The only vibration she'd felt was likely her own skin, trembling because it was *his* turn to ask questions.

The image of Kelley's smooth, tantalizing skin trembling was nearly too much to bear. "Moron," he muttered at himself as Kelley helped Jenny out of her seat. He had to clasp the icy orange juice glass in both hands before he could stand comfortably.

KELLEY WALKED JENNY back to KidClub. Shawn, too.

"See you later, Mommy," Jenny called to her.

"Yeah, see you later," Shawn said.

Kelley headed back to her office.

The man acted brazenly. As if he were a member of the family.

He hadn't invited himself to join them that weekend. Jenny had done that. But hadn't he realized it would be an imposition?

And why the heck was Kelley looking forward to their potential outing when she hadn't really agreed to it?

She'd asked him a few questions, too, to cut him off before he'd been able to return the favor.

But why didn't she believe his responses?

When she reached her office, her next patient had just arrived. Fortunately, it was a follow-up on a case from last week.

She saw several other patients, forcing herself to concentrate, to make sure that she did everything correctly in their diagnosis and treatment. But in between patients, her mind kept racing.

To Shawn Jameson. There was more to the man than a student working his way through school as a child-care worker. She was sure of it.

Too bad she didn't really know anyone in the UC psych department. Maybe she would call to ask about their grad student Shawn Jameson when she got the chance....

But even if she confirmed he wasn't a student, it wouldn't answer the biggest question of all—why was he here?

And why was he considering spending his free time with a little girl he saw every day and her divorced, rather boring mother? Never mind that she happened to find him too attractive. She wasn't about to let that show.

When she had sent her last patient on his way, Kelley sat back in her squeaking desk chair in her small office and thought.

Not about Shawn Jameson, she instructed her mind.

About Etta Borand and her claims that Kelley had prolonged her husband's illness.

About administrator Louis Paxler, who seemed to believe the woman. He should be behind Kelley, a doctor on staff at his hospital. But he clearly didn't consider her much of a doctor.

She thought about the other case she'd lost that day.

About her ex-husband Randall and his innuendoes, broadcast by his lover and sycophant, nurse Cheryl Marten.

And about the cases that had started it all—the Silver Rapids flu cases.

It was time that she poured over the files minutely, to understand what had happened.

Then she might be able to salvage her career.

At the time of the flu outbreak, she'd considered a theory and forced herself to discard it—then. But a few weeks later, a call she'd gotten from a friend, Dr. Wilson Carpenter, had sent her mind careening down the path it had barely tiptoed toward before.

Surely that possibility was too off-the-wall. She hadn't even wanted to think about it. But she *was* thinking about it, especially now. And that meant she had to study every shred of evidence for clues to convince her that stress was driving her nuts. But what if she *wasn't* crazy?

On impulse, she lifted her phone and punched in a familiar number in Silver Rapids. A number that had grown even more familiar over the last weeks because she had called it so much.

But had never gotten an answer.

As usual, the phone rang. And rang. And—

"Hello?" said a female voice.

Kelley sat up straight in her chair. "Hello." She clutched

the receiver. "This is Dr. Kelley Stanton. I'm looking for Dr. Wilson Carpenter. Who am I speaking to, please?"

"Oh, yes, Dr. Stanton. I got the messages you left on Wilson's machine."

Then why didn't you respond? Kelley wanted to ask. *And who are you?*

"I'm Deidre Krafson," the woman continued as if reading part of Kelley's thoughts. "I'm the receptionist at the medical office next door to Dr. Carpenter's, and my doctors asked me to keep an eye on things at Dr. Carpenter's while he's gone. I'm to refer medical questions to them and emergencies to the hospital."

"I see." Obviously, Deidre's instructions did not extend to getting back to a concerned friend. Kelley had been increasingly worried about Wilson and was sure her messages reflected it. It hadn't helped that his last call to her had ended so abruptly, or that he hadn't called back later to explain. "I'm glad I reached you now, Deidre. Do you know if Dr. Carpenter is all right? Where is he?"

"I really don't know. Who did you say this is?"

Trying hard not to lose her patience, Kelley identified herself again. "I'm an old friend of Dr. Carpenter's."

She *had* to talk to him. To understand what he'd tried to tell her. To run by him her own concerns, theories…and fears. He was the only one she could turn to now, for he was the only one likely to understand.

Unless she could find proof.

"Deidre, it's urgent that I speak with Dr. Carpenter."

"Do you have a medical emergency?" the woman asked. "If so, you should go to your nearest emergency room, and—"

"No!" Was she really that obtuse? Or was there some reason she feigned this ineptitude?

Kelley shook her head. Maybe she was becoming paranoid, after all that had happened.

"Sorry. No, I don't have a medical emergency. It's a…personal reason that it's very, very important that I talk to Dr. Carpenter. Can you give me his phone number?"

"I can't tell you more. I don't know where he is, and I don't think my doctors do, either. They just got an e-mail from him, asking them to keep an eye on things."

"Then, please, at least give me his e-mail address."

"Sure." Deidre rattled one off, then added, "But it won't do you any good, either. Dr. Carpenter hasn't responded to my doctors' latest e-mails."

."Thanks, Deidre." It was the same e-mail address she had for Wilson. He hadn't responded to any of her electronic messages, either.

Still, after hanging up, Kelley sent another e-mail to Wilson.

But with a sinking sensation, she realized this was probably another dead end.

Where are you, Wilson? her mind cried out. *Are you all right?*

She was afraid she wouldn't like the answer.

Chapter Six

Shawn waited until long past midnight to slip into the medical building adjoining Gilpin Hospital. The hospital staff might still be tending insomniac patients and emergencies, but no civilian would have an appointment at a doctor's office to have an ingrown toenail checked out or a wart removed.

He moved stealthily up stairs and down dimmed halls until he reached the sign that read, "Kelley Stanton, M.D., Internal Medicine." Of course the door was locked.

Of course that didn't keep him out.

Nor did he have any trouble opening her bottom desk drawer. He'd been a P.I. long enough to have lock picks for nearly every occasion.

But what did frustrate him was that, except for a checkbook, the drawer was empty. It wasn't checks he'd seen Kelley fumble with when he barged into her office with Jenny. She was hiding something, and he'd intended to learn what it was.

"Damn!" He closed the drawer.

He inspected the rest of the desk inside and out, thumbed through random folders in the file cabinet, but found nothing noteworthy. Scowling, he let himself back out of the office.

What had she done with the stuff?

At least being here this late wouldn't be a total waste. He had one more stop to make.

He headed for the administrative wing. As part of the hospital building, it was more likely to be occupied even at that hour. Fortunately, he ran into no one in the deserted corridors. But he waited near the entrance to KidClub, listening just in case. Once certain he was alone, he entered the burned-out records room.

Only when he was inside and had closed the flimsy plywood door—completely this time—did he turn on his flashlight.

He didn't honestly believe he could discover anything in the emptied room, in the dead of night, that the Fire Investigation Bureau hadn't already determined.

Still, he had to look, at a time when the lovely Dr. Kelley Stanton wouldn't burst in on him again.

She'd certainly been inquisitive today. Had he somehow blown his cover with her? If so, his assignment could still be salvageable. The direct approach might even work better with the intelligent lady doctor. *Hi, me arson investigator. You…arsonist?* Well, maybe not.

In any event, he looked forward to joining Jenny and her this weekend. It would be another avenue for studying his prey. Learning everything about his chief suspect.

The woman was frustrating him in more ways than one, damn it. He needed answers. He needed this case to be over.

He needed a brain transplant. Or at least a cold shower.

Right now, though, he had to absorb all the impressions he could, in this room where arson had wreaked destruction.

"Okay, Jameson," he whispered into the dimness. "Do your stuff."

First, he took a deep breath. The place still smelled lousy, like smoke and burnt things.

According to the report Colleen had obtained from the Denver Fire Department, they had received a 9-1-1 call around seven in the evening, from Dr. Kelley Stanton. That she called in the report did not, of course, preclude her from being the arsonist.

The firefighters had responded within ten minutes. Their primary concern was to protect life, so their first order of business was to ensure that no one remained in that wing of the building. Next step was to extinguish the fire. Fortunately, they'd done so before total evacuation was necessary.

Extinguish it? Yeah, with their equipment. Most of Gilpin was relatively new, constructed of code-compliant fire retardant materials and sprinklered. But the admin wing was the oldest part, the original hospital. Because there were no patient rooms here, the requirements might not have been enforced as stringently.

Shawn swung his light up toward the ceiling. A single sprinkler head, near a corner. Not enough to protect much more than one file cabinet. Certainly not enough for the entire room.

Next, he swung his light toward the floor. The burn pattern analysis in the report indicated that the fire had started in the center of the room. The floor was definitely blackened in the middle. As he moved the beam to the edges, not everything appeared as charred.

Fires that began in the middle of the room were unlikely to be electrical fires. Just in case, he used the flashlight beam to seek out what remained of the recessed ceiling lights. Most were still there, but their glass covers were either shattered or gone. He looked at the electrical outlets in the walls. One wall, the outer one, was now just plywood sheets, so that didn't help. Another wall was nearly decimated. The other two still stood, despite being charred. And, yes, they each had a couple of low-set electrical outlets, all intact.

The report indicated that the steel file cabinets had nearly melted. Hard to tell if their drawers had opened as the steel grew hot—or if they had been open before.

The speculation now was that the fire had been set in a couple of strategically opened drawers. That an accelerant was used. Lighter fluid.

Traces of tobacco had been found, as well as a cigarette lighter. As if the fire had been set by a careless smoker. That was why the initial take was that the fire had been an accident. Until the investigators looked more closely.

Kelley didn't smoke. But an arsonist didn't have to.

Cigarette lighters were small enough to fit in a man's pocket. Or a woman's purse.

Damn! Despite what he'd been told, Shawn didn't want Kelley to be the arsonist. She was a loving mother. A doctor who wanted to save lives, not put them at risk.

Or was that simply his fantasy?

She was suspected of medical malpractice. Cheryl Marten had even proclaimed that Kelley had been thrown off a case just the day before.

If she'd been negligent, why not hide the evidence in any way she could—like burning it up in a fire?

Growling, he continued his survey of the room. Quickly, but thoroughly. He needed to get the hell out of here.

More than that, he needed to continue to investigate. Ask questions. Interview witnesses without raising suspicions.

He had to expose the damned arsonist, whoever it was.

And if, in the end, Kelley was the guilty party?

Even when nobody was injured, *no one* should get away with setting fires.

KELLEY PULLED HER CAR into the Gilpin Hospital parking lot.

This wasn't how she had anticipated spending Saturday afternoon.

Not that she had wanted to take Shawn up on his offer to go see the latest blockbuster animated movie with Jenny. They'd made arrangements, but Kelley had had to call to cancel. Fortunately.

"Who are you kidding?" she grumbled to herself as she parked and grabbed her purse.

Her digital pager had beeped her a short while earlier with the emergency signal, and she had responded quickly. She was needed at the hospital, stat. Since it hadn't been a cardiac emergency, Randall was at home, so she'd dropped Jenny off.

She ran into the emergency room. Dotty Bailey, a longtime E.R. nurse, saw her and beckoned. She had been the one to call Kelley. "Fourth room," she said, a worried look on her face. "Looks bad. And—"

Kelley hesitated just a moment. "And what?"

"The resident on call treated her, but there's no improvement. I'm sure he did all he could, but Heather—the patient—is one of my neighbor's kids. Just graduated from college, has her whole life ahead... I want to make sure everything possible is being done. She's Dr. Younger's patient. I paged her, but she didn't respond, so I beeped you. Hope you don't mind."

"Not at all." But inside Kelley sighed. She didn't want to step on anyone's toes, particularly not Madelyne's. On the other hand, if she could help, then of course she would. "I'll go see her." Kelley tossed a smile at the older woman, who nodded. At least someone here hadn't been swayed by the rumors of Kelley's incompetence.

Or maybe it was Dotty's concern over this particular patient that made her take a chance.... No matter. Kelley would do all she could—as always.

Hurrying into the evaluation room, Kelley quickly realized the nurse hadn't overstated the situation. It did look bad.

The patient was a young lady, early twenties. Her face, beneath oily brown hair, was flushed from fever, and her eyes were glazed. Her arms lay limp on the white sheet, and Kelley noticed the red bumps covering them. What had caused the rash?

"Hi, Heather." Kelley flipped over a page on her clipboard to a fresh chart. "I'm Dr. Stanton, and I'm going to help you feel better."

The girl's thin lips twitched as if it were too much effort to smile.

"I don't have your information yet." A partial lie, for Heather Harrell's records were in a holder on the door, but Kelley wanted to start fresh. "Tell me what's wrong."

"Okay. I have mono."

"Mononucleosis?" Kelley repeated.

A slight nod. "I was feeling awful a couple of days ago. Tired, headache, a fever. I just graduated from the University of Colorado and moved back home while I look for a job, and my mom took me to Dr. Younger."

"Good choice," Kelley said. "And she diagnosed you with mono?"

Another brief nod. "She said I'd kissed too many boys." This time, the weak smile lightened her whole face, and Kelley realized the girl was probably pretty when not feeling awful.

"Yes, mono can be spread by fluids like saliva." Kelley smiled back.

"But she also said I'd just have to ride it out, that there's nothing that can be done to fix mono, only rest and treat its symptoms. So I stayed in bed, but my headache got worse, so my mom got me a stronger pain medication.''

''And what was that?''

Kelley wrote down the name of the common over-the-counter analgesic.

''And then this happened.'' Heather pointed to the rash that covered her arms. ''Mom brought me to the emergency room, and they told me it was an allergic reaction. They gave me a shot, but…well, I still feel awful.''

''Mmm-hmm.'' Kelley's mind raced. If the usual antiallergen shot hadn't helped, then maybe it wasn't an allergic reaction after all. Could Heather's illness be something other than mono?

''So you just graduated. Do you have a boyfriend?''

''Kind of. But he's fine. I checked with him.'' She sighed. ''By cell phone. He's up in the mountains, like I want to be. Again. Still.''

That got Kelley's attention. ''Still? Were you up in the mountains recently?''

Heather nodded. ''My boyfriend and I did a term paper together on some ecological issues that we had to research. We're both majoring in zoology, and I've already been accepted to veterinary school next fall.''

''I see.'' Questions swirled in Kelley's head.

''Well, hello!''

Startled, Kelley turned to see Dr. Madelyne Younger stride into the room. She was dressed in one of her signature purple lab coats, and she carried a chart.

''So, Heather, you've gotten into more trouble?'' she asked.

''Guess so, Dr. Younger.''

''Thanks, Dr. Stanton,'' Madelyne said. ''The staff found me, so I'll take my patient back now.'' She turned back toward Heather. "Now, didn't I tell you to stop kissing all the guys?"

With a sinking heart, Kelley wondered if Madelyne was going to stick by her original diagnosis.

"Heather has a rash, Dr. Younger," Kelley said. "She—"

"Right. An allergic reaction, right, kiddo?" She sat on the edge of Heather's bed and began her examination. When she had finished, she turned and appeared startled to see Kelley still standing there.

Her expression turned grim for an instant. "We're fine now," she said to Kelley. "Thanks."

Kelley knew she was being dismissed. She also knew that Madelyne's diagnosis of mono just might be wrong.

And she suspected she knew what Heather really had— something rare. Something dangerous. Of course, she could be mistaken. And if she were, it would only add to her being discredited here...

If she were right, she could save Heather's life.

"Dr. Younger, may I borrow you for a minute?" Kelley asked.

Madelyne did not look pleased, but she agreed.

Outside in the hall, Kelley saw Dotty hovering. She would have to be careful how she phrased things. She certainly didn't want to criticize her colleague, but her first charge was to help the patient.

The accordion of wrinkles at the edges of Madelyne's eyes had deepened, and without lipstick, her lips appeared pale and drawn.

"I don't want to butt in, Madelyne," Kelley said earnestly. And she didn't. Even though Madelyne had been butting in a lot on *her* cases lately... Kelley banished the uncharitable thought. It wasn't Madelyne's fault that patients heard unfounded rumors and asked that Kelley be removed.

"Then don't, kiddo. We're getting along fine."

"Good. But did you know Heather was on a hike last week?"

"Not really, but why—"

"But you had a monospot test taken, didn't you?"

"Sure." Madelyne looked affronted. That was one standard way to diagnose mononucleosis.

"Then no problem. Her blood test was positive for Epstein-Barr or cytomegalovirus antibodies?" Both were indicative of mono.

"She came in early after the symptoms developed. I'll order another test now, of course."

Which meant that the prior test had been negative for mono antibodies. And Kelley suspected that this one would be, too.

"I just had a thought. Why don't you have her blood checked for Rocky Mountain Spotted Fever, while you're at it?"

"Why would you think that?" Madelyne retorted, yet her eyes turned thoughtful.

"Rocky Mountain Spotted Fever?" Dotty had joined them. Kelley sighed inside. It was bad enough if she was wrong and made a fool of herself to Madelyne. But now her folly would spread with the rest of the rumors about her.

If she was wrong.

If she wasn't…

"Just because we live in the Rocky Mountains doesn't mean—" Madelyne began, her words instructional but her tone edgy.

"I know," Kelley interrupted. "The disease was first identified here, but it mostly occurs in the east. It's rare.

But there are a few cases here each year. And Heather was hiking in the woods. She might have been bitten by a tick. I didn't get a chance to ask her, but—''

"All right. I'll ask. And I'll check for Rocky Mountain Spotted Fever.''

Kelley chose not to explain that her father, a general practitioner, had had a patient nearly die from Rocky Mountain Spotted Fever when she worked in his office as a receptionist during her high school summer breaks.

Her father hadn't been much on bedside manner, even with his own family. In fact, the only reason he had permitted Kelley to work there that summer was to show her the miserable and mundane side of the practice of medicine, to nip in the bud her idealism and growing ambition to become a doctor herself.

It hadn't worked, to his fury.

But despite his antiquated ideas about a woman's role, his tyrannical behavior to family and patients alike, he had been an excellent doctor.

He'd saved that patient's life.

And Kelley, while in medical school, had read all she could about Rocky Mountain Spotted Fever and other diseases caused by similar kinds of microbes to rickettsia, which was not a virus but some sources considered to be a bacterium. She hadn't seen another case of this disease—until, possibly, now.

If she was right and Heather was left untreated, she could suffer severe kidney failure. Even shock. And death.

A while later, Kelley learned that the blood test had been positive for RMSF. Heather was given appropriate antibiotics, and began to improve almost immediately.

And she did admit to Dr. Younger that she had burned a tick from her arm while hiking with her boyfriend a week earlier.

At last, Kelley felt vindicated. She *was* a good doctor. But what was more important, she knew that she had saved a life.

"CONGRATULATIONS, Dr. Stanton," said Juan Cortes. The janitor shoved the mop he had been holding into the bucket in the open door to the men's room that he was obviously cleaning.

"For what?" Kelley asked. It was Monday morning, and, medical bag in hand, she was on her way through the admin wing to peek in on Jenny at the child-care center. Randall had had their daughter on Sunday, too, though he hadn't been scheduled to. He'd done Kelley the favor of watching Jenny at the last minute, so she didn't deny his request to keep her longer. Now, she wanted to see Jenny before getting to work.

Juan leaned against the hallway wall. His toothy grin raised the edges of his dark mustache. "You haven't heard? It's all over, how you figured out what was really wrong with that young lady on Saturday."

This place was like a small town, Kelley thought. Everyone knew everything about everybody else. "No kidding? Well, I'm just glad she's doing better." She had come in to check on Heather on Sunday and had found her sitting up in bed eating. That had been the best reward she could imagine. But she didn't mind if people heard she'd succeeded. Maybe the rumor mills would find someone else to pick on. Better yet, maybe they'd shut up.

"I'm glad, too," the janitor said. "And in your honor, I brought some cream-filled doughnuts today. They are in KidClub, as usual, but I didn't slice them up for the kids."

"Thanks, Juan." Kelley hadn't the heart to tell the kind man that neither her tastebuds nor her waistline were fond of cream-filled doughnuts. She'd have to cut off a small piece of one and eat it. That way, she could tell Juan how much she'd enjoyed it without fibbing much.

When she reached KidClub, she hesitated at the door to drink in the sight. Brawny Shawn Jameson had somehow shoehorned himself again into a seat at the small, kiddy-size table. He was surrounded by children who stared in awe over his arms and shoulders as he drew something. Jenny, beside him, pointed at something on his paper and chattered, as usual these days, about "an'mals."

As if he sensed her, he looked up. His eyes met Kelley's. From this distance, she couldn't make out his expression, yet it somehow seemed intense. She felt a flush rise without knowing why. "Jenny, look who's here," he said.

"Mommy!" Her daughter rose and flung herself into Kelley's arms. She hugged the small form and kissed Jenny's clean-smelling blond hair. "I missed you, Mommy," Jenny said.

"I missed you, too, honey."

"I know you had to go help someone so we couldn't see the movie, but Daddy took me. Cheryl, too."

"Oh." Kelley told herself it was just as well, that she shouldn't feel disappointed, but she did. But there would be other movies she could take Jenny to. And as to the other complications surrounding that particular animated film—

Shawn had extracted himself from his throng of young fans. "I'm glad you got to go, Jenny," he said. "Wish I could have gone, too."

Again his gaze met Kelley's. This time she was close enough to see the glint of irony in his sparkling blue eyes. And something else she couldn't put a name to. Didn't *want* to put a name to. If it was the same kind of lust that she had begun to feel for him, she didn't want to know. It would simply go to waste.

"Mommy didn't get to see the movie, either, Shawn." Consternation knit Jenny's small brow. Clutching Kelley's hand, she looked up at Shawn. And then her worry turned into a smile. "I know. You and Mommy can go to the movie together."

"Yeah, that's a good idea," Shawn said with a lazy smile that made Kelley's heart pump double-time. "Maybe Mommy and I can do something together like that."

"Er… We'll think about it," Kelley said, knowing that she really would think about it, more than she should. "I have to go to work now." She fled the child-care center, grabbing a small piece of cream-filled doughnut first, and started on rounds.

Her first stop was to look in on Madelyne's young patient. Heather was doing well, which pleased Kelley immensely.

In a while, she visited the floor where her embarrassment had occurred last week when she was replaced on another case by Madelyne. No matter what, she reminded herself, one success did not mean that her reputation was restored.

Or that it should be.

But she didn't really buy that. As she'd reminded herself often lately, she *was* a good doctor.

It didn't hurt that Dotty Bailey hurried up to her when she reached the nurses' station. A plump, smiling woman was with her. "This is Heather's mom," Dotty said. "She wanted to thank you in person for helping Heather."

The staff at the nurses' station listened with obvious interest as Dotty effused over Kelley's treatment of Heather, and the girl's mother thanked her over and over. "I've already sent a letter of thanks to the hospital for your good work," said Mrs. Harrell. "Right to the top, the administrator—Mr. Paxler."

Wonderful, Kelley thought. She wanted to laugh aloud

when Randall and Cheryl joined the group. They both added their commendations, though their smiles were puckered as if their words hurt.

When she glanced down the hall before entering her first patient's room, she noticed Shawn Jameson leaning on a wall, arms folded, watching her. A trickle of alarm passed through her. Jenny wasn't with him. And he didn't approach her. Was he following her? Why?

She entered the room, but made a mental note to ask the man that evening.

For a child-care intern, he was underfoot a lot. Without kids. Didn't he have enough work to do? She could think up more things he could do for the children's benefit if Marge had trouble assigning him responsibilities.

Later, when she returned to her office, she found paperwork sent by Louis Paxler regarding Etta Borand's claim on behalf of her husband. Feeling better than she had in a long time, Kelley called the administrator, prepared to tell him to instruct the Borands to go pound sand, but she deflated when she only got Louis's voice mail.

Still, Kelley breezed through the rest of the day seeing patients. A call from the mother of Jenny's best friend, Claire, put a damper on her good mood, for Janice Fritz invited Jenny to come over and spend the night. It would be the third night in a row that Jenny would not be with her. But it would be good for Jenny, and Kelley wouldn't even need to go home for anything, since Randall would have brought back Jenny's overnight bag. She agreed, hiding her sigh. It was her problem if she was lonely that night, not her daughter's.

She headed to KidClub early to make sure Jenny liked the idea and to spend time with her.

"Yes, Mommy!" Jenny, obviously thrilled, clapped her hands, which made Kelley happy she'd agreed.

While there, Kelley looked around for Shawn, determined to ask what he'd been doing earlier when she'd seen him in the hall. He came in a short while after her arrival. "Hi," he said in an offhand manner.

"Hi, Shawn," she returned. "Have a minute? I wanted to ask why you—"

"Just a sec." He bent lithely as if suddenly fully engrossed in tying a child's shoe.

Where had he been? She had the odd notion that he'd been wherever *she* had been. And that he was avoiding her questions.

"I saw you in the hallway in 2L," she said, referring to the patient wing where she had noticed him. "What were you—"

"Claire's mommy is here." Jenny tugged on Kelley's arm to get her attention.

Kelley glanced at Shawn, who appeared relieved at the interruption. For the next few minutes, she exchanged pleasantries with Janice Fritz. Kelley made sure that Jenny had her things in her overnight bag. Then, ignoring the moisture in her eyes, she watched them leave.

She met Shawn's gaze after they were gone. His eyebrows were raised, as if he were amused by her bittersweet reaction at seeing her child's departure.

"I didn't get a chance to finish asking you, Shawn," she began again. "I saw you in 2L, and later in the office building, and—"

"Seems as if I'm following you, doesn't it?" He made light of it, damn him. "Why would I do that?"

She flushed. "That's exactly my question."

"I'll keep you guessing. Care to help me clean up? It's nearly time to close KidClub for the day." He turned and confidently strode away in his cowboy boots.

He'd thought she was flirting with him!

If she'd had a pair of boots on herself, she might have gone after him and kicked him right where it would hurt most.

Needing to cool off, she walked briskly back to her office and spent the next few hours working with the door closed. She had brought back the files on the Silver Rapids epidemic in her medical bag that morning. She had taken them home over the weekend, but hadn't had time to study them.

Her review now didn't ease her temper. It simply stoked it further.

She digested the notes and the negative results of tests on blood and other bodily fluids, while letting her mind mull over what it all might mean.

She found nothing to show that *she* had done anything wrong. Yet the more she studied the files, the more the entire outbreak seemed wrong. How could nothing have shown up in the IFA tests?

There had been plenty of questions at the time of the outbreak, of course. But the initial furor had subsided along with the end of the epidemic. The two dead patients had been mourned and eulogized, and that had been the end of it. Maybe.

If only she knew where Wilson Carpenter was.

If only the idea he'd slipped into her mind hadn't ignited her already smoldering suspicions.

If only she had someone else to discuss those suspicions with.

If only…

She slammed the files back into the drawer and locked it. Was she right in keeping them there? Or should she keep them hidden at home even when she wasn't planning to study them?

She hung her lab coat behind her office door and put on the khaki suit jacket that matched her slacks. When she finally left her office, she regretted the loss of her earlier good mood. She regained it partially when she took a peek into Heather's room on the way out.

"She's doing great!" said the duty nurse, smiling at Kelley. "Thanks to you."

Kelley hummed as she headed for her assigned space in the parking garage.

Until the squeal of tires shrieked in her ear like the cry of a wild animal.

She looked up to see the huge, boxy form of an ambulance barreling right toward her.

Chapter Seven

Stepping from the garage stairwell, Shawn heard the vehicle's rumble before he saw it. He heard the shrill of skidding tires and began running, just as the sound was joined by a woman's scream. Kelley!

There. A few yards in front of him. He dove between two parked SUVs and, with a flying tackle, shoved her out of the way of the speeding vehicle just in time.

No opportunity for niceties. Though he managed to thrust his hand beneath her head so it wouldn't hit the unyielding floor, he landed on top of her.

He heard the breath rush from her, felt the jar to his hand as it cushioned her face.

He lay there for a moment, breathing heavily. Inhaling the usual parking garage fumes tempered by the sweet, clean scent of the woman beneath him. He might be crushing her, but her soft curves cushioned him.

He had an urge to stay right there but he couldn't. He hastily turned Kelley so that her face would not touch the floor, then rose and ran after the ambulance.

Too late. He saw its flat rear doors as it disappeared down a ramp. Noted the name "Gilpin Emergency" in big blue letters, and the ambulance's license number. For all the good that would do. He'd missed seeing who was at the wheel. "Son of a bitch," he muttered. He didn't know if the driver was a man or a woman. And he'd no doubt find, when he checked it out, that the ambulance was stolen.

He returned to where Kelley sat on the floor, knees bent, head in her hands. "Did I hurt you?" he demanded.

Her eyes were huge and dazed as they met his. "I... No," she finally said. "I'm all right. I think. But... Thank you."

He grinned wryly. "For tackling you? Any time."

"For following me—this time—and keeping me from being hit. Why would he speed like that in a parking garage?"

"He? Did you see the driver?" Shawn knelt and grasped her shoulders.

She blinked as she shook her head slowly. He wasn't sure if she was responding in the negative or still trying to shake off her befuddlement.

"Did you?" he repeated.

"No," she said. "But he had to have seen us. Why didn't he stop to make sure we were all right?"

"Yeah, why?" Shawn repeated, but he knew the answer. "Look, do you need to go back inside, get checked out in the emergency room or anything?"

She hesitated, and her eyes searched her body as if determining if everything was intact. Shawn followed her gaze, feeling a warmth ignite that was separate from the heat of his anger. She looked damn good to him.

"I'm fine," she finally said.

He silently seconded that, despite the dirt on the knees of her light slacks. "Good. Then you're going to get into my car with me, and we'll get out of here."

The muzziness in her gaze cleared at that. "No, I'm fine, really. I can drive. I need to get home."

"I know Jenny's not there and she's okay. And you don't need to get home. Not now."

"But—"

"Don't you get it? Some son of a bitch just tried to run you over, Dr. Stanton. Intentionally. And since he—or she—didn't succeed, he just might try again."

WATCHING FOR COPS, the arsonist sped away in the stolen ambulance.

Taking action like this, in anger, was a mistake. It wasn't on the agenda.

But neither was the improvement of Dr. Kelley Stanton's status at the hospital. She had saved a girl's life, and everyone was talking about what a great doctor she was.

Praise for Kelley Stanton could wreck the entire plan. And nothing could be permitted to stand in the way.

If Kelley couldn't be stopped one way, she would need to be silenced forever. But not yet.

Her reputation was still precarious. It could still be ruined.

The arsonist was smart. Even when acting on an angry impulse like this, there were no mistakes. No fingerprints or other evidence would be found when the ambulance was abandoned.

And if the arsonist's intention had actually been to strike Kelley rather than scare her, warn her...well, she would no longer be around to toy with.

But she was still necessary. Someone was needed to take the blame, and it was her.

Just wait, Dr. Kelley Stanton, thought the arsonist. *I'm not through with you yet.*

KELLEY CLOSED her eyes as she sat in the passenger seat of Shawn's big, blue SUV. She didn't want to think about what had just happened.

But that was all she could think about. That and the aftermath, with Shawn literally flying to her rescue, then flattening her to the pavement. Shielding her, even as he gently cupped her head to protect her.

She shuddered, and not entirely from revulsion at nearly having been run over. Surely it was just her relief that made her relive, over and over, the heat that had circulated through her, especially down below, as she had imagined she had felt the throb of Shawn's body....

She opened her eyes and shook her head at her own folly.

"You're shivering," he said from the driver's seat. He reached over and took her hand, holding it on the console between them. His was warm and large and felt much too comforting. And sexy. She imagined him taking his very masculine, long fingers, touching her places other than the back of her hand...

Frustrated divorcée, she taunted herself. Her near-death experience must have stimulated hormones long dormant—until she'd met Shawn. She wasn't about to act on them anyway.

She glanced at him. His wide forehead was creased in a frown of concern. It was his job to be concerned, she reminded herself—about children, not imaginative adult women.

"We're nearly at my place," he continued. They hadn't been in the car very long.

"Look." She pulled her hand back, though the gesture made her feel as bereft as if she were suddenly the only person in Denver. Being alone with him at his place was definitely not a good idea—not with the direction her thoughts were going. "What happened was an accident. No one has any reason to intentionally run over me. Please, just take me home. I'll lock the doors just in case and take a taxi to work in the morning. You don't have to worry about me."

He muttered something she couldn't quite make out. But it sounded like, "Yeah, I do."

"Pardon?"

He didn't respond. At first she thought it was because he had to concentrate on waiting for an iron gate to open into an indoor parking garage. He pulled into a space in the crowded garage, then turned off the engine as the gate closed behind them. And didn't look at her.

More was on his mind than what he'd told her. There was *always* more on his mind than he revealed, she was sure of it. "Do you know who was in that ambulance?" she asked a little too casually.

"No," he replied, not meeting her eye. "You're sure I didn't hurt you? No broken bones, or—"

"What aren't you telling me?" she demanded.

He shut up, and his sudden silence chilled her. At the same time, it made her curiosity run rampant.

"What's going on, Shawn?" she tried again.

He finally turned toward her with a blank expression that doused any residue of her earlier lust. What was he thinking, damn it? "This may be a mistake," he said at last. "But we'd better talk."

"About what?"

"The truth. About you. And—" He held up one large hand to keep her from interrupting as he finished. "About me."

She swallowed hard, knowing she'd been right to be suspicious. Knowing she wouldn't like what he said.

"Good," she said anyway, trying to sound as detached as he did. "Tell me."

"As soon as we get inside."

SHE SHOULDN'T HAVE BEEN surprised at the compactness of his apartment, or even at its sparse furnishings or shabbiness. He did, after all, claim to be a student, and students seldom had money for luxuries. His job as a child-care intern at KidClub probably didn't pay much.

Assuming he was just a child-care intern. Which she believed now as much as she'd have believed he was one of the animal caricatures he sketched.

The place didn't *feel* like him. Wasn't the sort of home she envisioned him in.

With his muscular build, his vests, jeans and cowboy boots, she visualized him in wide, open spaces. Even at that, she suspected she hadn't any idea of who the real Shawn Jameson was.

Or why he had really brought her here.

He gestured toward the worn green sofa, and she obediently sat down as he turned on the stuffy room's window air conditioner.

"Sorry I don't have much to offer to eat or drink." Like champagne and caviar? No, that didn't fit him. Steak fresh from a ranch, and a keg of beer? Maybe, but...

Barbecue. Yes, that fit, though she wasn't sure why. Spicy. Hot. With a well-aged bottle of Merlot, each sip slipping smoothly, sensuously, over her tongue, down her throat...

"That's okay," she said hoarsely. *You're here for answers, damn it,* she reminded herself. *Not sex games.* "I'm fine."

"I'll make some coffee," he said. "Decaf. We're probably both too hyped up for caffeine. I've got some good unleaded beans already ground. Okay?"

"Sure." She didn't think that real men admitted to drinking decaf, let alone to grinding beans. But there was no doubt that Shawn Jameson was a real man.

She waited alone in his compact living room, allowing herself to relax while listening to the comforting sounds of his puttering in the kitchen. In a short while, he was back.

"It's brewing. We can talk while we wait."

"About time," she retorted.

Sitting at the far end of the couch, he ran one hand through his dusty-blond hair.

He turned toward her, his firm jaw set. Had she once thought his blue eyes icy? Now they seemed to radiate an intensity that was disturbing. "Kelley, enough beating around the bush. I need answers from you. Now."

Taken aback, she said, "What about the answers *I* need?"

"Later. Soon as you're done."

"Tell me the questions, then." She tried to speak glibly, but to her surprise the words came out in a nervous croak. Why did he make her nervous? *He'd* promised *her* an explanation.

"Okay, here's a big one," he said. "Did you set the fire in the records room at the hospital?"

She glared, but his stare was unnerving. And unequivocal.

"No," she asserted, "I did not. Now, your turn. Why are you asking? Why would you care?"

"That's two questions. Hold on to them till you've responded to a few more of mine."

"Maybe," she said. Her hands were clasped uneasily in her lap, fingers twining as if she sought comfort from her own touch. For something more productive to do, she brushed futilely at the dirty scuffmarks on the knees of her slacks.

He watched her. She stared back defiantly as their gazes met once more. "Go ahead and ask," she finally said.

"Tell me about the Silver Rapids flu epidemic."

Her laugh came out as an incredulous snort. "In twenty-five words or less?"

"Right." This time, one side of his otherwise impassive mouth twitched, as if he waged war against a grin.

"You promise, if I tell you, that you'll explain why a child-care attendant wants to know about such things?" Not that she'd tell him everything. But with all his sneaking around, the other questions he'd asked, she had suspected for awhile that Shawn Jameson wasn't what he professed to be. Now she was sure—and she also thought she knew why. But she wanted confirmation.

He nodded solemnly.

"All right." She gave a rundown of how the first patients who had trickled into Gilpin Hospital from the small town outside Denver had turned into a deluge. How she had been the infectious disease specialist on call when the intake had begun. How she had done a workup on each patient, ordered tests, prescribed treatment. All the stuff she should have done over the week of the epidemic. "The tests showed influenza. And despite all the rumors I'm sure you've heard, I wasn't negligent. Period."

She watched his face. Despite his intense concentration on what she said, there was no indication as to whether he believed a word. She wanted some response, damn it. Some sign that would reveal whether he was like the people who pretended to accept her story but still spread lies about her. "Do you believe me?" she demanded.

"Is that all?"

"Yeah," she lied.

"Yeah?" Now she wished she hadn't gotten a reaction from him, for the one she got now was skepticism—how could he tilt just one of his blond brows that way?

She wanted to touch it. Smooth it... Get him to believe her. Believe *in* her.

"Where's the damn coffee?" she demanded, standing abruptly. "Isn't it ready yet?"

"I'll check." He rose, too.

"No." She realized she was contradicting herself. "Don't you dare leave this room until you tell me who you are and why you're asking so many questions."

Now, when she didn't want him to smile, he did. She wanted to shove his amusement right back into those perfect teeth. Down the long throat with the prominent Adam's apple.

"Okay," he said, "but it's one of those situations that if I tell you, you've got to keep your mouth closed about it or I'll have to close it for you. Can I trust you?"

"What do you think?" she retorted. Was he joking—or was it a real threat?

"Can I?" One stride brought him close to her. He gripped her shoulders gently in her long-sleeved blouse, but his hands burned right through, as if her arms were naked. His gaze captured hers, stared as if his hold on her was as accurate as a lie detector, and her eyes provided the reading. Maybe they did.

"Yes," she whispered. Then, much too hoarsely, she said, "Believe me..."

Time stopped. Everything seemed to stop—except for the needy sensations deep inside her as his mouth muttered something unintelligible, then lowered to hers.

Were his lips also testing her credibility? At first they were soft, exploring tentatively, nibbling. Tasting.

And then they were devouring hers. Had she passed his test?

She didn't care. All she wanted was more of him. She pressed closer, reveling in the sensation of his solid, hungry body against hers. Feeling the straining hardness at her belly. She moaned. Wanted more. Wanted—

He pulled back. His breathing was ragged, and he still held her arms. "Whoa," he said with a small laugh. "That's what I was told to say when it's time to hold my horses."

Bemused, she did nothing but stare for a moment. She blinked, then took a step away from him. She had to regain her composure. "What are you talking about?" she said, wishing her tone was more commanding than perplexed.

"Before we both do something we regret, I need to answer some of your questions."

"About time." She crossed her arms over her chest, as if to ward off the vulnerability she now felt. "Why are you so interested in me and my work? And the fire?"

"Because," he said, "I'm an investigator for Investigations, Confidential and Undercover. ICU is a private investigation agency, Kelley."

Her insides constricted. Oh, it was no surprise. She'd suspected something like that. But—

"I'm an arson investigator by trade," he continued. "Working for a client I can't disclose. Among other things, I'm at Gilpin Hospital to determine whether you set the fire in the records room, and if so, why. And now there's something else I need to look into."

"What?" Kelley was afraid to ask.

"If you are innocent, why did someone want to kill you tonight?"

"So you handled the epidemic just as you should have," Shawn said to Kelley a short while later, crossing one leg over the other as he pretended to relax into the corner of the sofa. "And that was the end of it?"

He knew she had more questions but he'd needed a break, so he had gone into the kitchen to pour their coffee. Now, he was back in his living room. Its smallness hadn't mattered before, when the place just contained him, but now his forced proximity to Kelley was disconcerting.

After that urge for a kiss had erupted inside him, he wasn't sure that even the full length of the Royal Flush ranch would have been enough distance between them to give him comfort.

"That was the end of it," she confirmed, but she took a sip from the white mug she held in her hands much too quickly.

Damn, but she was pretty, even when lying. Her auburn hair swept forward from her face as she tilted her head, its soft coppery shade an elegant contrast with the whiteness of the mug, and an appealing complement to the creamy shade of her blouse.

If he were to draw her caricature right now, though, he would lengthen her small, straight nose just a little, like Pinocchio when he first told a lie.

He had a hunch, however. Despite all he'd heard from Colleen, all he'd heard while hanging out around the hospital, he believed in this woman's integrity. She'd said he could trust her. Call him a fool, but he did.

He *had.* For if she hadn't the deep-down integrity he believed in, despite the lies he knew she told, he was busted. He'd purposely blown his cover, because he knew she suspected something and figured it was the only way to get her to be straight with him. Maybe.

Of course, he hadn't revealed the agency he really worked for. Colorado Confidential was too new, and too…well, confidential, to trust an outsider with knowledge of its existence.

Right now, he had to goad her. Maybe if he pushed her enough, she'd spill what was really on her mind. "So you had no reason to destroy those files."

"No, of course not."

"What about other files? What is it you're hiding?"

Her brown eyes widened. "What makes you think I—"

"Kelley," he said in an admonishing tone, lifting one hand from his own mug so he could wag a finger at her. "I *know* there's more you're not telling me. But like you told me I can trust you, you have to trust me."

"Why?" A storm crossed her face, causing her brow to wrinkle ominously. "You said you're checking up on *me*. To see if I set the fire, and why. Not that you're trying to figure out who *did* set it."

"Because, no matter what my orders, I do things my way." He grinned. "If you don't believe that, ask the Denver Fire Department. That's a good reason they're my *former* employer. We reached a mutual parting of the ways a while ago." He leaned toward her, serious once more. "Could be I'm putting my current job on the line, but I've a feeling you didn't set the fire. And I've learned, over the years, to trust my gut."

He nearly wanted to throw his filled coffee mug across the room when she looked back at him with tears in her eyes. Damn! He sure as hell didn't want to make her cry.

What had he said to get her all misty-eyed?

"Thank you," she said. There was such fervency in her tone that he wanted to take her into his arms again.

Of course he probably would have wanted to take her into his arms again even if she'd told him to go to hell. She'd felt damn good there....

"All right," she blurted. She stood, her back toward him. "It's not that I *know* anything, but there is more to the story." She pivoted to face him.

Her uneven breathing made her chest rise and fall in a syncopation that drew his attention to the enticing shape of her breasts beneath her businesslike blouse—and caused his body to stiffen in acknowledgment of how she aroused him.

"But you've got to keep your mouth closed about it," she continued, "or I'll have to close it for you." Her serious expression suddenly swelled into a ray of sunshine as she grinned at him, despite the remaining moistness in her eyes.

"Promise?" he asked, unleashing his own lascivious grin. Damn, but this woman turned him on, even when she was teasing. *Because* she was teasing.

She laughed aloud. "Down, boy." Her face sobered once again. She resumed her seat as far from him on the sofa as she could get. He resisted the impulse to scoot over. Close. Real close.

He read in her eyes that she was about to reveal something, and it bothered her.

"The epidemic kept us busy," she said softly. "It was terrible. So many people, and some of them very, very sick. There were two elderly people… One of them, Peg Ahlers, I got to know a little bit. She was so sweet and cheerful…and ill. She got worse. And then she died."

With no further thought of lust, of anything but soothing Kelley, Shawn reached toward her. She slid into his arms. Her voice was very low as she continued. "Afterward, I felt terrible, but tried to put it behind me—doctors have to do that to survive. But several weeks later, I got a phone call."

He knew that. Colorado Confidential had checked her phone records for the last few months and had noted the recent call from a phone booth in Silver Rapids. But he didn't know who had called.

She told him. "It was a friend from med school, Dr. Wilson Carpenter. He sounded—well, different. Upset. Said that some people who'd been ill were his patients, and he'd been talking to them. He wouldn't tell me more, though."

She was lying. Shawn could tell. Why?

"Since then, I haven't been able to reach him. It's as if he disappeared. The woman who's watching his office says he's out of town." She looked at Shawn. "Since you're an investigator, can you find out where he is?"

Wilson Carpenter. Shawn had no doubt that Colleen and the Confidential bunch could track down the mysterious, missing doctor. But what he told Kelley was, "I can try. What do you think he had in mind?"

She pivoted in his arms to face him. One slim, elegant hand was raised. "I don't know."

But you do know more than you're saying, he contradicted her in his thoughts. "Tell me the conversation," he said. "Exactly as you remember it."

"It's been a few weeks," she dissembled, "so I really don't recall it verbatim. But Wilson thanked me again for treating the patients. Said he was really sorry about the two who died, and asked about the test results for influenza. Said he'd just examined some of the recovered patients—routine stuff—which was what prompted him to call. But we'd discussed this before, so I wasn't sure what he was driving at."

"And that was all?"

She nodded. "He sounded nervous, hung up so abruptly that I wondered if we'd been cut off. Then when I called back to ask more questions, he wasn't around."

Did this Wilson Carpenter know something about what had caused the epidemic? Had he mentioned it to Kelley, and was that what she was hiding?

Did she know more—because she was part of it? He didn't want to think that. But, damn it, what was she holding back?

Still, a dialogue had been opened between them. He

wanted to rule her out as a suspect. Maybe he would be able to, once he actually got the entire story from her.

In the meantime, she had nearly been run over that evening. *Someone* must know what she knew, at least enough to consider her a threat. And that was something Shawn would pass along.

"COLLEEN?"

It was late that same night, but Shawn had had to wait until he had convinced Kelley to sleep in what passed for the bedroom in this joke of an apartment.

His joke of an apartment, where he'd gotten used to being alone again. As always. Despite the busy stretch with people forever around on the ranch. Would it feel like his place again after Kelley was gone?

Now he sat hunched over his shrimpy kitchen table, whispering into his cell phone.

"That you, Shawn?" his boss replied.

"Yeah." He'd reheated a cup of coffee in the microwave, and he took a sip of the dark, bitter brew.

"How did things go today?"

"Fine," he said, "as long as you don't count the fact that our chief suspect nearly got squashed like a bug by someone aiming for her with an ambulance."

"What!"

He loved to picture Colleen's face as he made his almost daily reports to her. And now that he'd begun sketching caricatures again, he concentrated on imagining her most prominent features—those arresting blue-green eyes of hers. The way she puckered her forehead in concentration. The way she was most likely grimacing at the phone right about now.

"I need a little help here." He laid out the facts as he knew them. "See if you can track down the ambulance, though I'll lay odds it was stolen. And then we need to track down a friend of Kelley's from Silver Rapids, a Dr. Wilson Carpenter.''

"Kelley, as in 'Dr. Stanton'?''

"That's the one.''

"Where is she now?'' Colleen's tone was suspicious, and rightly so.

"I couldn't let my chief suspect get murdered right out from under me, so right now she's asleep in my bed.''

"What!'' Colleen exclaimed again. "Jameson, you'd better—''

"Relax,'' he told her with a laugh. "I'm sleeping on the couch tonight.'' *More's the pity.* But he wasn't about to tell his boss he was lusting after their primary suspect.

Who just might not continue to be their primary suspect…

But he was acting prematurely, without all the facts.

"Watch your step, Shawn,'' Colleen warned. "If you can't be objective, we've other operatives who can step in.''

"Oh, but no one can do as good a job at being a nanny as me. You as good as said so.''

"Shawn…'' She drew out his name.

"Good night, boss,'' he said, then hung up.

Chapter Eight

Kelley was awakened the next morning when the bedroom light clicked on. Her exhausted mind registered the odd sound. Her light switches were silent, weren't they?

"Good morning, sweetie," she managed to groan without opening her eyes. Her early-bird daughter was often her alarm clock, but she'd slept so little the night before that she really needed more rest.

"Good morning, darlin'," replied a deep, amused voice.

Her eyes popped open and she wrapped the sheet around her as Shawn Jameson strode into the chamber that was smaller and shabbier than her bedroom. He proffered a mug of coffee. He was dressed in a gray, partly-unbuttoned Henley-style shirt and charcoal jeans. And he looked well rested, damn him.

"Thanks," she muttered ungraciously.

He smiled as his gaze slid down her. She felt her face flush. Why should she feel embarrassed? Though she'd taken off her suit and slept in her underwear, her strategic places were covered in the swirl of sheet around her. And if her hair was a tangled mess, her face pale and devoid of makeup, so what? That didn't seem to keep Shawn from devouring her with his eyes.

The heat from her face suffused lower. Much lower. It

was only then that she recalled in a rush exactly why she hadn't slept the previous night. And it hadn't completely been because she was in a strange room.

Yesterday, she'd nearly been run over by a speeding ambulance. She'd been saved by her daughter's day-care attendant, who turned out, not to her surprise, to be an undercover investigator trying to find evidence that she had committed the heinous crimes she'd been accused of.

She'd told him of the call from Wilson Carpenter to get his help, but not what Wilson had said—the part that really troubled her, that she didn't dare mention without backup. With no proof, it would only sound as if she'd made up one hell of an excuse for her inability to save two lives.

Of course the worst source of her insomnia was her contemplation of the fact that Shawn was in the next room, sleeping on his battered and undoubtedly uncomfortable couch, acting the role of gentleman. It was a role that did not suit him, notwithstanding that he seemed to don different personalities with ease, from uncomfortable child-care provider to inquisitive spy.

And, perversely, she hadn't wanted him to act like a gentleman.

She just wanted *him*. Emotionally. Sexually. *All* ways. Because her life had turned into one hell of a tangle, and she needed to take comfort where she could.

Fortunately, she wasn't a sex-crazed ninny, nor a woman who couldn't control her impulses. And so she had controlled her body. She hadn't left the room.

Her mind—well, it had raced out of control, but so what?

As the edge of the bed sagged with Shawn's weight, Kelley realized she had taken refuge by staring into her coffee cup. She took a hasty sip and looked at him.

''Okay,'' he said, ''I've another fact to stick into your file. You're not a morning person.''

"Yes, I am," she contradicted. "I just… Never mind." She couldn't explain why she hadn't risen as quickly as usual. "If you'll excuse me, I'll get dressed."

"Sure," he said. "If you need any help, holler."

"Of course," she muttered, though her insides grew molten at the idea of his helping her dress. Or undress.

At the doorway, he paused. "By the way, I was right."

"Are you ever wrong?" She sighed as he raised an eyebrow. "Okay, I'll bite. About what?"

"You can bite anytime you want. But what I'm right about this time is that the ambulance was stolen. I got a call this morning from my employer confirming it."

"Did they confirm who stole it?"

"Still checking, but I doubt they'll find evidence worth saving."

"Of course," Kelley repeated as the door closed behind him.

KELLEY INSISTED THAT Shawn drive her home so that she could change clothes. He didn't argue, but his insistence on checking her house before she entered made her feel both relieved and uneasy. Fortunately, everything seemed fine.

There was a message on her answering machine from Randall, asking her to call about their schedule for Jenny over the next couple of weeks. Kelley sighed. He'd be angry that she hadn't called back right away. But she knew he scheduled surgeries first thing in the morning on Tuesdays, so she wouldn't even try to reach him until late in the day.

Another message on her machine was from Janice Fritz. "I'll be taking the girls to KidClub early today, Kelley," she said. "I need to be at work early."

Reminded that she hadn't had her daughter for three

days, the first thing Kelley did when she and Shawn arrived at the hospital was to go to KidClub.

Jenny, in a denim smock dress and tights, was arguing with Claire when Kelley arrived. She couldn't quite understand the origin of the disagreement, though cereal flakes and pieces of doughnut littered the table and the floor beside it. Jenny burst into tears without explaining. So did Claire.

Kelley took her small, sorrowful daughter into her arms as Shawn tried to distract the other little girl. Kelley wanted to make it all better, whatever had caused the problem. "We'll talk about it tonight, honey, okay? I'll try to come for you early, and we'll have a good time tonight, I promise. If you want, I'll even let you help me cook dinner."

"Cookies?" Jenny asked hopefully through her tears.

"Sure, as long as we have a good balanced meal first."

"With lettuce and other green stuff with s'getti?"

"Something like that," Kelley said with a relieved laugh as she breathed in the scent of her daughter's soft, clean hair.

Jenny didn't exactly cry when Kelley left that morning after helping to clean up the mess, but she did cling to her mother and get misty-eyed again. She hadn't done that for days, since Shawn had begun occupying the kids with his caricatures.

A pang of remorse burrowed into Kelley's heart.

She glanced around for Shawn as she prepared to leave. His gaze was on her, but he was involved in a conversation with Marge Ralston. He held up one hand as if to tell her to wait, but she had patients to see.

"Now, you go over to Shawn, Jenny," she said, wishing she felt better about leaving. The child gloomily obeyed.

Kelley waved back toward Shawn and left, but not before she all but ran into Cheryl Marten. "Randall was here when

Claire's mother brought Jenny in this morning," she said. "He's not happy that you didn't call him back last night, and that you didn't tell him Jenny had an overnight at a friend's."

And that's why you're here? Kelley steamed inside. *To make sure everyone here knows that Randall is angry with me?*

"I was busy until late last night, Cheryl. You can tell Randall I'll be in touch later today. Do you want to give Jenny a good morning hug?"

"Er—Randall is waiting for me before starting his surgery this morning."

"Of course," Kelley said sweetly. She watched Cheryl leave, then chose a piece of apple from the treat box that rested in the usual place on the counter. She'd insisted that Shawn not stop for breakfast since they would arrive so late. He'd not been happy about it.

He'd also tried to give her instructions on how to act that day regarding the ambulance incident and to remind her not to treat him any different from the way she had before. And why should she? She'd never quite accepted that he was a college student anyway.

She was still nibbling on the fruit when she saw Juan Cortes pushing a large broom in a hallway near KidClub. She lifted it to show him. "It really hits the spot this morning," she told him. "Thanks. Our turn is Friday, remember."

"If that's what you want, Dr. Stanton," he said, a smile of pleasure brightening his face.

She began her rounds, stopping first to check on Heather Harrell. The young woman was doing much better. Her prognosis was excellent and she would probably be discharged from Gilpin in a day or two.

Kelley thought she couldn't have been more pleased. But

she was, a short while later, when another colleague on the floor asked her a question about one of his patients' symptoms.

A few weeks earlier, such a consultation would have been routine. Now, it felt as if she had grabbed onto a vine while sliding down a slippery slope toward hell and was swinging her way back to heaven.

She didn't even flinch when she found a message from Louis Paxler waiting in her office. Not that she wanted another meeting with the dour and difficult hospital administrator, but at least her reburgeoning self-esteem would allow her to stand up to whatever gripe he had this time.

Or so she thought. The first thing he said, after she'd settled in the designated chair across the desk from him, was, "Are you sleeping with that child-care worker Shawn Jameson?"

"What?" Kelley sputtered. "Who I sleep with is not your business, Louis." She ignored the scowl that knitted his thin brows together beneath his gold-rimmed glasses. "And why on earth would you ask me about Shawn? Is someone starting more rumors about me?"

Had someone seen her at Shawn's apartment? Or had they been spotted arriving together this morning? She hadn't noticed anyone in the parking garage when they'd pulled in, but that didn't mean no one had noticed them.

"Be careful, Kelley. Sleeping with your child's caregiver, a hospital employee, would be in poor taste." His jowls quivered in his righteous indignation.

Did Paxler know Shawn was an undercover investigator? Kelley sat up straight in her chair. She couldn't be sure what Paxler knew, and she had promised Shawn not to reveal his true reason for being there to anybody. He hadn't made Paxler an exception.

"What kind of strange idea do you have, Louis?" she

dissembled. "Why would you think Shawn and I have any interest in each other?" She cringed inside, knowing even as she spoke that she sounded defensive.

"I've got your best interests in mind, Kelley," Paxler said in a more reasonable tone. He leaned back in his tall leather desk chair. "There are circumstances behind his being hired that I can't reveal. But your getting involved with him could wind up hurting the hospital."

Kelley's facial muscles froze. Good thing, too, or her angry frown might have fallen into an expression of dismay.

Was Paxler suggesting that Shawn would cozy up to her to look for evidence of incompetence? Could Shawn have lied about investigating the fire?

Her tone was less acerbic when she spoke again. "Are you suggesting that Shawn's integrity is questionable? If so, Louis, why did you hire him to work around kids?"

He waved a hand. "I can't go into it. But watch your step, Kelley. Your every action is being noted."

"Right." Feeling dismissed—and wanting to escape—Kelley stood and headed for the door.

"Oh, and another thing."

Slowly, she turned back toward the thin, black-haired administrator.

"I've heard again from Etta Borand. She is giving us a chance to pay her a million dollars before she lets her attorney file a lawsuit for mistreatment of her husband. We're not going to pay unless we can negotiate a more reasonable sum. Still… Is there anything about that matter that you want to tell me?"

"Yes, Louis, there is." Kelley's dismay was trumped by irritation. "You said you have my interests at heart. If so, you'll stand behind me on this and everything else. I did nothing wrong in my treatment of Ben Borand. I did nothing wrong in my treatment of the Silver Rapids influenza patients. You should feel damned glad to have my services as a physician here.'' She glared at him.

''Oh, yes, you must be thinking of that little Rocky Mountain Spotted Fever matter.''

Little? Kelley opened her mouth to protest, but he continued, ''I talked to Madelyne Younger. She was pleased you found the solution. The thing was, the patient hadn't told her that piece of the puzzle, that she'd been hiking a couple of days before her symptoms first began to appear. If she had, I'm sure Madelyne would have diagnosed the disease right away.''

Madelyne didn't ask, Kelley wanted to shout. She didn't, though. Madelyne was her friend as well as her colleague. The disease was not an easy one to diagnose.

And Kelley could not force the administrator to recognize her abilities, she realized drearily.

''Right, Louis,'' Kelley said grimly, then left the office. Only then did she realize she hadn't found out the source of Louis's information.

How did he know she'd spent the night at Shawn's?

CONCENTRATE, SHAWN TOLD himself.

It was late morning. The other child-care staff were looking to him to keep the tots amused. And he was doing his usual bit of giving them a drawing lesson, the only way he knew to deal with them. He actually enjoyed it.

He'd already used colored pencils to sketch a panda and a moose with antlers that held drying laundry.

Except that all he wanted to draw was pair of sad and watchful brown eyes. Brown eyes that twinkled. A lovely lady, flustered as she wrapped herself in a bedsheet that might have hidden the flesh he longed to see, but did nothing to camouflage the soft, firm curves beneath....

"Here, Shawn," said Claire Fritz, who tugged at his sleeve as he walked around the table to see that all the kids were drawing. "I drew a octopus, wif' lots of legs."

He glanced down. *Lots* was the operative word. The stick creature she had drawn probably had several dozen limbs writhing around it. "Do you know how many legs an octopus has, Claire?"

"Lots," she repeated.

He smiled without correcting her. "Well, this is a really nice octopus," he told her, then continued around the table.

One boy had drawn a box he had labeled, "Gilpin," not a bad representation of the light brick edifice. Another had drawn a person with blue eyes. "This is you, Shawn," he said proudly.

Then Shawn got to Jenny's place at the table. She didn't look up. But there was nothing at all on her paper.

He knelt beside her. "What kind of animal would you like to draw today, Jenny?" She blinked rapidly, and when he put an arm around her he felt her shaking. "What's wrong?" he asked gently.

She didn't say a word.

"I'm in the mood to draw a...princess," he said. With colored pencils, he sketched a caricature of Jenny as he had once before, with a crown on her head.

"No!" Jenny stood and grabbed a crayon from the table. She drew jagged red lines over his smiling picture.

Shawn had a horrible suspicion he knew what they were intended to represent. Still, he had to ask. "What does the red mean, Jenny?" he asked casually.

Her eyes, as she looked up to face him, were huge, and her lower lip trembled. A large tear rolled down her face. "Fire," she whispered, and then she began to cry.

"SHE WOULDN'T TELL me more," Shawn said. He clutched a cold glass of iced tea, wishing he'd been able to spike it.

He wanted to reach across the cafeteria table and touch Kelley's arm in comfort but didn't dare. People around here talked too much.

Kelley's pale face looked stricken. He had called her to meet him here, for he wanted to tell her about Jenny's drawing when the child was not around.

Kelley's soft brown eyes blinked rapidly as if to hold back tears. "She added fire to a sketch of herself?" She sighed desolately. "I'm worried. What if she saw whoever set the fire that night, Shawn? Someone may have tried to harm me yesterday. What if it was the arsonist, and he knows that Jenny saw him?"

"Or her," Shawn said grimly, shaking his head. "We don't have a clue as to the arsonist's gender."

"Sure you do." Acid suddenly dripped from her tone. "Your agency thinks it was me." Her glare turned hard. "Did you try to talk to Jenny about the fire—to manipulate me into confessing that I set it?"

He stared at her, his blood suddenly running as icy as his tea. Where had that attack come from? And, damn it, he might not know how to work with kids, but he sure as hell wouldn't try to scare one like that.

Especially not Jenny.

"*Are* you confessing?" he asked coldly.

"Of course not." She lowered her voice. "But we both know why you're here. And I have it on authority that I'm still the focus of your investigation."

"What authority?" he demanded, also in a tone designed not to be overheard. Which was hard, when what he wanted to do was shout some sense into her. "Damn it, Kelley, have you been talking about my work with someone, after you promised to keep it confidential?"

Confusion seemed to war with defiance in her expression. "No," she said. "Not the way you think, anyway."

"If you've talked about it in *any* way, it's a problem. Don't you understand that?"

She rose but bent down so that her lips were near his ear. Damn it all, as infuriated as he was, her breath on the side of his face, tinged with the sweet scent of the soft drink she had been sipping, made him crazy with lust.

"I understand more than you think, Shawn," she whispered. "I understand that you still believe I'm capable of setting the fire, and that I am therefore capable of having botched the treatment of those flu patients enough so that some died. And I understand it's your job to find out the truth, no matter what it takes for you to get the information. But what you need to understand is that I will not allow you to use Jenny. If you want something from me, ask *me*. And if I hear that you interrogated my daughter to try to get her to reveal why she drew fire, I *will* ruin your cover. Do you understand?"

Without allowing him to respond, she hurried from the cafeteria.

KELLEY PRACTICALLY RAN down the halls toward KidClub.

Had she been right to heed Louis's warning about Shawn? Or had she, in her fear for her daughter, overreacted?

One thing was certain—Shawn had his agenda, and she had hers. As an undercover investigator, no matter what he was truly investigating, it was his job to try to ferret out the truth—as he perceived it.

Despite his saving her life yesterday, she couldn't be certain that he had exonerated her from setting the fire.

And though she didn't understand why, she had the distinct impression that Shawn particularly despised arsonists.

She'd no doubt that he was good at his job. Stubborn. Tenacious. Qualities she found appealing.

She found *him* appealing. But she would not allow him to railroad her. She was innocent.

As innocent as Jenny…

Once she reached the admin wing, she stopped. How should she approach Jenny without upsetting her more? How could she get her daughter to explain her reason for slashing fire onto Shawn's drawing without interrogating her?

She still had no answer when she walked into the child-care center.

Marge Ralston, in the middle of a group of kids, spied her at the door. The curly-haired manager hurried over, a big, false smile on her face. "Hi, Kelley. Glad you're here."

Shawn had said he had put the picture away with Jenny's approval, without showing it to anyone else—a surprise for Mommy, they'd agreed. Did Marge know about it?

If so, she didn't mention it. She had another reason for being glad to see Jenny's mother.

"I'm sure it's just a phase," Marge said, "but Jenny's being a holy terror today. She's been yelling and pinching and throwing things—everything from crayons to snacks. It's not even lunchtime yet, and she's had two time-outs."

What was wrong with her sweet child today? "I'm sorry," Kelley said. "I'll talk to her."

She saw from the corner of her eye that Shawn had entered KidClub, too. He loomed beside her. She practically felt how tense he was with anger.

She thought of their closeness last night. How his arms had enveloped her. Their kiss…

Come off it, Kelley, she commanded herself. This man's investigation could hurt her. And Jenny.

"Hi, Shawn," she said a bit too cheerfully. "I know you have that picture you wanted to show me. Why don't you get it for me now? I'm here to take my daughter to lunch."

"And I—" his soft, sensuous breath on her ear, as he whispered into it, caused her to shiver. Or was it his words? "—intend to find out the truth."

REMEMBERING SHAWN'S comment a while later, as Jenny and she sat in her daughter's favorite fast-food restaurant, Kelley shuddered.

Then she steeled herself. *She* intended to find out the truth, too. The real truth.

She wanted to hug her daughter. To run away with her. But that would not teach Jenny anything positive. Above all, Kelley wanted to be a good role model for Jenny. They would stay, as long as her daughter appeared to be in no danger.

As for danger to *her,* well, the more she thought about it, the more certain she was that the whole ambulance incident had been an accident.

The sullenness Jenny had shown when Kelley first approached her at KidClub had all but disappeared. Jenny seemed excited about their midday adventure. For now. But Kelley had to handle this just right. Without scaring Jenny.

"So how has your day been so far, sweetheart?" she asked.

Her daughter dipped a French fry in ketchup and popped it into her mouth without answering.

"Did anything new happen at KidClub today?"

"No," Jenny replied, but this time she glanced up at Kelley with a wary expression on her small, fragile face before she began to smoosh the ketchup around in the fries' cardboard container without trying to eat anything.

Holding her breath, Kelley reached into her purse and

pulled out the picture Shawn had handed her. She unfolded it carefully. "Shawn gave me this. Do you know who this is?" She pointed to the caricature of a smiling, familiar face with a crown on her blond hair.

Jenny nodded solemnly. Her eyes were huge. "It's me."

"Shawn said that the red stuff is—"

"It's fire, Mommy," Jenny whispered, her gaze darting around them.

"Does the fire still scare you?" Kelley asked carefully. "I know it scared me, especially when I found you near it, but we're safe and sound now."

Jenny nodded, but she did not look convinced.

"Remember the nice counselor we've gone to see? She said it's a good idea to talk about things that scare us. Do you want to talk about the fire now? Or anything you saw the night the fire started?"

"No, Mommy." Jenny hesitated. And then she ate another French fry.

Kelley wouldn't push her now. But she'd think of a way to bring it up again later. For Kelley knew something had made her daughter draw flames that day.

Somehow, she had to learn what it was.

Chapter Nine

Okay, Shawn told himself as he watched the second hand on the KidClub wall clock meander in its eternal circle. It hadn't slowed. Clocks didn't do that. But he had a job to do. A different job. And until—

"Watch me, Shawn," shouted Jenny. Kelley had brought her back from lunch a while ago. The kid had been a pistol all afternoon, alternating between stubborn refusal to heed directions and stony silence when he tried to start a conversation with her—one intended to lead to an explanation of her disquieting defacing of his artwork. Most particularly, what Jenny had seen that night.

Like her mother playing with matches?

No, someone else. Shawn wanted it to be someone else.

To his dismay, as soon as he looked over at Jenny, she started doing somersaults in the play area, right where a couple of other girls were having a pretend tea party. "Jenny, no!" He unwound his long legs from beneath one of the kiddie tables where he'd been giving a drawing lesson, but not fast enough. Of course Jenny's feet smashed loudly into the plastic cups and saucers.

And of course both girls began to cry.

Marge Ralston hurried in from the next room as Shawn swallowed his dismay while trying his damnedest to com-

fort the shrieking kids and keep Jenny from doing another
somersault out of spite. "What's going on here?" Marge
glared as if he'd been the one to cause the chaos.

"Glad you're here. I need a potty break." Without looking back, he strode from KidClub.

And stopped outside the door, guilt sticking a poker up
his back. This *was* part of his job.

Besides, he had to be here when Claire's mother returned.

With a deep sigh, he walked back inside. "Sorry," he
said to Marge as meekly as he could muster. He helped her
right the upended tea party. And he was the one to give
Jenny her third time out of the day.

Damn, but it felt like hell to do that, to watch the cute
kid sit defiantly in a corner. She was hurting. He knew it.
But he couldn't get her to talk about it.

Maybe Kelley would get something out of her later. But
Kelley wasn't here right now.

And the kid was her mother's daughter—pretty and appealing and cagey. Even at age three, she kept secrets of
her own.

When Jenny looked over her shoulder at him and a tear
rolled down her cheek, he nearly lost it. He clamped his
hands into fists so tight they hurt, to prevent himself from
dashing over to give her a great big hug.

As if he really knew about child psychology. But he'd
been instructed that kids who misbehaved had to endure
the results of their actions.

"You've something on your mind today, don't you,
Shawn?" Marge joined him at the doorway where he stood
with arms folded. The child-care coordinator spoke in a
soothing voice, and when he looked down she regarded him
with a sympathetic smile that hinted of flirtation. "You're
usually so good with the kids."

Implying that, today, he was the pits. Which was the truth.

And he had no intention of flirting back with Marge, no matter how nice she was.

He knew the drill about no conflicts of interest, and nevertheless was already being taught the hard way of the folly of caring about someone on an assignment.

His primary suspect.

"Yeah, I've something on my mind," he said.

Like, I have more work to do, I'm in a hurry, and today, when I have some real questions to ask, I have to wait.

Then, realizing how whiny and immature his thoughts were, he grinned ruefully at the curly-haired brunette. "The kids are teaching me as much as I'm teaching them." Without giving her more opportunity to comment, he motioned to a couple of boys, and they all joined the girls at their pretend tea party—after Shawn promised to read them an adventure story when they were done.

And when he did, he made certain enough time had passed that Jenny could join them.

He remained in KidClub's main room, keeping an eye on the door. When Janice Fritz, Claire's mother, appeared, he excused himself from the squawking kids and joined her at the entry. "Can I talk to you?" he asked. "It's important."

"Sure." She looked nonplussed as Shawn ushered her into the hallway.

Janice, who wore her dark hair in a ponytail, looked barely out of her teens and wore no wedding ring. All Shawn knew about her was that she worked in the hospital pharmacy and that she had a well-behaved daughter who liked to draw skunks. She wore a white smock over white slacks.

"Is something wrong with Claire?" she asked immedi-

ately. Her eyes were large and pale in color, and she wore
no makeup except for bright lipstick.

"No, she's fine. But Jenny Stanton has been acting up
today." He did not intend to mention the lines she'd drawn
depicting fire. The fewer people who knew about it, the
better—especially if Jenny had seen the arsonist. No way
would *he* endanger the child.

"Jenny? Poor thing, she's been through a lot, hasn't
she?"

"Yes," Shawn agreed, leaning a shoulder against the
wall as if he were relaxed. Despite the number of people
walking down the hall, he stayed focused on Janice. "Today she's seemed more upset than any day since I've been
here. Did she say anything to you this morning that might
explain why?"

Janice's ponytail swayed as she shook her head. "Not at
all."

"Did you see anyone or anything this morning when you
brought her in that might have upset her?"

Her narrow forehead puckered as she mulled over the
question. "I got a call at home last night that I needed to
be here earlier than usual this morning." She shook her
head more vehemently this time, and the edges of her ponytail grazed her smooth, rosy cheek. "I wish I'd known
before, or I'd have had Jenny sleep over a different night.
As it is, I had to get the girls up early. And when we got
here—" Her eyes lit up and she snapped her fingers. "We
did see her dad and Cheryl Marten, the cardiac nurse who's
his assistant. They didn't see us at first. They were right
outside the parking garage involved in a…discussion with
Dr. Madelyne Younger."

Shawn didn't let his excitement show. "A discussion?
Did you hear what they were 'discussing'?" Her hesitation

suggested she'd softened her initial characterization—argument.

Again she shook her head. She obviously used her ponytail to punctuate her thoughts, and it was beginning to annoy Shawn.

"No," she replied. "But why do you need—?"

"Did you know I'm majoring in child psychology?" The lie now tripped easily from Shawn's lips. "It's why I've got an internship at KidClub, and I want to understand Jenny's behavior, see if I can help her."

"Oh. I didn't know that. Anyhow, no, I didn't hear what they were talking about. Jenny's dad spotted us and came over, and that was that. Except…"

"Except?" Shawn prompted.

"Well, Cheryl and Dr. Younger came over to say hi, too. The two of them seemed…well, as if they wanted to avoid being near each other. Cheryl fussed over the girls, but Jenny hid behind me until Dr. Stanton—Randall—pulled her out." She looked up at Shawn. "Do you think that made Jenny upset enough to act up today?"

"Could be," Shawn said. He hid his disappointment. Nothing she'd said gave him any indication as to what might have made Jenny think of the fire.

Except that Kelley had said that Cheryl had signed Jenny out of KidClub that night, then left Jenny there and blamed it on Kelley.

Cheryl, of course, had told him just the opposite.

He wanted to believe Kelley. But he needed to learn the truth.

"And there was nothing else you saw or heard when you brought the girls in?"

"No, though Jenny did say something about being there too early. I figured she was unhappy because she was awakened too soon." She looked up at Shawn hopefully. "Do you think maybe she was just tired? That sometimes makes Claire act grumpy.''

"Could be," Shawn agreed. But it still wouldn't have explained her drawing the fire.

He thanked Janice and followed her back into KidClub, where she signed Claire out.

He now had a couple of leads to follow up.

Merely seeing Cheryl probably hadn't caused Jenny to draw fire, even if she blamed her father's ''friend'' for leaving her at the child-care center that night. She'd seen Cheryl many times since then, and she had never before sketched flames.

But she'd seen her father, too. Was it their location that had troubled her? Their argument with Madelyne Younger? Had she seen Madelyne since the fire? Probably. But the doctor hadn't been around KidClub while Shawn was working there.

All of a sudden, Shawn decided he wasn't feeling well.

"So, WHAT SEEMS to be the problem, kiddo?" asked Dr. Madelyne Younger. She leered at him, eyeing him up and down suggestively. "You look in tip-top shape to me."

Shawn laughed. "Looks can be deceiving."

He'd had the internist paged a short while before. Thankfully, she'd still been around. She'd agreed to see him in her office.

The oak desk in the compact and austerely furnished room was immaculate. Nothing was out of place anywhere else, either.

Funny. He'd imagined the colorful and outspoken doctor would choose colorful and outspoken surroundings, too.

They sat on stiff wooden chairs around a glass-topped coffee table, empty except for two teacups—real and fragile this time.

Shawn didn't think much of herbal tea, but the stuff Madelyne had offered actually had some taste—sharp lemon and tangy melon, an odd but flavorful combination. The citrus-and-sweet aroma filled the small room.

"Actually, though," he told the doctor, whose short, platinum hair suggested she was older than middle-aged, "you're right. *My* health isn't the reason I needed to talk to you."

"Whose, then?"

"Little Jenny Stanton's."

Her eyes widened so much that the wrinkles at their corners all but disappeared. "What's wrong with her?" She scowled and drove her fists hard into the pockets of the purple lab jacket that she hadn't removed, despite being off duty. "That vulture of a nurse who's got her talons in Jenny's dad isn't getting to her, is she?"

"Cheryl Marten?"

"None other." She spat out the words as if her tea had suddenly turned insipid. "That b—er, witch has been pretending she likes kids. But no doubt about it, if she gets Randall to marry her, the first thing that'll go is Jenny." She shrugged. "Which isn't exactly a bad thing, you understand. The tot would be a lot better off if her mom got sole custody."

"Do you think Kelley Stanton is a good doctor?" Shawn figured he'd push the questions as far as he could under the guise of a concerned caretaker of the "tot."

"Of course." The words exploded from Madelyne. "Though that has nothing to do with her mothering ability. I take it you've heard the hospital scuttlebutt, though why it would get to the ears of a child-care attendant—no offense, Shawn, but it really isn't your business how Dr. Kelley Stanton practices medicine."

Oh, but it is, Shawn's thoughts contradicted.

Just like it was his business to find out why, after the way they'd gotten along last night, Kelley was acting today as if he'd sprouted horns and a forked tail.

"I know," he said smoothly, "but if her concerns affect her daughter, that's my business." He proceeded to describe the day with Jenny, as he had with Janice Fritz. "She wasn't with her mother last night, but she wasn't with her father, either."

"She saw her daddy when Claire's mom brought her in this morning," Madelyne said. "Did Jenny tell you?"

Ah, the exact opening Shawn was looking for. "No, but I did ask Claire's mother whether she knew of anything that might have set Jenny off this morning. She said she saw you talking with Dr. Randall Stanton and Cheryl Marten, but didn't know why Jenny would get upset about that."

"Me, neither," Madelyne said.

"What were you discussing?"

"A case." Her tone, and her belligerently outslung lower jaw, suggested to Shawn that she had no intention of saying more.

"Which case?" He kept his own voice ingenuous, as if he were driven by sheer curiosity.

Madelyne sighed and rose. Her bleak expression indicated she didn't want to talk about it further. "Let's just say we were talking about Kelley. Randall keeps—well, never mind about that. I'm sure you've heard how Kelley saved the day with that Rocky Mountain Spotted Fever patient. There's a lot of good in how Kelley practices medicine."

"And a lot of bad?" Shawn suggested.

She reeled on him. "I didn't say that."

But she didn't deny it, either.

"Look," she continued as she paced the area rug on her

wooden floor. "I've been a physician a lot longer than Kelley, and even I fail to catch things. I really thought that kid had mononucleosis. Classic case. Only it wasn't. Kelley got it right, maybe saved the kid's life." She stopped pacing and faced Shawn. "Stuck me where it hurt—right in the old professional pride. But we all make mistakes sometimes. And that's why we encourage our patients to get second opinions."

Shawn was skating on thin ice, but there was a question he had to ask. "Do you know of any situations where Kelley made mistakes? Like, in her treatment of the Silver Rapids flu patients?"

"If you want to believe rumors, go ahead," she said angrily. She visibly got hold of herself, but the leer she turned on him this time looked forced. "And if you don't intend to show me any part of your anatomy for a diagnosis, this session is at an end."

But Shawn realized, as he left Madelyne's office, that she hadn't given her opinion about whether Kelley's treatment of the flu patients had been wrong.

And that might have been an answer in itself.

"DID JENNY SAY anything?" Kelley asked Shawn.

It was much later than she'd planned to get to KidClub to pick up her daughter. She had been delayed by a last-minute appointment with a patient whose mild, ignored cold had turned into severe pneumonia requiring immediate attention.

Now it was six-thirty in the evening. Time for KidClub to close. She was the last parent to pick up a child.

And she'd come in to find Jenny sitting in a corner. According to Shawn, it was her second time-out that afternoon. Her fourth that day.

Guilt danced through Kelley like a demented demon,

making her want to weep. Of all days to be late, when she knew her daughter was hurting…

"She didn't say much," Shawn replied to her question in a low voice. Jenny had been told to stay put for another two minutes. She was looking over her shoulder so sadly that Kelley had to quash the urge to dash over to comfort her. At least she probably couldn't hear what they were saying, but Kelley was glad Shawn was taking no chances.

Leaning on the sign-out desk beside her, he looked beat. His broad shoulders appeared to have deflated, and dark circles underscored his reddened eyes. Somehow, though, he still looked like a hunk. One who needed a good night's sleep.

The kids must have gotten to him.

Jenny must have gotten to him.

He confirmed it. "Unless what you're asking is whether she decided to practice her loudest singing at naptime. Or whether she yelled until Claire shouted they weren't best friends anymore, and then they both cried."

Kelley's smile was bittersweet. "That's not what I meant."

"I know." He shook his head. "I did some other checking, to try to figure out if anything upset her today." He described how he'd questioned first Claire's mother, then Madelyne. "I didn't get much, only that Janice had to bring the girls back especially early this morning, and that Jenny saw Randall, Cheryl and Madelyne together near the parking lot and they were most likely arguing."

"About…?"

Shawn's blue eyes opened a shade wider.

"Me?" Kelley guessed.

"That's what I gathered."

Kelley could imagine the gist—Randall badmouthing

her, Cheryl seconding what he said and Madelyne defending her.

Only—she had stepped on Madelyne's toes over the Heather Harrell case. If she hadn't, Heather could have sickened further. Maybe even died.

Madelyne wasn't the type to hold grudges. Was she? But if the argument had been about Kelley, her friend and colleague would have been the only one likely to take her side.

Randall and Cheryl certainly wouldn't.

"Thanks for checking," Kelley told Shawn. "I only wish…" His gaze caught hers. She sensed sympathy and something more.

Something she refused to allow herself to identify.

"So," Shawn said, straightening so that she again had to look up to see into his face. "Where are we going for dinner?"

Kelley blinked in astonishment. "We?"

"After last night, I'm not letting you out of my sight this evening. Jenny, either. And if she starts talking about what upset her, I want to be there."

"I'll take care of Jenny," Kelley said stiffly. "And we'll be fine. Both of us." But now that Shawn had reminded her of the incident that hadn't really left her thoughts all day, she saw again in her mind the ambulance speeding toward her….

Recalled how Shawn had saved her.

Recalled that Louis Paxler had known she'd spent the night in Shawn's apartment.

She didn't really think Shawn had told Paxler she'd been there. But now that she knew for sure that his agenda was to draw information out of her, some of which she wasn't prepared to reveal, she had no intention of spending any more time in his presence than she had to.

Especially since she yearned to. To tell him all, to let

this undercover investigator take care of everything, including her.

Yeah. He'd take care of her all right.

And she'd wind up in prison—of one sort or another.

Shawn Jameson clearly liked to be in charge. And Kelley
knew just what it was like to have a man like that in her
life.

"You want to take a chance with your safety? Jenny's
safety?" He sounded incredulous, as if he couldn't believe
she was turning down the offer of his chivalric presence.

"I'll be careful. And we don't really know it wasn't an
accident, last night."

He snorted derisively. "Yeah, someone stole an ambulance and *accidentally* sped it right toward you."

"Could be."

"Kelley, look."

Uh-oh. She was about to get the "be reasonable" speech.
She'd heard one like it every time she'd dared to contradict
Randall, as if he were the only one whose opinion was
rational.

She'd heard something similar during those rare times
her mother had dared to defy her father.

She wasn't her mother.

But she was *a* mother. Jenny's mother.

For her daughter's sake and her own, she needed to take
care of things herself.

"We'll see you tomorrow, Shawn," she said, only nar-
rowly preventing herself from wincing at the look in his
eyes. Anger. She only imagined the hint of hurt.

She headed toward the corner to collect her daughter.

"Kelley? It's shawn."

He had been watching as one light after another blinked
out in the Stanton house, a cozy brick residence snuggled

into a pleasant suburban community. Only a single light remained on now—the one in what he presumed was Kelley's bedroom.

"I know. I recognized your voice. Not to mention your SUV sitting right outside my door. Your cell phone has static."

"You could hear me better if you let me come in."

"I'm getting ready for bed now. Jenny's asleep, and—"

"Did she talk about the fire?"

A pause. "No, not even to her therapist, though we both encouraged her."

"I'm sorry." And not just about Jenny.

He was sorry he hadn't been able to check out the house before they went inside, though everything seemed fine now. And he was sorry he was sitting here, all cramped up in his vehicle, when he could be there, watching Kelley get ready for bed....

Yeah. Right. That definitely wasn't on her agenda. And it shouldn't be on his.

"We're fine, Shawn. Go home."

"You're not fine," he shouted. Damn. That would get him nowhere. "Do you have a security alarm you can turn on?" He knew the answer already. He'd checked out her house that morning while she changed clothes. "Do you at least have a weapon?"

Another pause. "Good night, Shawn." Her voice was shaking. Damn again! Now he had frightened her.

Which was good. If she was scared, maybe she'd let him in.

Maybe she would finally talk to him.

"Do you?" he repeated.

A click, and then the remaining light turned off.

But Shawn was certain that Kelley wouldn't be sleeping. Any more than he would.

THE ARSONIST DROVE BY.

Not in an ambulance this time, but in a very ordinary car, one no one would notice. At an ordinary speed, too, like any other resident hurrying just a little to get home at this hour.

But the arsonist saw Shawn Jameson's big blue SUV sitting outside Kelley Stanton's house. Saw a form in the driver's seat. Jameson, of course.

Shawn Jameson, who wasn't all he seemed. The arsonist knew. Would have known anyway, even if the damned investigator hadn't been asking so many questions.

It didn't matter. The answers couldn't be found so easily.

The arsonist had followed them yesterday, too. Had seen Kelley go to Jameson's home. And not come out. A useful fact to throw into the mix.

For the arsonist wasn't through with her reputation. Not yet.

Next time, it would definitely, irrevocably, be ruined.

Chapter Ten

Another day was well underway. Rounds were over.

So was round umpteen with Louis Paxler.

Kelley's shoulders slumped as she headed back to her office. Her whole body slumped. She felt so exhausted, it might as well have been midnight instead of early afternoon.

She felt as defeated as if she'd lost another patient. Of all the verbal battles she'd had with Louis Paxler, this had been the worst.

But that didn't mean her fights for the day had ended.

She returned to her office to find Shawn there, staring out the window. Holding a disposable coffee cup in one large hand.

She resisted the urge to throw herself into Shawn's arms. Especially when he turned to face her.

Comfort was obviously not at the forefront of his mind. But something was. And she didn't want to know what.

"Hi," she said. "How's Jenny?" She stood with one hand on the knob of the door she'd closed behind her. If her office didn't turn out to be a haven this morning, she would have to leave it. Fast.

"I'm sure she's fine." He was dressed in a vest she

hadn't seen before—rich brown suede over his navy shirt. His jeans showed no wear. Not the same clothes he'd worn yesterday. They looked good on him, though. He looked very…male.

Her hormones began to ooze, but she controlled them.

''Then you didn't come here from KidClub?'' She hadn't seen him there that morning when she'd brought Jenny in. She hadn't asked about him, either, despite how curious she had been.

She'd looked for his car when Jenny and she had left the house that morning, in case he'd watched over them all night. She shouldn't have been surprised to see he wasn't there—but she was surprised at how disappointed she'd felt. Obviously he'd gone back to his place to sleep. Leaving Jenny and her vulnerable to the phantom ambulance driver.

If something had happened last night, Kelley would have had no one to blame but herself.

''No, I haven't been to KidClub this morning.'' His tone was level, but there was an edgy undercurrent she didn't understand. ''I had a meeting. With my boss. My real boss.'' The expression on his face was bland. All except for his eyes.

They had turned so chilly that she hugged herself.

''I see.'' She didn't, really. But his meeting obviously hadn't gone well. And the tentative warmth they had shared two evenings ago had apparently disappeared totally. She felt tears threaten but forced them away.

''Damn it, Kelley, I told you the truth about why I was here because I figured you'd trust me. But you haven't told me anything I can use. I'm in deep doo-doo for playing a hunch that didn't pan out. For trusting *you*.'' He slammed the coffee cup down on her desk. Fortunately, it wasn't full, for nothing sloshed out of the plastic lid.

"What's wrong?" she demanded with more force than she thought herself capable of at that moment.

"Only that my employer's miffed that I blew my cover. I'd have gotten away with it if I weren't still short on results, thanks to you."

"What do you mean?" Her tone was shrill. She didn't need this discussion. Not now. She had already survived one knock-down-drag-out this morning. Again she considered fleeing. But where would she go? Instead, she made herself cross the room casually and sit behind her desk. She was wearing a rose-colored silk blouse and a black skirt that didn't quite reach her knees. She tugged at it, wishing she'd worn something to cover more. She felt exposed after her earlier argument.

"I don't know what you want from me," she continued calmly, though she heard the quiver in her voice. "You're here to investigate the fire. I didn't set it. And to figure out if I did something wrong in treating those Silver Rapids patients. I didn't." To her dismay, she nearly sobbed aloud. She swallowed. Hard. "I didn't," she whispered rawly.

He studied her with those ice-blue eyes of his as if speculating what was in her mind. "I'd like to believe that, but I know there's more you haven't told me. And until you do—"

The dam of emotion that Kelley had erected inside her by sheer force of will collapsed. Her breathing deepened. So did her rage. "I don't have to," she shouted. "You'll hear about it. Everyone will hear about it."

"Hear about what?" He approached and leaned over her desk. Digging at her with his words. His glare.

"What Paxler told me. He says someone found a chart

misfiled in another patient's records. He showed it to me, said it was for one of the Silver Rapids patients—Peg Ahlers, one of those who died. The chart indicates that I said to hold off on antibiotics, to see how the symptoms continued to manifest themselves, because tests on other patients had shown the pathogen was a virus and antibiotics don't help viral infections. But antibiotics can stave off other infections when the patient's immune system is weakened, so it could have been malpractice not to medicate her. And because this one little sheet survived my torching the records office, word will get around that there's proof I fouled up. My career is over.''

He was around the desk so quickly that she pulled back in alarm. To no avail. He leaned over, grabbed her shoulders. ''Are you admitting that you set the fire?'' His face was so close to hers that she felt his warm breath, inhaled the scent of his recently drunk coffee.

''I might as well, right? The paperwork is there to prove I messed up. I killed my patient. Maybe both of the ones who died. So the fire was for nothing, wasn't it?''

''Kelley, tell me—'' His tone was ominous, but no more menacing than his fierce expression. He spoke one word at a time. ''Did. You. Set. The. Fire.''

''No,'' she shouted. ''I had no reason to.'' A laugh bubbled up from somewhere inside. Hysteria, she diagnosed, stepping back from herself. *Be clinical, like a good doctor should.*

A good doctor. She *was* a good doctor.

''You see,'' she continued, practically spitting her words into his face, ''Louis wouldn't let me see the paper. I don't know where it came from. It was a lie. I didn't treat Mrs. Ahlers different from the others. And it didn't come from my charts. My files.''

"How do you know that?"

She wrested her arms away. *Don't do anything out of emotion,* her detached mind told her. *You may regret it later.*

But her anger was too far gone to consider all the possible ramifications. She stood. Walked to the file cabinet. Found the folder marked "Myles." Extracted the key.

She returned to her desk, opened the locked drawer, and pulled out the armful of files.

"They didn't burn." Her voice was ragged, but no more so than her emotions. "I'd stolen them first, so they didn't burn."

Hot damn! Shawn hadn't stopped grinning. It was better than he could have hoped for—the actual files. Not just reconstruction by memories faulty and false.

Wouldn't Colleen be pleased?

Him, too, of course. Not that he'd understand all the medical stuff likely to be in them, but soon he would dig in and figure out all that led up to the fire. Maybe get enough to rule Kelley out once and for all.

Or find enough in there to ensure she remained suspect number one.

All he had to do was start looking. Soon.

But first, he had to let go of the woman in his arms.

He wasn't ready to do that. She felt too good.

Kelley had ended up there after her revelation. He hadn't intended to urge her off her chair and tight against him. But she had been so defiantly sad. So fragilely strong.

So contrarily enticing.

Now, she clung to him as if he were her salvation instead of her tormenter. Not a great idea. But she felt so good, small and supple and curved in all the right places. Dressed in a blouse and skirt and all female, despite her responsible profession. And smelling like antibacterial soap and woman.

Arousing his protective instinct. Arousing *him*.

But there was no time or place for that. Now or ever.

His grin disappeared.

"It'll be okay," he lied into her fragrant hair. "I'll take the files to my agency's office. Even if anyone suspected they still existed, no one will figure I have them. And—"

She was out of his arms, facing him with hands on her hips, anger warring with fear on her face. "No," she said.

"But we need to find out what happened. If there's any possible tie-in with the fire."

"You won't be able to tell from those files," she said. "All you'll be able to do is see who the patients were, the tests that were run on them and the results, the treatment prescribed. I can't let them out of my possession, especially now. I have to show somehow that the chart Paxler has is a forgery."

Damn. This wouldn't be easy—especially since he saw Kelley's point. She had her own butt to protect, and the files could be her only shield.

"My people can analyze handwriting, even ink. If we get the paperwork Paxler has, they can compare it, determine if it's a forgery." He saw her stiffen at the "if." He should have been more positive. He sighed. "Kelley, one way or the other the truth needs to come out. I don't think you did anything wrong. You certainly didn't set the fire to hide these files, and I don't think you set it at all. But if you keep hiding things, how can we clear you?"

The rebelliousness in her ramrod-straight posture lessened just a little. "We?" she repeated scornfully, as if she doubted she'd heard him right.

He nodded. Slowly. For he knew now that his number one arson suspect hadn't had any motive to start the fire. Unless, of course, she'd been threatened, or Jenny had. Or Kelley had been coerced, blackmailed or even bribed. But Shawn had seen no indication of anything of that sort, no physical evidence and nothing in Kelley's demeanor, though he couldn't completely rule them out yet.

Still, he'd come to figure that if he were sick, there was no one he'd like more to treat him than Dr. Kelley Stanton.

Wise or not, justified or not, he believed in her.

"We," he repeated. "Let me help you, Kelley."

HIDING IN A NOISY CROWD kept anyone from hearing most cell phone conversations. Still, Shawn kept his voice low.

"C? It's me."

"Yes, Shawn? It's only been an hour since our last meeting. Miss me already? Or did you want me to chew you out some more?"

He ignored the sarcasm in his boss's voice—especially since she really had reamed him but good at the ICU office that morning for his lack of progress in the case.

Good thing she couldn't see his smug smile. But he was damned pleased he had something positive to report. Finally.

Though how helpful the new evidence was remained to be seen.

"Hang around in Denver tonight," he said. "I don't want to draw any suspicion to Dr. Stanton or myself, but get some of the troops rallied, prepare them to analyze some files, will you?"

"What files?"

"The infamous Silver Rapids flu files."

He heard her intake of breath. "But they were destroyed in the fire."

"Not."

Silence. Then, "Get here soon, Jameson. Understand?"

He flipped his cell phone closed. Good thing, too. He had just reached KidClub. And heard crying inside.

He looked up at the ceiling. He looked down at the floor. He straightened his shoulders as he faced the closed door, then hesitated, looking around for an excuse not to enter.

He met the eyes of some stranger passing by who grinned, as if reading his mind.

Give me strength, he prayed, then went inside.

And was enraged by what he found there.

"WHAT DO YOU MEAN you blame Shawn?" Kelley slouched in the kitchen, her weight resting on her hip against the sink counter.

She felt as if she could hardly stand at all, especially since the linoleum floor was damp, as if it had just been mopped.

Marge Ralston's arms were crossed over her characteristic paint-spattered smock. As she shook her head, her short, curly hair vibrated. "You know, though the guy says he's studying child psychology, I have to wonder."

If you only knew. "What did he do?" Kelley tried to remain patient, but all she knew was that Shawn had called her a few minutes ago to come and calm Jenny.

When she'd gotten here, her daughter had been hysterical. She'd held Jenny and comforted her and gotten her settled down. The poor little thing had been so exhausted that she fell asleep almost immediately on one of the floor mats they used for naps.

Shawn was still in the next room, watching over her. The

expression in his eyes would have made a lesser person quake.

Not Kelley. But she wanted to get him alone. Soon. So she could figure out exactly what happened.

She doubted Marge understood much.

"The thing is, something obviously upset her. Shawn wasn't even here when whatever it was set her off. She started throwing things again, really made a mess of some kids' breakfasts. Then she grabbed some paper and crayons and began making jagged red lines on other kids' drawings."

Fire again! Oh, no. Though Kelley felt the blood drain from her face, she waited for Marge to continue.

"She was screaming. I tried to get her to stop crying but she was so upset. Then Shawn came in, saw what was happening, and he grabbed her—gently, mind you—but he tried to get her to talk. And when she didn't, he let his frustration show and she got even more hysterical."

"I see. I'm sure he meant well, but..." She didn't need to stick up for Shawn. She knew his agenda.

If *she* hadn't set the fire, someone else had.

The fire still upset Jenny, and Kelley still didn't know if she'd seen anything that night.

"Speak of the handsome devil," Marge muttered as Shawn strode into the kitchen, boots clumping rhythmically on the floor.

"Stephanie is watching the kids," he told them, naming another child-care attendant. "I told her to especially keep an eye on Jenny, to let us know if she so much as blinked. Or if anyone else comes in."

His grim expression suggested that the presence of other people concerned him even more than Jenny's blinking. Why?

"Marge, for me to figure out what got Jenny so upset, I need to know everything that went on before she started crying." His voice was calmer now, as if he was once again playing psychology student.

Which was probably better than telling the child-care coordinator the truth, which could really freak her out. It still freaked Kelley out, even though he'd promised to help her.

Of course, she might be beyond help, at least around here.

"I don't actually know what upset Jenny," Marge said, distress written in her eyes. Which was telling in itself. She *was* distressed. Every other time Kelley had seen her in Shawn's presence, she'd overtly flirted with him. "A few people were around here who usually aren't, though."

"Who?" Shawn pounced on the question, which worried Kelley.

Marge gave a rundown that included Randall and Cheryl, Louis Paxler and a woman Marge didn't recognize who sounded like Etta Borand. They'd all seemed to be discussing something vociferously. Madelyne Younger had joined them, too. "And—" Marge glanced nervously at Kelley "—when the strange woman left, Mr. Paxler seemed relieved, but he looked at the others and said something I didn't quite hear about heads about to roll." Her expression grew startled. "Could that be it? Kids take things literally, and maybe Jenny thought heads would actually roll."

Could be, Kelley thought, feeling her heart grow sluggish with defeat. Especially if... "Did my name come up in the conversation?"

Marge frowned. "Mr. Paxler did say 'Dr. Stanton,' but since Dr. Randall Stanton was there, I assumed he meant him. But if Jenny thought that either of you was about to lose a head…''

"Neither of them is," Shawn asserted. "But we need to make sure Jenny understands that."

Kelley agreed.

"I'll call you as soon as she wakes up," he told Kelley. "Then you can take her home."

But as he walked Kelley to KidClub's door, he whispered into her ear, "We'll all leave then. Be sure to get the files ready to go. Stick them in your medical bag, whatever, to obscure them. I've someplace I need to take Jenny and you—and them."

Chapter Eleven

Kelley's mind flopped like the screen of an electrocardiogram gone mad.

Shawn had driven Jenny and her straight to the office of his private investigative agency ICU. Now, they were back in his SUV. As he had before, he kept looking into the rearview mirror and the side mirrors. A lot. Kelley suspected he was not only driving defensively against other drivers, but defending against anyone who might be following them, as well. But why?

She wanted to discuss everything with Shawn, but Jenny was wide awake. "Where are we going?" Kelley asked.

"A surprise," Shawn said. They had stopped at a light, and he turned to wink at Jenny, who giggled in delight.

Her daughter might like surprises, but Kelley didn't.

At least Jenny had calmed down since leaving KidClub. Now she acted like a normal three-year-old. One who wasn't terrified, thank heavens. But what had bothered her before? Kelley had to find out.

She needed other answers, too, to questions she couldn't ask right now.

"That Becky was certainly a whiz at making quick photocopies," she said. She gestured toward her medical bag, on the floor beside her. It contained copies of the patient files. The originals were to stay in the ICU offices.

"She made me a copy of my hand," Jenny piped up from the back seat.

"You're sure they won't lose the originals?" Kelley whispered to Shawn. "I mean, if I need them to prove my story, I'd hate for them to be missing."

"Believe me, Colleen will not allow anyone to lose anything," Shawn reassured her.

The ICU office was in downtown Denver, not far from the U.S. Mint. According to Shawn, Colleen Wellesley, the head of the agency, had chosen the location by design. She had wanted to ensure that its employees stayed focused on turning out perfect results, time after time. And, of course, on making money.

Kelley had met the attractive, slightly older Colleen. Then there'd been the men in cowboy gear—one, Michael, was Colleen's brother. Another, Ryan Benton, had been tall and quiet.

There had also been an attractive young woman named Nicki, who'd apparently sensed how overwhelmed Kelley felt. She had shared a lot of warm glances with Michael Wellesley. "Don't mind this gang," she'd told Kelley. "I just met most of them myself not long ago. There are others, too. But don't worry. They may bite, but it doesn't hurt a bit."

Kelley hadn't felt reassured, especially when Colleen very persuasively tried to talk her into leaving the Silver Rapids patient files. What had convinced her was the way Colleen had gone over them, page by page, before getting them copied. Had discussed all the patients' symptoms and the results of their tests. As if understanding it all mattered to her. As if the *truth* mattered to her.

She'd deferentially asked Kelley to explain the medical

indications. Kelley described how all the patients had been
tested for viruses and had been found to have a strain similar to influenza type A. Despite treatment with antiviral
medications and a mild antibiotic to prevent further infection, the patients had developed symptoms. She'd had their
blood checked for bacterial infections as well in the IFA
tests. The results had been negative.

And yet, something had seemed…well, off, to Kelley.
She'd changed the meds, which had seemed to help most
patients. And she'd made notes about her concerns. But
with nothing to go on but gut feeling, she'd had to let her
questions drop—even after the two deaths. She'd made
light of her disquiet when explaining the files to Colleen.

Wilson's call had brought it all back and then some, but
that wasn't in the patient files, of course.

In the end, Kelley prayed that the resources this group
undoubtedly had could help to clear her. As long as they
didn't decide to railroad her, as someone at Gilpin Hospital
was already attempting to do. And because she'd kept copies of the files, it would be harder for the ICU clan to
modify them.

She knew Shawn had already asked them to help find
Wilson. So far, they hadn't been successful. And until Kelley could discuss her suspicions with him, she would keep
them to herself.

"Here we are," Shawn said, breaking into Kelley's rev-
erie. She glanced out the windshield and smiled. They'd
stopped in front of an old-fashioned saloon that had been
turned into a museum and steakhouse. "Hope my *pardners*
have big appetites tonight. We're going to eat like cowboys.
Okay, Jenny?"

"Okay, Shawn."

A WHILE LATER, Kelley sighed in relief as they pulled up
in front of her house. Dinner had been excellent. So had

the company. Shawn had played the cowboy role—drawl, boots and all—to the hilt with Jenny, who had loved it.

So, in fact, had Kelley.

He'd tried to get Jenny to talk about all she'd done that day. When she'd started to get upset he'd stopped, thank goodness. But there was still no answer as to why Jenny had acted up.

The day had seemed abysmally long. Kelley was ready to get Jenny to bed, and to turn in, too.

Not that she expected to sleep.

She reached for the door handle. "Thanks for everything, Shawn." Dinner, at least. The jury was still out on whether she should thank him for introducing her to the ICU team. That would depend on whether their investigation helped or harmed her.

"You're welcome," he said as he got out of the car. Kelley was used to opening doors for herself, but by the time she reached for the handle, he had beaten her to it.

She smiled as she stood, her eyes locked onto his. Something arced between them. Something that made her belly—and below—liquefy like lava. "See you," she whispered.

"Yeah," he said so huskily that her knees nearly buckled. "Yeah, you will," he continued more forcefully, drawing his eyes away. "I'm coming in." He stood with his hand on the door to the back seat so she couldn't retrieve Jenny.

Her mood changed so fast it dizzied her. "Don't you wait to be asked?"

"Not when the choice is either inviting myself in or spending another night twisted into pretzels out here." He tapped his SUV.

"You don't need to do, either." She tried to reach around him for the door handle.

He again blocked her. "Yeah, I do."

"Why? Do you think I'll sneak out and start another fire?"

The infuriated glitter in his eyes told her she shouldn't even joke about that. "Could be. Or could be you were nearly run over a couple of nights ago, and today something scared your daughter. Plus, though Colleen could have kissed me for bringing in those files, she'd be all too happy to castrate me like a steer on her ranch if I lost a suspect while zoning out at my apartment in front of late night TV."

"What do you mean, 'lost'?"

Instead of answering, he pulled open the back door and unhooked Jenny from the seat belt in the child seat they'd transferred from Kelley's car. He lifted her out. "So, Jenny, what's your favorite bedtime story? I'll bet it has animals."

"Uh-huh," Jenny said with a big nod.

"Good, 'cause I'm going to read it to you." Without giving Kelley time for further protest, he headed for the front door.

Damn controlling man! She wanted to shout something nasty at him. But not in front of Jenny.

And what if they *were* in danger…?

She opened the deadbolt without another word, only to hear Shawn say, "You still need to get an alarm."

Kelley flicked on the light in the entryway, her lips pursed in fury at his presumption.

And in fear? What if someone could get in?

What if she was allowing herself to get spooked, just to play into Shawn's controlling hands?

In spite of herself, she found herself waiting. Listening. But no one leaped out at them.

This was her home. Everything would be fine here.

But Shawn still checked the place out, then returned to the entry where Kelley waited with her daughter.

"Jenny, honey, go to your room and start getting ready for bed," Kelley said, scooting her daughter down the hall in that direction. She turned back to Shawn. "Thanks again, but it's really time for you to leave now." The brightness of her tone, assumed for Jenny's sake, belied the determined set to her jaw as she regarded him icily, waiting for him to go.

"I don't think so." He walked down the hall instead of toward the door.

"He's going to read me my favorite an'mal book," Jenny said from in front of them.

They were ganging up on Kelley, and she didn't like it. "Shawn can read you your book," she finally conceded. "Then he's going back to his home. Aren't you, Shawn?"

It was a question she shouldn't have asked. He clearly regarded it as a challenge, and the answer was written in the stubborn amusement in his cool blue eyes. "We'll see," he said.

Kelley hurried Jenny through her usual routine of bathing, changing into pajamas and brushing her teeth. She leaned against the bedroom wall while Shawn and Jenny laughed over the antics of a talking dog in one of Jenny's favorite stories. They both seemed to enjoy themselves.

She, too, found herself enjoying Shawn's mellow baritone as he read the humorous tale. Watched how the obviously strong man gently hugged her daughter. How this man who normally seemed ill at ease with kids let down his guard with Jenny.

Soon, the story was over. Jenny yawned. "'Night, Shawn."

"Good night, Jenny. See you in the morning."

But not here, Kelley's mind told the intrusive man. She glared it at him, too. A corner of his wide mouth quirked, as if he heard her thoughts and they amused him.

She nearly melted as he gave Jenny a big hug and kiss, and her daughter, wearing a big, sleepy smile, kissed him back. The scene was so sweet and domestic that a deep yearning bloomed inside Kelley, wrapping around her heart and squeezing. If only she could provide Jenny with a happy bedtime like this every night. If only it could be with someone like Shawn…

Hardly, the wisest part of her brain sneered. He didn't seem the domestic type. And he'd been sent to investigate her.

They walked down the hall in silence. When they reached the entry, Kelley put her hand on the doorknob. "Thanks again," she said. "As you can see, we're fine here. I'll lock the door behind you. Maybe I'll even consider getting an alarm system."

"Kelley, I'm staying."

"No!" Expecting this, she expressed her outrage in her tone and then glared at him. He hadn't bothered yet to ask if he could stay. He'd *told* her.

The thing was, a part of her perversely wanted him to stay.

Perversely wanted *him.* Here. In her home. Now.

Shawn Jameson was the best-looking hunk of male sexiness she had met in a long time. Probably forever. But it wasn't just his looks that attracted her. He was so kind to Jenny.

And though he wanted something from Kelley—confessions of misdeeds she couldn't give—he was kind to her, too. And protective. But what was he expecting to defend them from here? Renegade ambulance drivers? Menacing forgers who slipped false pieces of paper into hospital files?

She didn't want to feel protected by this man, but she did. And insanely, incredibly attracted to him.

All the more reason to make him leave. Now. Before she let another domineering man try to convince her she had to obey his every command. He wouldn't succeed, of course. But she wouldn't even give him the chance.

She began to unlock the deadbolt, but he stayed her with a firm grip on her wrist. "Put on a pot of decaf, okay? I've a feeling we're about to have a long talk."

"Put it on yourself!" she exploded as this last order put a match to a very short fuse. "The kitchen is right down there."

He looked at her with a tawny brow raised quizzically. An instant later, as she followed his quick, sure stride down the hallway of her house, she realized that this man, with his damned commanding manner, was getting his way after all.

"So, DO YOU WANT to explain why you're suddenly acting like I'm a loathsome disease you want to eradicate?"

Ignoring the compulsion to leave since he clearly wasn't wanted here, Shawn had made himself at home in Kelley's compact but well-supplied kitchen. He had found ground coffee, though not decaf, in the freezer, and a six-cup coffeemaker on the gold tile counter. He'd poured water into the carafe at the spotless stainless sink, but had had to ask where to find filters. They were unsurprisingly in a cabinet with other paper products.

He started the coffee brewing, then planted himself deliberately against the counter, facing her.

Arms folded, she stared as if he'd suddenly broken out in hives. Her knee-length black skirt vibrated, demonstrating how much she trembled.

"Does what I'm thinking matter?" she growled in response to his query.

Maybe it was trite, but the woman sure looked beautiful when she was mad. Of course, Kelley looked beautiful all the time.

And damned if he was going to take her into his arms, as he wanted to do, when he had no idea why she was so furious. She'd probably scratch his eyes out. Or some other equally vital part of his anatomy. She clearly wanted nothing to do with him, which was fine with him. It had to be.

"Take a breath, Kelley," he made himself say softly, "and—"

"Don't tell me what to do!" She turned away and sat at the small pine table in the corner. When she looked up again, she'd wilted. "Please leave." Her voice was hoarse. A plea.

If he were a gentleman, he'd obey. But in his current incarnation, he was a cowboy and an undercover operative. There was no gentleman in that equation.

He slid a mug beneath the stream of brewing coffee to take half a cup, then returned the carafe to its place and sat down in a chair facing her.

"Sorry, Kelley, but I'd be worried about your safety. Yours and Jenny's."

"What is it you're really concerned about?" Uneasiness shadowed her soft brown eyes.

"Damned if I know. But something bothered Jenny today and she won't talk about it. And though I tried to make sure we weren't followed, if someone knows you're with me and we went to the ICU office, that someone could get a bit perturbed."

"*What* someone?"

"If I knew, I'd take care of him—or her—and wouldn't worry you about it."

"You're talking in riddles, Shawn." Kelley sounded exhausted. She looked exhausted. So what if she wanted nothing to do with him? He wanted to take her into his arms so much now they ached.

Instead, he rose and got her a cup of the fully brewed coffee. When she took it from him, their hands touched. She didn't pull away. He felt more scorched than if he'd poured the steaming liquid over himself.

He was the one to remove his hand from hers. She reddened and took a sip of coffee.

"It's like this," he told her gently. "Either you're paranoid, or someone is out to get you."

She laughed mirthlessly.

"No joke," he said. "If you didn't set that fire, then someone else did and is willing to let you take the blame. I now have good reason to believe you have no motive to commit arson. Meantime, you've been blamed for bad doctoring. When you started to redeem yourself with that Rocky Mountain Spotted Fever diagnosis, somebody didn't like it one bit."

Kelley's eyes no longer looked tired as they widened in surprise. "The ambulance incident was because people were, for once, acknowledging I did something right? That's far-fetched."

"Far-fetched is my business. So's 'what if.' Bear with me. You're in the proverbial doghouse again, what with that chart from the Silver Rapids flu file being found." He held up his hand. "I know it was probably manufactured, but its existence means you're Dr. Do-wrong again. That could be good for your health, if not your reputation. However, what if someone has figured out who I am and why I'm there?"

In fact, Louis Paxler did know who he was—sort of. But he hadn't seen the administrator that day and had no reason to think Paxler knew of the continued existence of the Silver Rapids patient files, or that they were now in the possession of Colorado Confidential.

"Plus," he continued, "until we know why Jenny was so upset, I have no intention of letting her—or you—out of my sight unless I'm sure there'll be no equivalent of a speeding ambulance tonight. Or another fire."

"Here?" Kelley blanched.

"Who knows? Just call me overly cautious."

"I'll call you a realist," she said with a sigh. Then she added scathingly, "And a man."

He smiled at her quizzically. "You say 'man' as if you're swearing a blue streak."

She shrugged a slender shoulder in a movement that stretched her blouse tighter over her small yet curvy breasts, making him even more aware he was a man—and she was, most definitely, the opposite sex.

"I hate it when a man gives me orders," she said. "I'd rather be told reasons for a demand, then given a choice."

"Sometimes there is no choice."

"There's always a choice." She glared a finely honed dagger or two. Then she stood and started to busy herself with a paper towel, cleaning a counter that was already pristine.

"Why do I think I missed the first act of this play?" He rose and took her shoulders from behind. He'd only thought she was trembling before. Now he felt the shudders wracking her.

"What's wrong, Kelley?" he asked in alarm.

Her expression, when she pivoted to look up at him, was filled with such pain that he felt it stab through him, too.

"I'm sorry," she said. "You did miss the first act of this play. And the second."

"Fill me in." He held her close against him, waiting for her to pull away and tell him to go to hell.

Instead, after a minute, she began to talk, her breath heating a spot in the center of his chest. "It's not just you. I'm tired of being told what to do, how to live, what to think. And being punished if I fail to act like a good little girl."

"Who hurt you, Kelley?" he demanded roughly into the sweet fragrance of her hair. "That s.o.b. Randall?"

She shrugged. "It doesn't matter. And it's not anything you want to hear."

"Tell me," he insisted, "and I'll fix it."

"Spoken like a man. But there's no way you or anyone else can fix it." But with a little more coaxing, she did tell him what he wanted to know. Even though she was right. There was nothing he could do. Except listen. And hold her.

Speaking against him, as if to herself, she described a bummer of a childhood, in which her domineering father had insisted that Kelley's mother be a perfect, storybook wife with no mind of her own. "She did everything just right. She was an ideal mother to my sister and me, kept an immaculate house, entertained with flair whenever he wanted, chauffeured, scheduled, whatever. But if she ever dared ask to do something she wanted, he shouted her down and told her what a miserable excuse for a wife she was. She believed it. And when she no longer had the role of mother, too—when my sister and I were grown and out of the house—she left him. Us, too."

"Then she did get away? Good for her."

Kelley yanked herself free with a bitter laugh. "She committed suicide."

"I'm sorry," he whispered, trying again to draw her close.

"Did I learn my lesson?" Kelley continued as if she

hadn't heard him. She stood rigidly, fists clenched, staring over his shoulder as if at the ugly specter of her past. "No. I married a doctor, like my father. That part was okay. But the doctor was Randall, who was already considered the best damned cardiologist at Gilpin Hospital—maybe in Denver—while I was in med school. I couldn't believe someone so preeminent could care for a nobody like me. When he asked me to marry him, I was in ecstasy. Of course he told me not to specialize in cardiology. Women weren't good in specialties requiring so much knowledge. Internal medicine—well, that was all right. Until I had Jenny. He wanted the mother of his child to stay home and specialize in that. He demanded that I quit practicing medicine and become a perfect wife." She laughed aloud. "Sound familiar?"

"You're not your mother, Kelley," he said quietly, his hands itching to pull her close again. He wanted to soothe away every hurt she had ever felt. And not only to comfort her.

To hold her. To touch her.

"No," she said, "I'm not my mother, though the hell of it is I wondered if he was right. But I fought it, because I intended to be a good role model for my daughter. I told my husband no. So he divorced me."

"No great loss." Shawn could have slugged himself in the gut. Talk about a male blurting something insensitive. But instead of getting angrier, she laughed.

"No great loss," she agreed. She took a deep breath and shook her head. Her auburn hair shimmered in the artificial light of the kitchen. "Anyway, I don't take orders. It's as simple as that." She didn't appear angry anymore. Just defiant.

And sexy as hell, as she stood with her hands on her

hips as if daring him to give her one more order. He felt challenged.

And turned on. Very turned on.

"Go to bed with me, Kelley," he said. "Now."

Her eyes widened. This time, when she laughed, it sounded nervous. And sexy. From way deep in her throat. "Was that an order?"

"No, a plea. From a man who's in agony from wanting you."

He didn't think why or how he'd begun to burn with desire for her. One moment she'd been spilling her guts, and he'd wanted to kiss her and make her feel better as he did with tots at KidClub. But she was not a child. Oh, no. And the kisses he wanted to share with her would only churn up his own aches.

Something inside him—his conscience? His common sense?—demanded what he was doing. Sex with a suspect? It had to be one of his profession's biggest taboos.

And yet, if he really still suspected she was an arsonist, he wouldn't—couldn't—be doing this.

Would she say no? He'd learned not to let rejection bother him…sort of. But with this woman, he wondered if he could stand it. Her gaze searched his, even as her full, ripe lips parted, and she gnawed her lower one—just as he wanted to do.

"I don't stand for possessiveness," she said huskily. "When men have sex, they want to own the woman they bed. But if I go to bed with you, it's because I want to then. And I may never want to again. Understood?"

"Understood." Shawn heard the hitch in his voice. He wondered whether he could close the short distance between them without limping, he was so hard.

He didn't have to. In moments, she was in his arms.

"We can't stay in here," she said, looking up at him

with eyes that flashed with desire so fiery that he felt the conflagration spread inside him. "And we'll have to be quiet so we don't wake Jenny."

"Of course." He bent down to kiss her, but she wasn't finished talking.

"You won't get territorial?" she murmured against his lips.

"Not me," he assured her, pulling back to look her in the face. Her angelic, devilishly delicious, heart-shaped, heart-stopping face. "One thing I'm not is territorial."

"Really?"

"Yeah. When you were a kid, you learned about men giving orders. When I was a kid—well, no home, no family and definitely no territory." Still... The idea of some other man touching her...he'd have to get over it.

She looked stricken. "Tell me about it."

"Another time," he said, and took her back into his arms.

Chapter Twelve

Kelley held Shawn's hand as she led him toward her bedroom.

Was this a mistake? Maybe. He was still a controlling man. But though he hadn't told her so, he didn't act now as if he still considered her suspect. Instead, she felt more as if he protected her. Cared for her. Was she delusional? If so, she wanted it to go on—at least for now.

She stopped at Jenny's room and glanced inside. Fortunately, her young daughter slept soundly. She closed the door nearly all the way, leaving it slightly ajar so she would be able to hear if Jenny cried out.

Her craving for Shawn turned every nerve in her body into raw need. Was there a medical term for such intense, explosive desire? At least she knew exactly what the cure was—Shawn.

She hesitated inside her bedroom door, scanning the room anxiously as if through his eyes. She'd moved into this house with Jenny two years ago, after the divorce. It was the first time any man had seen her bedroom. Except the movers, of course, and the men who had laid the thick, cream-colored wall-to-wall carpeting.

What would Shawn think of it? Not that it was all frills and femininity, but the wallpaper was riotously floral, and she had placed leafy green potted plants along the walls, on shelves, atop her pine dresser and chest of drawers.

The room even smelled fresh and green.

She'd wanted plants before, but Randall had been allergic.

What if Shawn—?

"This is great." He pulled her close so her back nestled against the solid, sexy planes of his chest. "I've always imagined making love in a jungle." He pushed closer, and she could feel his hardness strain against her buttocks. "The wilder the better."

Laughing huskily, Kelley pulled away to face him. Lord, but not touching him piqued her desire!

Quickly, she turned to close and lock the door behind them so Jenny couldn't walk in on them. But her daughter, even after the fire, always slept through the night. No matter what else went on, Kelley would still be listening for her child. "I'm not sure how to do wild," she said looking at Shawn once more, "but I'm willing to learn."

She barely had time to take another breath before his mouth closed over hers—ravenously. Wildly.

She kissed back with fervor that astounded her. Her tongue flicked rhythmically in a natural dueling duet, one where both combatants were glorious winners.

She used her hands to pull his head even closer. His fingers combed through her hair and downward, over her back, clasping her behind. He dipped so his face was even with hers, and his hands explored lower, centering beneath her skirt. Between her thighs. And upward.

Kelley gasped, even as Shawn groaned her name. And stroked her there outside her sheer, light undergarments. Harder. Deeper.

Wild? That didn't describe the half of her longing for more.

When she tried to shut off the light, he stopped her. "I want to watch you," he growled. The idea of making love not in the dark, but with every sense in play—watching *him*—enflamed her even further.

His hands snaked around, cupping her breasts over her blouse. Inching their way between buttons. Inside her shirt. Inside her bra. Rubbing her nipples till they yearned for more.

She tugged at his jeans as they tripped together toward the bed. Her skirt fell to the floor. Her blouse and bra. Her slip.

Her panty hose took longer.

And then they were on her bed, atop the thick, soft coverlet. Flowered, of course.

She watched as he removed his shirt and boxers. Her eyes slitted in lust but she refused to close them. She wanted to see every muscular contour on his hard and angular male body.

To observe his very thick, very aroused erection that stoked her own fires. Melted her. Moistened her, as he touched her even more there, where her desire was centered.

She had to touch him, too, but after a moment, he took her hand. Stopped her.

"We'll do it slow next time, Kelley," he said through gritted teeth. "I can't wait."

"Me, neither," she managed to whisper.

She heard the rustle of a plastic wrapper and smiled approvingly at his readiness and caution. And then he was pressed against her. It had been so long that she felt small and tight and very, very needy. When he hesitated, she thrust her hips so that she took him inside fast.

There was a shock of pain, yes, but the shock was mostly the rapture in having him there. Pulsing and thick and hard.

"Are you—"

She didn't let him finish but grabbed his neck, pulling his face down so she could kiss him, taste him, even as she rocked her hips upward, urging him to move.

The rhythm he began was slow only at first, but in moments it accelerated and crescendoed. Quickly. But not so fast that it left Kelley behind.

She cried out, even as his groan heralded his release. He stiffened in her arms, then crumpled onto her in a delightful, spent, supple heap.

Kelley must have fallen asleep, for the next thing she recalled was a kiss. Soft and sweet and gentle at first.

Until she came fully awake and joined in.

And realized they were still in her bed. Still nude.

The lights were on, and she looked at him. And saw that his need had returned. *Really* returned.

Desire once more danced through her.

This time, they took their time.

As they did the time after that.

SHAWN WOKE EARLY. He always did.

Today, he had more reason.

He didn't stir at first. Instead, he watched Kelley.

Her hair, gold-flecked and fiery, lay tousled on pale green sheets. Her eyelashes were so long, they nearly touched her high cheekbones as she slept, and their auburn shade, like her hair in a more intimate place, proved her hair color was natural.

She was natural. There was no artifice in her lovemaking. She held nothing back.

His groin stirred at the mere thought of last night. He stifled an irritable mutter at himself. No time now. He would leave soon, before Kelley had to awaken Jenny.

Not that a child that age would understand, but neither

would she know to avoid mentioning at KidClub about how Shawn stayed at her house last night.

No need to embarrass Kelley. Or make his job harder.

For now, he just watched Kelley. She breathed deeply, rhythmically raising and lowering the top sheet, which had slipped to the swell of her breasts. He had a momentary urge to pull back the sheet farther, to get one more glimpse of the firm mounds and their sweetly appetizing nipples.

Her eyes popped open. They widened as if in surprise to find him there, then narrowed to catlike, contented slits. "Good morning." Her husky whisper poured over him, hardening him. As if he needed more to raise his desire to fever level.

"Good morning." He tried to sound cool but failed miserably. "Time for me to leave."

"Oh." The disappointment in her voice made him grin. "What time do you usually wake Jenny?"

She raised up to look over his shoulder at the clock he'd noticed on the bedside table behind him. The sheet slipped farther.

"I didn't realize it was so late. Sometimes she even wakes me." Kelley sat up, holding the sheet in front of her. "You're right. It's definitely time for you to leave."

But before Shawn got dressed, he checked to make sure the bedroom door was still locked—and gave Kelley one heck of a kiss to remember him by.

KELLEY DIDN'T REGRET a moment of what she had shared last night—and this morning—with Shawn. But the glow faded a little as she hurried to get herself and Jenny dressed. She let Jenny pick her own outfit for the day, a Minnie Mouse T-shirt over peach knit slacks. But that did not help her daughter's difficult mood.

Kelley had already donned her own black sleeveless shell

and soft gray pantsuit. As they got ready to leave, Jenny, grumpy and on the verge of a tantrum, made it clear that she didn't want to go to KidClub.

Kelley had patients scheduled all day, after rounds. And the only way she could try to learn what had upset Jenny yesterday was to take her back, try to get her to talk.

Besides, honoring a tantrum only encouraged more.

Kelley finally got Jenny into the car. As she drove toward the hospital, she saw another vehicle pull close behind.

Her heart skipped a beat until, in her rearview mirror, she recognized a familiar, utterly handsome male face grinning at her.

Shawn had left her house, but he hadn't stopped watching over them. The thought warmed her and made her grin right back.

As they passed through their residential neighborhood into one that was more commercial, Kelley remembered this was Friday. "This is the day we promised to buy morning treats," she told Jenny.

They stopped at a convenience store she'd scoped out. It sold presliced fruit as well as doughnuts.

Unsurprisingly, Shawn joined them inside. Jenny's grumpiness evaporated as he lifted her high into the air. "Good morning, princess," he said. "Isn't this a coincidence?"

"What's a c'incidence?" Jenny asked as he set her back on her feet.

"A very happy surprise."

Kelley noted he wore a blue shirt, not the one she had all but ripped from him last night. Did he keep a change of clothes in his car in anticipation of evenings like that with other women? The idea made her crazy.

But he was an investigator. Undercover. He had to be prepared for any situation, like all-night stakeouts, right?

It was not something she wanted to ask.

A while later, Jenny ran into KidClub with Kelley and Shawn following. Shawn held the box of doughnuts and Kelley the bag with fruit. She watched for Juan Cortes on the way in, but the janitor wasn't in sight. It was later than he usually brought the treats in for the children. Since she hadn't followed his example, she wondered if he would ever allow her to treat again.

She cut the doughnuts into small pieces acceptable to the kids' parents.

"We runned into Shawn at the store," Jenny proudly told her friend Claire, as the kids gathered around to make their choices. "It was a c'incidence."

Kelley smiled at Shawn as her daughter was asked to explain the big word. "See you later," she told him. Then, kneeling to give Jenny a goodbye hug and kiss, she said, "Have fun, sweetheart. And listen to Shawn."

When she stood up again, she found herself staring longingly at him. Too bad she couldn't get a goodbye hug and kiss from him, too. Both amusement and desire glimmered in his blue, blue eyes. He looked as if he understood and shared her thoughts.

How had she ever thought those eyes cold? Today, they were the color of a sun-warmed pool that tempted her to jump in.

Maybe later…?

Marge Ralston walked into the room. Kelley gave her a hearty, "Good morning," and prepared to flee, in case the evidence of how wonderfully she had spent last night was legible in the smile on her face. "See you later, Jenny," she called. "See you later, Shawn," she said more softly. She felt his gaze envelop her as she headed for the door.

Kelley lingered long enough to wrap an uncut chocolate-covered doughnut with peanuts in a napkin as she left.

Which was fortunate, for as she entered the medical center's nearly empty elevator lobby, she saw Juan.

"I apologize for being late." She handed him the doughnut she'd brought especially for him.

"No problem." He smiled, then used his large front teeth to take a big bite of the rich confection. "Excellent." He chewed and swallowed. "I just bring them early because I have to get here early." He wiggled the mop handle he balanced in his other hand. "The better to finish early, you see?"

"Sure. So if it's all right, Jenny and I will treat again next Friday."

"Okay. Thanks." Finishing his doughnut, Juan turned away and began mopping with long, experienced strokes along the linoleum floor.

But Kelley had a thought. Juan had been in on the hospital gossip on that rare day when she'd been lauded for her diagnosis of Rocky Mountain Spotted Fever. He'd known also of the ebb to her reputation due to claims of ineptitude in the Silver Rapids cases. Maybe he'd know if more was being said, courtesy of exalted administrator Louis Paxler and his unearthing of the troublesome forged document.

"Juan, have you heard any more rumors about me in the last day or so?"

He turned, a puzzled expression in his wrinkle-bound brown eyes. "Rumors? I don't think so." His grin turned up the edges of his trim mustache. "Have you shown up one of the other doctors again?"

"No," she said with a laugh. And then she sobered. "Someone warned me that a less complimentary rumor might be starting, so I was just wondering."

Juan shrugged one husky shoulder beneath his gray uniform shirt. "If I hear anything, I'll tell you. But I only learn when I overhear the doctors and nurses talking. They don't tell me what's on their minds.''

As soon as Shawn could reasonably take a break that morning, he headed for the sidewalk outside Gilpin Hospital. His cell phone worked best there, and people generally bustled by and were therefore unlikely to overhear what he said.

A breeze as soft as summer wafted around him, and when he looked up and beyond the closest buildings, he imagined the clouds scudding toward the distant Rockies.

He mulled in his mind how to extract answers from Colleen without revealing anything he intended to keep private. Like his night with Kelley.

His very memorable night…

The mild late-August morning suddenly grew as hot as if the afternoon sun had been pelting down all day. Shawn, impatient with himself, pushed in Colleen's phone number.

''It's me,'' he said with no preamble when she answered. ''Has anyone gone through those files yet?''

''Yeah, but we haven't had them a full day.'' Colleen wasn't the defensive type. Instead, irritation scorched her tone.

''In other words, you haven't found anything helpful?'' He watched as a teenage girl in a striped hospital volunteer pinafore pushed a wheelchair along the sidewalk, a wizened older gentleman slouched in it.

''So far, it appears as if the Silver Rapids flu patients simply got sick. Then they were brought to the hospital, admitted, treated, and got well—except for the two older ones who didn't survive.''

''No common threads other than that they were in Silver Rapids at about the same time?''

''A couple went out to eat, a few were at the town's

casino, that kind of thing. It may be significant, but we need to check further. I'll let you know if anything helpful crops up.''

''And that friend of Kelley's—Wilson Carpenter? Nothing new on him?''

''It's also been less than a day since you last asked me that. You know we've excellent resources for tracking missing persons, but this guy seems to have vanished. And since he's apparently been in touch with the doctors' office next door, he's got to be alive. So—well, we'll keep on it, too.''

''Thanks, Colleen.''

''Yeah.'' She paused. ''You know, I think I like our chief arson suspect. I'm glad I got a chance to meet her.''

''Sure.'' Shawn wasn't sure how to respond.

''You think she's innocent?''

''I've told you that's my current thought. Except for someone trying to run her down with a stolen ambulance, I've seen no indication of direct threats, and no suggestion of blackmail or other coercion. Without something along that line, she's got no motive, since the Silver Rapids files didn't burn. And so far, you haven't found anything in them she'd want to hide.''

''Right. Sounds too pat, doesn't it?''

''What are you driving at?'' His ire scraped into his voice.

''Nothing.'' Colleen's tone was so sweet it nearly gave him a toothache. ''And did you act as her bodyguard last night?'' She didn't sound as if she meant a hired protector.

''Yeah. She and her daughter survived the night. Talk to you soon, Colleen.''

He shoved his cell phone door closed on her laugh.

BY THE TIME KELLEY went to pick up Jenny that night, she dared to hope Louis Paxler had decided to keep this latest bit of evidence against her to himself. Thank heavens.

Maybe she had convinced him it was false. Or maybe he didn't want to reveal it for the hospital's sake. No matter. What counted was that no one, not even Randall or Cheryl, confronted her about more proof of her supposed ineptitude.

She visited KidClub twice—mostly to check on Jenny, she told herself, since her daughter had had such a difficult afternoon the day before.

The fact that she saw Shawn didn't hurt, either.

Everything seemed fine.

That night, he stopped in again to make sure they were all right. And stayed.

The next day was Saturday, on a weekend in which Kelley had Jenny. They all spent it together.

And Shawn stayed the night.

When they awakened together, long before daylight, Kelley dared to ask him what he had meant once, when he'd alluded to growing up with no family, no roots. She'd wondered about it a lot, when she wasn't preoccupied with other things—like making love with him.

"I'm not one for pillow talk," he grumbled, pulling her tight against his naked body.

"Tell me." Her desire was stoked yet again by his nearness, his obvious arousal, but she wanted to know.

"It's no big deal," he said, then proceeded to tell her a story that was, to the contrary, a very big deal.

It explained who he was. Why he had become a firefighter, then an arson investigator. And why anyone who set fires was, to him, the lowest form of monster.

"We lived in an apartment building when I was seven," he said, his voice as neutral as if he talked about a trip to the supermarket. But his eyes—oh, all the pain of the world was in his eyes.

"Seems the owner was losing money—too many loans, rents too low, that kind of thing. But he had lots of insurance. He chose a time midafternoon, when most parents were working and kids were in school when he started the 'accidental' fire, then ran around knocking on apartment doors screaming for anyone there to get out. I was at school, but my folks had been up all night with my younger brother, who'd had a bad earache, and didn't hear the bastard...."

They'd died.

Shawn had no other relatives, and so he was brought up by a foster care system that, if not cruel, was at least indifferent. "I dared once to get a crush on one of my 'sisters,' but she set me straight fast." He spoke so matter-of-factly against Kelley that she wanted to cry. "I was nobody, to her and to the rest, just a kid with no real family."

"But—"

He continued without letting Kelley express her sorrow for the poor, rejected little boy he'd been. "Except for one of the 'dads' they set me up with for a few months. A real cool dude. Taught me how to draw caricatures. After that, I got my revenge on all the jerks in school who made fun of me for not having parents, all the teachers who gave me lower grades when I couldn't bring in folks to discuss my 'lack of achievement' with them. I'd just make them look on paper just as they did in my mind—a bunch of horses' behinds." He laughed, even as tears rushed into Kelley's eyes.

This time, when they made love, it was soft and sweet. It didn't make up for all Shawn had experienced, Kelley knew. But she wanted him to know that she cared.

DAYS MELDED TOGETHER. The weekend was soon over. So was another week at the hospital, in which nothing new blotched Kelley's reputation.

Apparently, nothing either helpful or hurtful had turned up in the files she'd lent to ICU, either, for when she asked, Shawn seemed perturbed that they'd still found nothing to point to the arsonist. He didn't say what else they were looking for, and she didn't ask.

If they found evidence of what she suspected, would they even tell her? But until she had something other than a gut feel, and an allusion from the still-missing Wilson Carpenter, she wouldn't stretch her neck out that far.

The next week at Gilpin Hospital was relatively calm. No new rumors. Not even any new outbursts from Jenny.

No rampant ambulances.

That also meant there was no need for Shawn to spend every night protecting Jenny and her. But she was definitely glad he was there. In her bed.

The next weekend was Labor Day. Randall had Jenny for two of the three days. Kelley spent them with Shawn, telling herself it was only sex. But what incredible sex it was!

During that time, Shawn hardly ever issued any orders. She almost wished he would, as that would give her an excuse to get away from him.

For she was falling in love with him. And that could not be good.

But on the Tuesday after Labor Day, Kelley realized she should not have let down her guard. Become complacent.

About anything.

LOUIS PAXLER'S smile appeared to Kelley as if he had eaten something that didn't agree with him.

He sat behind his vast mahogany desk. Kelley, at his direction, occupied one of the leather office chairs.

The other was occupied by Etta Borand, dressed in a gaudy yellow pantsuit. The gray-haired virago's expression was smug. She did not look at Kelley.

Louis had beeped Kelley only a few minutes earlier. Her digital pager had given his extension, and she had responded. Louis's receptionist Hilda had told her she was wanted for a meeting right away. Now Kelley knew she should have refused. Said she had an emergency. Anything.

"Mrs. Borand is here as a courtesy, Kelley," Louis said. "She brought me these." He lifted a small but menacing-looking pile of papers from his desk and waved them. They looked like legal documents. The complaint against the hospital no doubt.

And against her. For malpractice.

"I see." Kelley was unsure how to react. Inside, dread, thick, icy and debilitating, turned her stomach. Maybe it was time to get her own lawyer. Or at least notify her malpractice insurance carrier.

"They have already been filed with the court, and will be officially served later today." Etta's light tone suggested she was discussing a delicious recipe rather than something that could seal Kelley's fate. She rose, and the motion caused the gold bangles at her ears to sway. "Our lawyer didn't think it a good idea for me to come here, but I decided to give you a final chance to settle this matter amicably."

She smiled first at Louis, then at Kelley.

"No? Well, I suspect you have things to discuss." She flounced from the office.

Kelley watched as the door shut, delaying as long as possible turning back toward Louis.

"This is going to be damned expensive, Dr. Stanton,"

he exploded behind her. "I ought to make you pay every penny."

Forcing serenity she didn't feel onto her face, she looked at him. His pallor contrasted starkly with his dark brown hair. Maybe this would cause him finally to go gray. Or maybe it would simply prove he dyed his hair. Not that it mattered to Kelley.

Could the hospital legally do that? She didn't know. She tried inserting bravado into her voice. "The hospital is insured, isn't it?"

"That's not the point. With claims like this, rates go up. Plus we'll lose valuable time with people having to testify in court. There's administration. Dealing with our board of directors." He rose, and though he wasn't very tall, she felt him loom over her like a prophet of doom. "I haven't acted as fast as I should about the file material I found, Kelley. But it accounts for the flu patients' altered blood tests. And now with this lawsuit, you need to know that I'm considering suspending you from practicing at Gilpin Hospital."

"Altered? But—" Kelley bit down hard on her lower lip. The pain kept the moisture that shot to her eyes from falling. And kept her from questioning him further, fruitlessly.

"I'll let you know what I decide," Paxler said, dismissing her.

KELLEY THOUGHT of running to KidClub to cry on Shawn's shoulder. She needed to see him. But first, she needed to get hold of her emotions. She wouldn't want to scare Jenny.

And the idea of leaning on any man for something that was her problem... "No way," she whispered as she walked quickly toward the medical wing and her office.

When she got there, her shared receptionist wasn't in sight. Good. She didn't want to explain her overwrought state, particularly not to someone who might be linked to the Gilpin Hospital rumor circuit. She hurried into her office.

And stopped.

She nearly smiled. Shawn was there, behind her desk. When she needed him.

She crossed the room quickly. "I'm so glad to see you," she said. "That woman Etta Borand was in Louis's office, and then Louis mentioned—" She halted as fast as if he had slapped her.

In a way, he had.

Shawn's eyes were that icy blue she recalled from when she had first met him. His wide jaw was set, his lips straight and hard.

She swallowed to get hold of her emotions. "What's wrong?"

"I found these in your desk." He waved some papers.

She straightened, glaring at him, her indignation overpowering all other emotions. "Number one, I don't know what 'these' are. Number two, who do you think you are to go into my desk without my permission? Did you break the lock?"

"No, I didn't break anything. Opening the unopenable is just something I do, when necessary. And these were in a different drawer anyway."

"You—"

"I got back the original Silver Rapids flu files from my office today," he interrupted coldly, "and thought I'd put them where they would be safe, in your desk. I didn't know you hadn't given me everything."

"But I did. I…" No use protesting. He obviously wouldn't believe her. "All right, then. Tell me what you found there."

"I haven't had time to analyze them yet, but there are

some loose pages that indicate the flu was actually a combination of virus and Q fever. That you may in fact have intentionally given patients the wrong treatment to hide the disease and its origin.''

Kelley blinked, then sat down in the nearest stiff desk chair. ''I don't know how you came up with that, except… I had a theory, Shawn, about what the illness was and how it could have affected so many people. I didn't tell anyone because it was so bizarre, so impossible. And the blood tests I ordered didn't confirm it. That's what I wanted to talk to my friend Dr. Wilson Carpenter about, since his call made it seem possible that he was thinking the same thing. That's why I took the files. And then Louis just said—''

''And what is this bizarre theory of yours?'' Ice-coated blades shot from the voice of the man whose tone, before, had caressed her.

''I wondered whether the Silver Rapids epidemic had a human origin. Whether its pathogen was manufactured, perhaps in an act of bioterrorism. If I'd had any proof, of course, I'd have gone to the authorities. But everyone around here thinks I'm incompetent anyway, so I wanted evidence before I made a fool of myself.''

''You wondered? You wanted proof? These papers indicate you were part of it. I even bought your 'poor little me' story before when you claimed someone stuck counterfeit papers into a file Paxler found. But this, in your own locked drawer—'' He extracted a paper from the sheaf in his fist. ''This one even gives you direction on when and how to start the fire. You are the arsonist, Kelley, and that I can't forgive. Did you decide on your own to keep the files, in case you needed insurance against your coconspirators? You sure sanitized what you gave to me, but there's some good stuff here. I can't tell yet who else is involved. But I'll find out.''

And with that, papers in hand, Shawn stomped from the room.

Chapter Thirteen

Kelley stood for a moment, in shock.

Those papers indicated she had set the fire? Under some-one's direction? She should have demanded a look at them. But what good would it have done? She'd no doubt they contained what Shawn said they did.

Shuddering, she lowered herself into the nearest chair. Her own tiny office suddenly seemed like hostile territory.

What was happening to her?

The Silver Rapids epidemic must really have been man-ufactured. Shawn and his ICU people thought so, too.

Damn it, why hadn't he told her?

You didn't tell him your suspicions, either, retorted a nasty thought in the recesses of her mind. She ignored it. That was different. She had been protecting herself.

What else did Shawn know that he had kept from her?

Someone had to have put the papers in her desk. Some-one who wanted to discredit her. Probably the same some-one who'd fabricated the chart Louis had found.

Because that someone didn't want her to blow the whis-tle on her theory?

But it wasn't just *her* theory. She knew that now. Shawn and his group also suspected more.

And Louis had mentioned altered blood tests. Could they

have been altered to show the negative results for antibodies? If that were true, it would support her hypothesis.

Yet she still had no proof. And Shawn wouldn't help her. He didn't believe her. He thought she was involved.

He thought she'd set the fire.

A horrible thought struck her. Had he gotten close to her, made love to her, so that she would let down her guard? So that he could interrogate her, get her to spill all about her purported conspiracy?

He was a man, wasn't he? A damned, controlling man. She should have expected something this contemptible. She should have *known*.

Pain slashed through her as sharply as if she'd been ignited by a fireball. She'd allowed herself to care for yet another man who hurt her. But she would get through it. Somehow.

She forced herself to rise. What should she do now? She paced, considering her options. None was good.

It would be easy to fall apart. To simply run…

No. She had to get control of this situation. She had to fix things for herself.

She had to.

But not here. She needed to get away. Go home, to think. To strategize.

At least, she thought wryly as she hurried toward KidClub for Jenny, things today couldn't get any worse.

Only she was wrong. For when she arrived at KidClub, Jenny was in the middle of a screaming fit.

Marge, nearly at wit's end, was trying to calm her. She ran over to Kelley, a large paper in her hand.

"She's so upset, Kelley," Marge said. "Look what she's drawn today, over and over."

The page had one large brown line down the middle. It seemed to have whiskers.

But the rest of the paper was filled with jagged red and orange streaks.

Fire.

SHAWN HAD HEADED for the ICU office after finding the paperwork in Kelley's desk. He put the new materials into a sealed envelope and directed office manager Becky Morris to have it messengered to Colleen, who'd returned to the Royal Flush. Better yet, Becky could take it herself.

Shawn needed to return to Gilpin Hospital. He still couldn't completely blow his cover there, though he figured his assignment was nearly over.

Back in his SUV, he drove with his hands clenched as tightly on the steering wheel as if they had Kelley by the throat.

Kelley *was* the arsonist. Not because she wanted to hide evidence of her negligent treatment of patients, but because she was involved with covering up the origin of the Silver Rapids flu. And as suspected, the outbreak was probably tied in with Colorado Confidential's major case—the kidnapping of the Langworthy baby. But how were the flu and the possible biological experiments at the Gettys sheep ranch related to the kidnapping?

Damn!

Why would Kelley set the fire but keep incriminating papers? So that no one would look for evidence? Because she could somehow use the material against some coconspirator? Or blackmailer? Could she have been a victim of some kind of threat or coercion after all? Someone had tried to run her down with that ambulance.

Or had that been only for show, staged by one of her fellow schemers to throw him off the track?

He still had too many questions. But whatever the answers, he should have known better than to get involved

with a suspect. Getting close to *anyone* was out of line for
an undercover operative. But for him, of all people, to get
close to a suspected arsonist…

An *actual* arsonist. He was a total fool for letting himself
wonder whether a future with her and her daughter was
possible, falling in love with—

Where had that come from? Love? Hell, he didn't even
know what it meant. And he was damned if he would allow
himself to feel it for the duplicitous Dr. Kelley Stanton.

In the hospital parking lot, he simply sat for a moment.
He had to question her further, but since he'd tipped his
hand, it would take finesse.

How would he handle her now?

He still didn't know by the time he reached KidClub.

So maybe it was just as well that he had time to think
about it. Kelley had picked up Jenny and left.

THEY WERE AT A PLAYGROUND. Jenny sat beside Kelley on
a park bench in the shade of a tall, fragrant pine tree. She
leaned against Kelley, refusing to go play.

At least she had calmed down.

"Would you like me to push you on a swing, sweetheart?" Kelley asked, her heart shredded from her small
daughter's obvious pain.

"No, Mommy." There was such sadness in Jenny's
sweet and solemn face that Kelley could hardly stand it.

Jenny had shrieked and carried on from the moment Kelley had strapped her into her car seat, and Kelley had decided to drive to one of Jenny's favorite places. At least
that had calmed her.

This park was near an elementary school—the one her
daughter would have attended in a few years, if they had
still been around.

But they wouldn't be.

Kelley liked it here, in this pleasant Denver suburb, but now they would have to move.

The best case would be to someplace far from here that Kelley chose. The worst case...? She could wind up in prison if Shawn's accusations of arson and worse gained momentum. And Randall would get sole custody of Jenny.

She couldn't think about that now.

"Honey, I want to know why you were so upset at KidClub today. Please tell me."

Jenny's head shook in a vehement "no" that mussed her pale blond hair.

"You'll feel better if you do."

Again, a shake of the head. This time, two tears rolled down her cheeks.

Responsive wetness pooled in Kelley's eyes.

"Do you want to talk about the fire?" she asked. "Or the pictures you drew?" She'd left them at KidClub, with their jagged red lines and odd, shaggy brown ones.

"No!" Jenny leaped off the bench and stood facing Kelley, her hands on her small hips. If Kelley hadn't been so concerned for her, she'd have smiled at the very adult pose.

She stooped and hugged her daughter tightly. "It's okay, sweetheart. Everything will be all right." Her vow was as much to herself as to Jenny.

She only hoped it was true.

LATER, KELLEY REALIZED her bed had never felt so lonely.

For the umpteenth time that night, she rose, flicked on the light and slipped a light cotton robe around her. She looked through a crack in her closed draperies at the street in front of her house.

No big blue SUV in her driveway. Or parked nearby. And why should there be? Shawn had played her protector—or at least pretended to—as long as he'd thought she needed protection.

Now, he was certain she was one of the bad guys.

And she was certain he was…what? She'd given up conjuring epithets to hurl at him if he dared to appear.

Which he wouldn't.

Right now, she had decisions to make. Alone.

Without the interference of her attraction—former attraction—to Shawn.

With the best interests of her daughter at the forefront.

What had hurt her? Why was she drawing such alarming pictures? Had she, after all, seen who set the fire? How could they know, if she refused to talk about it?

How could Kelley protect her?

What would happen to her if Kelley wound up in prison?

Kelley closed her dampening eyes. No use crying or worrying now. Time enough for that tomorrow.

But one thing was for certain. She'd spent too much time with her head down, hoping she'd simply be able to practice her profession.

She had to go out with a bang.

A loud one.

SHAWN DIDN'T EVEN TRY to sleep that night. Instead, he paced his damned puny apartment. He'd figured it was tiny before, but he could barely fit six good strides into it, the way he was going. He'd stripped down to his boxers hours ago, after losing count of the push-ups he'd done to work off excess energy.

It hadn't been enough.

He pitied the guy with the flat below him. He'd probably get complaints in the morning. But that didn't stop him.

Damn. He'd had plenty of time to figure out how to deal

with Kelley. Plenty of time to realize he'd handled it all wrong with her. Some smooth undercover operative *he* was.

He shouldn't have confronted her with the damning evidence. Instead, he should have been subtle. Told her that the ICU team had determined there were papers missing from the files. Did she know anything about them?

And if she said no, *when* she said no, he could push harder till she admitted that she'd sanitized them. That she'd—

Lied. About everything.

Hell, he'd even assumed that, with all their lovemaking, she had feelings for him. But that had been part of her deception.

"Irrelevant, Jameson," he muttered. "Keep your mind on the job." And not on the way his groin throbbed painfully every time he thought about Dr. Kelley Stanton. Or the way his heart ached even more.

Damn.

"Okay, pea-brain," he continued. "Concentrate."

Before he'd left KidClub, he'd gotten an earful from Marge about how Jenny had acted up that day. She'd shown him more pictures that the little girl had drawn.

Jenny's pages contained a few straight brown lines that turned fuzzy at the bottom, and jagged ones, like those she had smashed onto drawings made by the other kids and him.

Red lines that must mean fire.

He of all people knew how terrifying fire could be to a child. And he hadn't even experienced it himself.

He'd only had his whole life affected by it.

Had Jenny seen the arsonist?

And had it been Kelley, as the papers he'd found indicated?

Damn it, he hadn't wanted it to be her. Still didn't. But

arsonists always pushed his hot button. "Hah, hah," he muttered. "Funny, Jameson."

Kelley had told him that the materials Louis Paxler accidentally found in another patient's file were false. Planted to frame her.

Maybe. Maybe not. But if it was true, then maybe she hadn't hidden pieces of the files in her locked desk drawer.

Maybe someone else had.

That same someone who had allegedly stuck the pages into the other patient's file.

Might Kelley in fact be innocent of everything? Or was he again thinking with the wrong part of his anatomy?

"Damn it, Kelley," he groaned aloud, and, sitting on the sofa, plopped his head into his hands.

THE NEXT MORNING, Kelley prepared, as she walked with Jenny to KidClub, what to say to Shawn if he was there. She would be as cool as he once was. Cordial but remote.

She had dressed in one of her favorite professional outfits, a deep green pantsuit that went well with the auburn highlights in her hair. Not that it mattered, but she wanted to look her best that day.

Jenny wore a pale blue T-shirt with lacy trim over blue jeans. She looked adorable. Despite her behavior at Kid-Club yesterday and the frightful drawings she had made, she pranced beside her mother as if eager to face the day. Kelley was grateful for that, at least. She would have left Jenny with a sitter if she'd been able, but the kind neighbor who usually helped in a pinch was out of town.

Kelley wasn't eager for this day to begin. But what she'd planned had to be done.

Maybe she should wait and see what happened before confronting anyone. Maybe Louis's threat of suspension wouldn't be imposed, or she could scare him into backing off. Maybe—

"Get real," she told herself. And prepared herself for battle.

At least one thing went right, to start with. Marge Ralston greeted the children that day. Kelley didn't see Shawn. That should have made her feel better, for she'd been concerned that facing him first might make her lose her nerve for the rest. "Have a happy day, sweetheart," she told Jenny and gave her a kiss.

Jenny clutched her hand as if preparing for one of her farewell scenes, but, seeing her friend Claire, hurried inside.

Kelley breathed a sigh of relief. *Two* things had gone well.

She waved good morning to Juan Cortes as she passed him near the entrance to the medical office building, not stopping to talk.

She went to her office. Unlocked her desk, to see if anything else had been planted to implicate her in something even more nefarious, like spying against the U.S.

The bottom drawer was empty. Apparently Shawn had taken back the Silver Rapids flu files, along with the "missing" pages he had found.

She took off her suit jacket and replaced it with her white lab coat. She had rounds to do.

Madelyne Younger was in the first room Kelley visited, seeing the patient in the other bed. They walked into the hall together. "You look awful, kiddo," the older doctor said, her hands in the pockets of her purple lab jacket. "What's wrong?"

"You mean the hospital grapevine hasn't passed along the latest?"

Madelyne's grin scrunched together the lines radiating from her kind eyes. "Are you accusing me of being a gossip? I resemble that remark," she quipped. And then she grew serious. "I haven't heard details, but there is a rumor circulating that you're on the big guy's least favored persons list again. Is he gunning for you?"

"Well, he's not exactly my best friend. That Etta Borand visited yesterday brandishing court papers." Kelley reminded Madelyne about that nasty situation, shaking her head. "My days here are numbered, Madelyne. I'm not harboring any illusions about it. But I know a few things about some other people around here, and I won't just go quietly."

A look of consternation passed over Madelyne's face. Or maybe Kelley just imagined it. "Go get 'em, kiddo," Madelyne said with a grin.

"I will," Kelley replied, pumping up her determination. It was the only thing she had left.

AFTER KELLEY HAD visited most of her hospital patients, she ran into Randall and Cheryl, as she'd hoped to.

"May I talk to you both?" She tried to insert the right touch of defeat and plea into her tone. Randall in particular would respond. The more groveling she did, the better.

Little did he know.

They found an empty patient room. "What's up, Kelley?" Randall demanded. "Make it quick. I have surgery scheduled later this morning."

She leaned against the nearest of the two patient beds, attempting to project dejection. Which wasn't hard. She wasn't exactly full of optimism. Just determination.

Cheryl, in a shocking pink smock a size or two too tight, did not try hard at all to hide her condescending, smug smile. She stood near Randall beside the closed door, as if asserting her territory.

Kelley ignored her as she addressed her ex-husband.

"Have you talked to Louis since yesterday about…about my status?"

Randall, impatient, had crossed his arms over the stethoscope that hung around his neck. He stared down his prominent nose at her. "You mean that he's considering suspending you? I didn't hear it directly from him, but, yes, I've heard."

"Have you heard why?"

"Something about that Borand claim, isn't it?"

Kelley nodded gloomily. "Right. It's going to court." And then she straightened and looked up directly into Randall's face. "Of course if it does, I'll have to tell the truth—that there are entirely too many postoperative cardiac cases around here that develop infections."

"What?" That got his attention. Randall's eyes widened, and he looked at her as if a dummy used for practicing cardio-pulmonary resuscitation had suddenly begun to yodel.

"I wonder if it's something to do with the surgery itself," she said calmly as Randall's hands clenched in fists at his sides. Could his silvery hair have gone more gray that quickly?

"Since I believe it's a possibility, I'll have to say so when I'm under oath."

"This is preposterous," Randall shouted. "If this is a ploy to get me to vouch for you and prevent your suspension, forget it. I'll never—"

"It's not a ploy," Kelley said calmly. "Of course, I'm more inclined to think it's the postoperative care from the cardiac nursing staff. Right, Cheryl?"

"Don't you dare accuse me," the nurse sputtered. But her face, beneath its model-perfect makeup, had lost color.

"I'm not accusing anyone," Kelley said in mock dismay. "I wouldn't want to do that to all my kind supporters here at Gilpin Hospital. I mean, I'm sure neither of you started the rumors that I did something wrong with those Silver Rapids patients…did you?'' She touched her chin and looked up in feigned pensiveness. ''I wonder if those rumors might have been started to hide the negligence of some others on Gilpin's staff. Or maybe the downright intentional ignoring of our strict anti-infection policies. Would you know anything about that?'' She looked pointedly at Cheryl, whose pale blue eyes looked shocked—and nervous.

''Cut it out, Kelley,'' Randall roared. ''No one in the cardiology department did anything to cause any infections, including Mr. Borand's problems.''

''And do you think I did something wrong there?'' she demanded. ''Since you performed the surgery, you must have reviewed his files. Did you see anything in them that indicated I committed malpractice?''

''Not that I recall,'' he said, obviously reluctant.

''I, on the other hand, remember having questions about some procedures, including postop,'' Kelley went on. ''Genuine concerns, and I relayed them to Cheryl. Right?'' She looked at the nurse. ''So that it wouldn't happen again. My notes should have been in the file.'' Which made Kelley wonder why Louis hadn't brought them up. Why *she,* and not Randall or Cheryl, was being blamed.

Because Randall was the hospital's star surgeon, wielding all the power of the big bucks his renowned skill brought in?

The notes should come out in the lawsuit, at least, if they hadn't been destroyed in the fire. She thought Ben Borand's case was recent enough that his records hadn't been filed yet, but she wasn't certain. And if they had been destroyed…could Cheryl have been the arsonist?

"She didn't tell me her concerns," Cheryl said to Randall. But her tone didn't seem even to convince him.

"I'll look into it further," he muttered, giving Cheryl a chilly glance before returning his gaze to Kelley. "In the meantime, what is this nonsense about the Silver Rapids cases? I had no involvement. The symptoms suggested influenza—an infectious disease matter, not cardiology."

"Maybe," Kelley acknowledged, "but someone has been trying hard to discredit me by criticizing my handling of those cases. They've even planted false documents in my office. Know anything about that?"

"Of course not." Randall sneered. "How would I?" He looked like—well, like Randall. And Kelley accepted the unlikelihood of his guilt.

But Cheryl was another matter. If Kelley were speaking to Shawn, she would definitely suggest he investigate the nurse as an arson suspect.

Cheryl didn't meet Kelley's gaze at first, and when she did, defiance radiated from her like a meteor shower pelting the night sky. "You're blowing smoke to protect yourself," she accused.

Maybe, Kelley thought, but that smoke seemed to be swirling around a certain nurse in this room.

"I have another matter to attend to right now," Kelley said. "But don't be surprised if you're both required to testify in the Borand matter. Or if you're sucked into the Silver Rapids mess, too." She gave them a sweet smile and left.

SHAWN HAD GIVEN Marge Ralston a lame excuse about why he couldn't work at KidClub that morning. She hadn't bought it, but what could she do? Fire him? His job there was nearly over anyway.

Clad in a black T-shirt, jeans and his ever-present boots,

he quietly stalked the halls of Gilpin until he located Kelley. He heard parts of her argument with Randall from the nurse's station outside the closed door.

When the door to the room opened, he ducked around a corner but glanced back quickly enough to see the direction Kelley headed, her shoes clicking her brisk pace on the polished linoleum floor.

He heard another argument inside the patient room as he passed to tail Kelley. Sounded like Randall Stanton and Cheryl Marten were having a lover's spat. Or something.

He wished he'd heard the details.

But right now, Kelley was his target.

"I KNOW I DON'T HAVE an appointment," Kelley said to Louis's receptionist, Hilda. Usually she got along with the woman, but today she had no intention of following the niceties usually associated with being granted an audience with the hospital director. Often, when she came in to see Louis but he was unavailable, Hilda would page her when Louis had some time open up, but today Kelley knew he was there. He had to see her.

Unconsciously, though, she felt for her pager. It wasn't in her pocket, where she usually kept it. With her thoughts so scattered, she must have left it in her suit jacket, back in her office. Even if no one wanted her services, she was on call and couldn't be without her pager. She'd retrieve it later.

After her meeting with Louis.

"It's important," she insisted to Hilda.

While in her office before, Kelley had considered what to say. How to say it. But nothing profound had come to her.

Except to focus on one little piece of the puzzle that Louis had suggested. Maybe it was just a bit of information she hadn't heard before. But just maybe it meant something more.

"I'm sorry," Hilda huffed, "but—"

Kelley ignored the frowning older woman and burst into Louis's office.

He emerged from his private washroom, arms folded above his protruding gut. His suit jacket was off, his green print tie askew. "I don't recall seeing you on my schedule." He scowled.

"No, but I've got some questions for you." She decided to start with the easy ones. "Why is Mrs. Borand gunning for me and for no other medical staff? I doubt you'd have shown her the files, assuming they still exist, but did you see my notes about her husband's postop treatment?"

"Kelley, you're overwrought. I have an appointment soon. Why don't we set up a time—"

"Sit down, Louis." She gestured toward the wheeled leather throne he used as a desk chair. "I'll want to see those files. Maybe they don't exonerate the hospital, but they exonerate *me*."

"I didn't see anything like that. And—"

"Did you remove some files but plant others?" Kelley knew that hurling unsubstantiated accusations probably wouldn't help her. But it certainly felt good. "Or—" She deliberately lowered herself into one of the chairs facing him. "Louis, what do you know about the Silver Rapids cases?"

"Nothing. Except, of course, that there is some evidence of your treating those patients ineptly." But he stroked the extra skin beneath his chin nervously.

"But yesterday you mentioned altered blood tests. What did you mean?"

She had never seen anyone's face grow so pasty so fast. "I never said anything like that," Louis stated. His eyes shifted about the room, not meeting hers. "You're just reaching, Kelley."

Kelley took a deep breath. The altered blood tests *were* a piece of information she hadn't been given before, but now she guessed the reason—no one knew about them.

No one except the person who had altered them.

While exerting his self-importance, leveling accusations, Louis had made a slip.

"If the blood tests were altered, that would give a lot of credence to some suspicions I have about the so-called flu," she said slowly. "And Dr. Wilson Carpenter's. Do you know him?"

"No. Who's he?"

"A friend. He called a few weeks ago, very nervous, and suggested that Q fever microbes were included in the pathogen that infected the Silver Rapids patients. Then he disappeared. Did you have something to do with it?"

"You're crazy." Paxler rose, eyes huge and furious behind his gold-rimmed glasses. But she saw his Adam's apple work nervously up and down his throat. "You're just trying to save your own skin by making ridiculous accusations."

"Could be. But who could more easily plant that 'missing' chart in another file than you? And no one would question the chief administrator visiting my office—to plant additional files there. What about those blood tests, Louis? Did you substitute samples to make sure no Q fever antibodies showed up in the patients' IFA results?"

"What are you talking about?" he blustered. But the rapid blinking of his eyes indicated she just might be right. "I never... I didn't sign on for that."

What was he saying? She didn't take time to sort it out. "I'm talking not only about framing me," she said, standing to lean over the desk in confrontation. "But also committing arson. I think you set the fire, endangering everyone in this hospital. How were you involved with the epidemic, Louis? What were you trying to hide?''

''You'd better leave,'' he demanded, though his face was white beneath his dark-brown hair. ''And consider yourself on suspension. Now.''

It was her turn to blanch, though she had anticipated this. ''I'll get reinstated by the next administrator,'' she bluffed. ''Once you're found guilty of setting the fire, you'll be gone a lot faster than me.''

''Get out!'' He pointed toward the door.

''See you in court,'' she shot over her shoulder as she left. She slammed his door behind her.

Thank heavens, she thought a moment later, that Hilda wasn't at her usual post. She gripped the edges of the receptionist's desk and leaned over it, trying to catch her breath.

Trying hard to keep her nausea under control.

Sure, it felt good to be on the offensive for a change, accusing others of things that she had been accused of, if not officially, at least by innuendo.

But it wasn't *her*. And it took a lot out of her.

She felt as if she had stirred up a whole apiary of bees' nests that morning. She just hoped she wasn't the only one who got stung.

She righted herself, smoothed her lab jacket over her green slacks, and prepared to leave.

She had taken a few steps into the hallway when the gunshot sounded.

Chapter Fourteen

Shawn had followed Kelley into the admin wing. He figured she was heading toward Louis Paxler's office.

He became certain of it when Hilda, Paxler's secretary,
skittered around the corner like a frightened shrew. She
nearly ran into him. "That Dr. Stanton—Kelley Stanton.
She's screaming at Louis as if she's come totally unglued."

Hilda seemed unglued, but Shawn refrained from saying
so. "Let's go see if we can help," he soothed.

Then he heard the gunshot.

He thrust the woman out of his path and raced toward
the administrator's office.

Kelley stood there, hand on the doorknob. Was she getting up the nerve to go back in—or had she just come out?

He glanced down. She held no gun. But that didn't prove
anything.

"What happened?" He pulled her out of the reception
room, for danger likely lurked inside the office.

"I—I just came out after speaking with Louis, and I
heard... Was it a shot?"

"Sounded like." No time to decide if she was the
shooter. If she wasn't... "Stay here," he commanded,

wishing he was armed. But he wore no weapons for this assignment. Too dangerous around kids.

Despite his order, Kelley trailed him back into the reception area. He wasn't surprised. But didn't she realize that, if she wasn't the shooter, somebody else was?

"Get down," he ordered. Her brown eyes were huge and bewildered. Yet for once she obeyed, sinking to her knees beside the desk.

"Police," he shouted outside the closed door to Paxler's office. No one inside would know he lied. He slammed himself down and against the wall, half expecting a volley of shots.

Nothing.

"Mr. Paxler, are you okay?"

Still silence.

"I'm coming in. I'm unarmed. I just want to make sure you're all right." When he still heard nothing, he motioned to Kelley to keep still, stood, and shoved the door open with a powerful kick. He somersaulted into the room, making himself a moving target, just in case.

No one shot at him.

He drew himself quickly to his knees and looked around.

"Damn," he said as he saw the body lying faceup on the floor.

He heard a gasp from the doorway. Kelley stood there, a perfect target if the suspect remained in the room.

Except it seemed there was only one suspect present, and he wasn't shooting anyone…else. Red blood oozed through Louis Paxler's very dark hair, and a small gun lay on the floor, near his slack hand.

It appeared that Mr. Paxler had tried to commit suicide.

Tried. Unsuccessfully. For when Shawn drew close and

pushed two fingers alongside the man's neck, he felt a very shallow pulse.

"Get a team from the hospital E.R. here right away," he shouted at Kelley. "And then call the police."

In the meantime, Shawn, trained in first aid by the Denver Fire Department, did what he could to keep the man alive.

"IT'S MY FAULT," Kelley whispered as the trauma team worked on Louis Paxler.

She stood in the hall with Shawn, near enough to see the activity, yet out of the way. Most of the hospital staff was being kept away by the police, but Shawn and she, potential witnesses, had been told to stay.

Shawn's expression was as blank as if he was a store mannequin. More so, for mannequins were often constructed to look pleasant. There was no hint of cordiality, no hint of humanity, as Shawn regarded her with expressionless blue eyes. He didn't even lean against the wall. His unyielding posture emphasized how much taller he was than her. His arms were folded stiffly against his T-shirt-clad chest.

If Kelley had wanted to throw up before, now she felt it even more. She loved this man, despite every morsel of rationality she had forced herself to digest. But to him, she was merely a suspect.

One who may have caused another person to try to take his own life.

"Why do you say it's your fault?" Shawn prompted when she forced herself to shut up. He might have been asking why she had chosen corn flakes for breakfast, but his studied neutrality made it clear what he was thinking.

"I didn't shoot him," she retorted, stiffening her shoulders. No matter how she felt, she didn't want to look defensive. "But I think I drove him to suicide."

"Why do you say that?"

Kelley described their confrontation. "I'm sure he knew more about the Silver Rapids epidemic than he let on. Why else would he have let slip a reference to altered blood tests?"

"What's their significance?"

"I'd felt certain there was more to the epidemic than even a mutated influenza virus, but the blood test results didn't support my suspicion. But if they'd been altered— the real results must have shown Q fever antibodies."

"You suspected the patients had Q fever?"

She nodded. "My suspicions were revived when I received Wilson Carpenter's call. That's when I grabbed the files, but soon after that the fire happened and the rumors about my negligent treatment of patients started flying. I wasn't about to vocalize my bizarre ideas to the hospital's chief administrator then, not without proof."

"I see. So in your scenario, why would Paxler set the fire?"

"Because he thought the files were still there. And he had to hide descriptions of the disease symptoms. Maybe there was even evidence that the blood tests were tampered with. Blood types could have been mismatched with patients. And... Didn't your investigators mention that some of the people had gone out to eat in restaurants, or visited the town's casino?"

"Yes," Shawn acknowledged, "but it was a lot of locations. There wasn't a pattern."

"Except that they were all in Silver Rapids on the same afternoon. The disease organisms were most likely disseminated within that time frame, but at different Silver Rapids locations. What if Louis knew where, and notes in the files pinpointed them?''

Shawn's pensive expression lifted his dark blond brows. "You could be right," he said slowly. "Paxler's involvement would make sense. Gilpin is the biggest major hospital on this side of Denver. It's no big jump to anticipate that really sick patients from small towns to the north, like Silver Rapids, would be brought here. And if there was a need to hide the disease's origin, who better than the hospital administrator? He'd know you were a good candidate for scapegoat since your ex-husband likes to dump on your abilities. If files needed to disappear, that same administrator would know how to get rid of them. Too bad, for his sake, that he didn't check first to make sure they were where they belonged that night.''

"Then you believe me?" Joy flooded through Kelley as if a menacing storm cloud had suddenly dissipated from the top of the complicated mountain her life had become. The man she cared for so deeply just might, after all, be on her side.

Only... The balloon of her billowing emotions burst as she reminded herself that he *hadn't* believed her before. He'd thought her an arsonist. Maybe even got close to her, made love with her, to catch her.

Then, he'd thought he *had* caught her in a complicated plot.

She'd tried to tell him that someone was trying to frame her. Someone had hidden those pages in her desk to incriminate her, and he had chosen to ignore her explanation.

"We'll need more evidence," he cautioned. But he had said *we*.

Foolish relief at his apparent support must have affected her mind. She certainly didn't forgive him for doubting her before. Yet she realized that if they hadn't been in a major crowd of people, if what was happening around them wasn't truly a matter of life and death, she might have thrown herself into his arms.

"Dr. Stanton?"

Kelley turned at the male voice. One of the police detectives who'd flashed his ID earlier approached her. His somber demeanor fit the funereal appearance of his dark suit.

But that did not mean that Louis Paxler wouldn't survive. She hoped.

"Yes, I'm Dr. Stanton," she told the detective.

"Is this yours?" He held out a small digital pager packed in a sealed plastic bag.

She bent to regard it more closely. "Possibly. Everyone at the hospital is issued one like it. Is my name on it? I put it on a sticker so it would be returned if I ever lost it."

"Where'd you find it?" Shawn had moved so that he was at her side. On her side. It felt wonderful.

Except that, at the detective's reply, she felt him pull away once more.

"We found this under Mr. Paxler," said the detective. "And, yes, it has Dr. Stanton's name on it."

SHAWN WATCHED KELLEY'S bewildered expression—real or feigned? "I didn't drop my pager when I was in there," she said. "I didn't clip it on this morning."

"When did you last see it, Kelley?" Shawn asked.

"I don't remember. I'm fairly sure I left it in my office. But…" Her eyes widened in shock.

"You think I shot him?" she asked the young detective, whose credentials identified him as Lt. Darrick.

The thought had replanted itself deep in Shawn's mind, too—like a leech that would not die.

"We're looking into all possibilities."

"But he shot himself, didn't he?" Kelley looked at Shawn for confirmation.

He figured she wanted the truth. "Guys who tried to commit suicide with guns usually eat the barrels or shove them against their temples. It's pretty hard to miss, but Louis's wound suggests someone else did it."

Kelley flinched. Shawn resisted the urge to take her into his arms. *Be objective, coach.* He at least had to appear objective, if he'd any hope of being taken seriously by Darrick.

"But couldn't he have changed his mind?"

"Maybe." Shawn hoped, for Kelley's sake, that her idea would be supported by the wound's entry angle.

She turned back to Darrick. "Whoever shot him must have planted the pager." She looked at Shawn. "This could be part of the plot against me."

Shawn involuntarily met the detective's eye. Darrick didn't know anything about Kelley's recent problems, so he clearly thought she was paranoid.

And quite probably the shooter.

"We'll figure it out, Kelley." But she apparently thought he was humoring her, for she glared at him.

"Yeah, we will," she said. She looked at Darrick. "Is there any word on how Mr. Paxler is?"

"Not yet." He glanced down at the notebook in his hand. "I'll need to talk to you further, Dr. Stanton." He glanced at Shawn. "And I don't know who you are."

Shawn flashed his ICU credentials. "I'm involved in an investigation at the hospital," he said. "Of course I'll be glad to cooperate."

"Of course you will," Darrick said.

Shawn didn't like the detective's smug grin but left it

alone—for now. And watched as Darrick took Kelley aside to interview her.

He really didn't want to believe she'd done it. He *didn't* believe it.

But looking at the situation objectively, he could see where someone like Darrick could believe it.

She had plenty of reasons to be mad at Paxler. At best, he had threatened her career. Helped make her look like an inept doctor. Tried to pin the blame for the Etta Borand lawsuit on her plus the patient deaths in the Silver Rapids flu epidemic.

At worst, he was involved with the plot to spread the Silver Rapids flu himself, had possibly tampered with blood tests and set the fire, and had tried to implicate Kelley.

Paxler knew Shawn was here to find the arsonist, and that Kelley was a prime suspect. But he didn't know that Shawn was looking into a connection to the Silver Rapids flu epidemic, for it had farther-reaching importance—a relationship to the kidnapping of the Langworthy baby.

What if Paxler did know more about the epidemic?

What if he didn't, and the original reason Shawn had come was true—Kelley had done it all?

She already said she felt guilty about Paxler's attempted suicide.

What if she had good reason?

"Damn it, Kelley," he muttered. He wouldn't believe it without proof.

And while she was being interviewed by the police, Shawn would look for evidence to clear her.

KELLEY FELT EXHAUSTED as she dragged her way back toward KidClub through the nearly deserted halls of Gilpin Hospital.

She'd had her receptionist cancel all her appointments that afternoon. The day had passed so quickly, especially during her interrogation by Lt. Darrick, that it felt as if she had somehow accelerated hours into seconds. At least it was over. Once she had picked up Jenny, they would leave for home.

Maybe for good.

She'd had so many confrontations that day that she wished she'd lost track of them the same way she had lost time. She hated confrontations. Yet she remembered each in painful detail.

Her verbal duel with Louis might have led to his suicide attempt.

If it *was* a suicide attempt.

How had her pager gotten there? Best she could remember, she had left it in her office, so anyone with access there could have picked it up.

Even Shawn.

She sighed as she turned the corner into the admin wing.

She couldn't believe that of Shawn, even though he didn't trust her. He appeared to believe she could have shot Louis.

That hurt worst of all.

Despite what he thought—feelings apparently shared by Lt. Darrick—she hadn't hurt Louis. For one thing, she didn't own a gun.

Louis did, though, and Darrick said he kept it in his office. Kelley hadn't known about it. As if Darrick would believe that any more than the rest of her story.

Around the corner in the KidClub corridor, she saw Juan Cortes at the far end of the hall. He came toward her, leaving his cart behind.

She sighed. Wasn't it Wednesday? She really didn't care who brought morning treats on Friday this week. She would just hand the janitor a few dollars and ask him to do it.

But fruit and sweet rolls were not what was on his mind. He faced her, his dark eyes troubled. "Did Mr. Paxler really try to kill himself?" His tone was hushed, though nobody else was around to hear.

"Ah, the eternal, infernal Gilpin gossip machine strikes again," Kelley murmured.

He looked confused. "Pardon?"

"Never mind. Officially, no one knows whether Mr. Paxler shot himself or someone else did, Juan. But it appears to be a suicide attempt, and it's still uncertain whether he's going to make it."

"Oh, that's terrible." He sounded genuinely upset, as if he cared what happened to the hospital administrator. Kelley suspected that the status-conscious Louis had probably never spoken to Juan, except maybe to tell him what messes to clean up. But Juan was a kind and caring man. Why else would he have been so determined to bring treats to the children?

"Yes, it's awful," she acknowledged. "We all need to pray for him." She began to edge around, but Juan touched her arm.

"Dr. Stanton, there's something I need to show you."

"What's that?"

He looked down at the floor, as if embarrassed. "I heard the rumors that you set the fire."

She closed her eyes for just a moment, wanting to break something. "Of course." It wasn't enough that everyone from patients to colleagues knew she was accused of incompetence. The maintenance staff knew it, too, and that she was suspected of arson.

"The thing is... Well, I was cleaning in the old records room before. We were told the fire department and insurance company gave permission to get it restored, so I was sent there to work. And...Dr. Stanton, I found something I think you should see."

Kelley stared at him. "Did you find evidence the arson investigators missed?" The way things had been going, it would probably be something else planted to implicate her. Still, she'd need to know so she could deal with it.

"I'm not sure, but I wanted to show you before I told them."

"That's kind, Juan, but I'm not sure it'll help me." She wasn't sure *anything* would help her now. Especially if Louis died without explaining how he had been shot.

"Please, come look." He seemed to be growing distraught. A frantic look had come into his eyes. "I need to show you."

"All right." She followed him down the hall. When they reached Juan's cart, he wheeled it before him.

The yellow police tape was gone, and the former plywood door had been replaced by a real one.

They went inside, Juan still pushing his cart. He stopped and closed the door behind them.

The room looked much as it had before, when she had been here with Shawn. In fact, Kelley couldn't see that any cleaning had been done on the blackened floor and walls.

"What did you find?" Kelley asked, unsure where he could have located anything in this room the arson investigators had emptied weeks ago.

Only then did her eyes light on the mop fastened onto the cart.

The straight mop handle, with the fuzzy cleaning head on the bottom.

Straight. Fuzzy.

Jenny and her pictures of the fire!

Kelley tried hard not to let the revelation show on her face, but it was too late.

"Here's what I want to show you," Juan said, aiming a large black gun at her heart.

SHAWN STOOD OUTSIDE in the parking lot talking to Colleen on the phone. It was probably the fourth time just that day. "You find anything yet?" he demanded.

"Nothing since the last time you called five minutes ago." His lady boss was obviously royally peeved.

"It's been a couple of hours, C, and I can't accept that Kelley shot Paxler. I still don't even buy that she set the fire. She accused Paxler, and then he wound up shot."

"Possibly self-inflicted."

"Possibly not. There are lots of entrances to his office. Look, C, give me something more to tie Paxler to the flu."

"We're looking, Jameson. Meantime, do your job. Even if you can't talk to Paxler, aim your investigation in his direction. Of course…"

"Of course what?"

"Of course, don't be surprised if following his trail leads you right back to your lady doctor."

He swallowed the nasty language that shot up his gullet. "I thought you liked my lady doctor, as you call her."

"That's the hell of it, Jameson." Colleen's voice had grown quiet. "I did. Her and her daughter. Anyway, keep at it, and good luck."

Shawn resisted the urge to grind his cell phone into the sidewalk. He headed back inside.

He wanted to talk to Kelley.

He *needed* to talk to Kelley, for his own peace of mind.

And because…because, no matter how bad things looked, he didn't believe in her guilt.

She had been interrogated all afternoon by that too-dedicated detective, Lt. Darrick. All the while, Shawn had needed to talk to her. To be with her, to plumb her for answers.

To hold her.

When he got back inside, to Paxler's office, he felt like pounding a fist into the wall.

Her interrogation was over, which was good.

But she was nowhere around.

And that was bad.

KELLEY SAT ON THE FLOOR where Juan told her to, her legs stretched in front of her. She held in her hands papers that could have been from the Silver Rapids patients' files.

Could have been, but weren't.

"I don't understand," she told Juan. "Did you forge these?"

"Could be." His voice was hard now, no trace of accent…no trace of humanity. Strange how his ethnicity was now unclear. All she knew was that he had black hair.

But, as with Louis Paxler's hair color, that could be as false as his janitor persona.

"What do these say?" She had to keep him talking. For when he stopped, he would kill her. She was sure of it.

What she didn't understand was why.

"They contain your very pitiful, very apologetic notes as to why your treatment of those patients was substandard."

She cringed at the horrible laughter in his voice. She wished he would go back to his earlier tonelessness.

"You are so terribly sorry that those patients died," he continued, shaking his head slowly. He still pointed the gun at her, even as he extracted a bottle from the bottom of the garbage can on his cart. "Now things are closing in on you. You tried accusing Louis Paxler, and when he made it clear he would ruin you, you shot him with his own gun and made it appear to be a suicide. But he survived. He may even be able to talk. Too bad you dropped your pager as you shot Louis, though it was handy that you left it in your office for me. Anyhow, it's over. You have to end it all." His deep, loud sigh was a horrible mockery. "So sad. Paxler will die anyway. And I will be so upset by all the terrible things that happened here that no one will be surprised when I leave soon, never to be heard from again."

"I...I still don't understand." It was difficult to talk, she was shaking so badly. She didn't want to die. *Jenny.* What would her daughter do without her? Randall as her guardian, with that horrible witch Cheryl as her possible stepmother. No!

And Shawn. She would never have the opportunity now to convince him she was innocent of everything—except loving him.

For she *did* love him, despite the fact that, even if she lived, they'd have no future together. He was a controlling man. He hadn't trusted her.

"Please." She carefully rose to her feet. Her voice trembled but she strengthened it by sheer will. "If I'm going to 'kill myself,' I'd like to know why."

The gun stayed trained on her, though he let her stand as he moved awkwardly to soak a rag with liquid from the bottle. A sedative? A poison? No matter. If he used it on her, she'd be at his mercy.

Could she somehow deflect his attention?

"Why?" he repeated. "It doesn't matter."

"It does to me," she insisted.

He shrugged. "Why not? At first, my employer simply needed a patsy so that no one looked too closely at the Silver Rapids flu victims. You were an easy target. So was your esteemed Mr. Paxler—even more than you."

"How?" Kelley asked, confused.

He didn't answer but continued, "Thank your highly regarded ex-husband for making you the perfect one to blame. He already enjoyed publicizing that you were a less than capable doctor."

"He's wrong!"

"The innuendoes were enough. You were 'it' in our game. Easy, with your kid in childcare, to make you the arsonist, too. You had reason to be in the area. And someone as bad a doctor as you sure wouldn't want anyone to find the files that kept track of your mistakes."

"And why were they really destroyed?"

"Come off it, bitch," he said, approaching her menacingly. "You know I didn't destroy them, thanks to you. We only just learned about it a few days ago because of some inquiries being made in Silver Rapids." He was so close now that she imagined she could feel the cold hardness of the weapon leveled at her chest. "I heard they were hidden in your desk drawer all this time. I planted some other damning papers there, but it was too little, too late. You made me look bad to my employers. Which is one reason this is going to be a pleasure."

He moved so fast she didn't anticipate it. He shoved the rag toward her face, at the same time grabbing her hair with the hand that held the gun. The sweet odor of ether gagged her. He was going to render her unconscious. All the easier for him to set it up as if she had committed suicide.

Not if she could help it.

"The police will smell the ether," she gasped, turning her head despite the pain as her hair was yanked hard. Better that than unconsciousness. "They'll find traces in my blood."

"So what?" His voice was so close, so ugly in her ear. "It'll be better if it looks like you did it yourself, so it's worth trying to set up. But whether they look that close or not, you'll still be dead."

This would be her only opportunity. Bracing herself on the floor, Kelley let herself go slack. Then, as his grip eased, she raised one leg and kicked it back with all her might, aiming the heel of her pump toward Juan's groin. As she moved, she screamed.

The sound of gunfire resounded not from a distance this time, but from very close.

At the same time, a pain as excruciating as fire shot through Kelley's head.

Chapter Fifteen

"Kelley!" Shawn had shoved her aside as he'd leaped into the room. He'd had to get her out of his line of fire.

She'd hit her head on the wall and gone down.

Shawn prayed he hadn't hurt her badly. But right now, he had to finish neutralizing Cortes or they'd both be toast.

The janitor lay doubled over on the floor. He clutched his groin with his left hand. Blood seeped from his right arm, which he held against his chest. Despite the excellent kick Kelley had landed on the s.o.b., he'd kept his gun, a lethal-looking 9 mm, pointed at her.

He still held it. Unsteadily, but Shawn couldn't be certain he wouldn't raise it and fire.

"Drop it, Cortes." He aimed his pistol right between the guy's eyes. He had retrieved it from the car while talking on his cell phone with Colleen.

Kelley moaned behind him. Damn! He wanted to run to her. Cradle her in his arms. Make sure she was all right.

But that had to wait.

"Go ahead and shoot," Cortes said. "I'm as good as dead anyway."

"Not until I get answers," Shawn growled.

He heard a noise behind him but didn't move. "Police!" shouted a voice that had become familiar only that day.

"What kept you, Darrick?" Shawn glanced behind him to make sure the cop had drawn his weapon and had the room under control. Only then did he put the safety back on and hand his weapon to Darrick. "It's licensed to me," he said. "I used it to keep this piece of feces from shooting Kelley."

Without waiting for further reaction, he hurried to Kelley and did as he'd ached to before—took her in his arms. Her eyes were focused, her pupils the same size. No concussion, but she rubbed the back of her head with her hand.

"Are you all right?" he asked gently, conscious of the sounds of the police taking charge of Cortes behind him.

"More or less." She threw her arms around him and pressed her face against his chest. He wanted nothing more than to keep her there, under his protection, forever. "Thank you," she whispered.

"Kelley, I—"

She didn't let him finish. "I know you didn't believe me, maybe you still don't, but I didn't have anything to do with the fire or the epidemic. I—"

"Sssh," he said, softly nuzzling her fragrant auburn hair. "I know. In fact, I think I knew it all along."

She smiled wryly up at him. "Of course you did." Yet despite her obvious skepticism, she didn't pull away when he bent his head and kissed her delectable, willing lips.

DESPITE THE ACHING throb at the back of Kelley's head where she had hit the wall, she reveled in Shawn's kiss. Treasured it.

For she knew it was undoubtedly the last.

Shawn had saved her life. Again.

Now his assignment was over. He would leave soon.

And she would feel as if she'd had cardiac surgery and been put back together without a complete, beating heart.

At least she had been exonerated from the charges of arson and complicity in whatever had caused the Silver Rapids epidemic. Maybe.

For with so many false accusations leveled against her, evidence planted to implicate her, who knew what Juan Cortes would say now?

Shawn helped her to her feet, kept his arm around her. She didn't want to lean against him, but it felt so good. "Are you up to answering more questions for the police?" he asked.

She nodded, wincing at the pain. But she wanted to get it over with.

Shawn stayed by her side this time as she described her encounter with Cortes. She answered questions from a different detective, for Darrick was busy with Juan.

"I need to get Jenny," she told Shawn when they were done. Hurrying with her, he accompanied her to KidClub.

It was just past closing time. "I'm sorry," Kelley told Marge.

"That's okay. Another teaching intern is in a back playroom with Jenny. She's the last child here, but I figured you'd be awhile. I knew what was going on, sort of. But did you really shoot the janitor?" She looked at Shawn.

He appeared endearingly embarrassed as he nodded brusquely.

"Mr. Cortes would have shot me otherwise," Kelley said, coming to Shawn's rescue. She wondered why the cool, macho investigator seemed suddenly bashful.

Maybe his stint as a child-care worker had softened him, just a little.

It certainly had affected her.

"Oh, hi," said a voice from doorway. It was Cheryl Marten.

Kelley sighed. This had been one hell of a day, and it wasn't over yet. "Hello, Cheryl," she said. She glanced over the nurse's shoulder. "Is Randall with you?"

"No. I'm meeting him later, but I'm here to check on Jenny." Her tone was chirpy—a little too cheerful? Kelley noticed that her overly made-up cheeks were as pink as the flowers of the nurse's smock she wore.

"She's fine," Marge said, and directed Cheryl toward the room where Jenny was.

"Thanks." Cheryl took only a couple of steps beyond the sign-out desk and hesitated in front of Shawn. She looked up at him, though for a change she didn't appear flirtatious. If she were, Kelley wondered if she had enough self-restraint left to keep herself from accosting the voluptuous, slutty nurse.

Not that she had any claim on Shawn.

"You know," Cheryl continued, "I heard that Mr. Paxler... That he tried to kill himself. Is that true?"

Whatever had made Shawn uncomfortable disappeared before Kelley's eyes. He was again cool. The consummate investigator. He crossed his arms over his broad chest. "Do you know of any reason he'd want to commit suicide?"

Cheryl took a quick step backward, as if he'd threatened her. "How would I know that?"

Shawn shrugged. Kelley loved the steely glint in his blue eyes—since they weren't aimed at her. "I don't know. How *would* you know that?"

"If you intend to say hi to Jenny," Kelley said to the woman's back, "please go ahead. I'm ready to take her home." Not that she wanted to rescue Cheryl, but she wanted to get her daughter and leave.

"Sure," Cheryl said, turning toward Kelley. "Kelley, I heard… Were you talking to Mr. Paxler before he shot himself?"

Kelley was puzzled about what Cheryl really wanted—it didn't seem to be to check on Jenny. She followed Shawn's example. "Where did you hear that?" she demanded.

Cheryl gnawed with perfect teeth on her full bottom lip. There was a shiftiness in her eyes, an unwillingness to meet Kelley's gaze. Why?

"I heard some E.R. nurses talking," Cheryl replied. When Kelley didn't say anything else, she continued, "I can't help being curious. Everyone around here is. Did Mr. Paxler say anything while you were talking to him?"

Before Kelley decided how to respond, Shawn stepped in front of her. "Like what, Cheryl? Are you worried about something?"

"I—I'll go check on Jenny now." She took a few steps toward the other room.

Shawn's voice stopped her. "From what I understand, Mr. Paxler will be fine."

Kelley looked at him in surprise. She hadn't heard anything about Louis's condition. Maybe Shawn hadn't, either. A good investigator often told lies to get information, after all. She'd learned that from him.

"The police intend to ask him not only if he shot himself, but also if there were others with reason to shoot him," Shawn continued. He was suddenly so close to Cheryl that if she'd struck one of her usual poses, her chest would touch him. Instead, she shrank back.

"I didn't shoot him," she said tearily. "I only wanted to protect Randall."

Kelley wondered how long it would take her thick eye shadow to run. And then, to Kelley's amazement, Cheryl sank onto one of the small children's chairs. A tale poured out of her about how she had been colluding with Etta Borand in the lawsuit against Kelley.

"Her family needed money. They were underinsured, and her husband's hospitalization was expensive. If someone was blamed for the infection he caught, I didn't want it to be Randall." She looked up at Kelley. "I'm sorry," she sobbed. "That was why I left Jenny alone here the night of the fire. I'd already taken any harmful references from the files—which were burned anyway. But that night, she was asleep. I was only going to be gone a few minutes to meet with Etta, you see?"

Kelley didn't see at all. But she bit her tongue to avoid interrupting the woman's story, for she sensed she hadn't heard the whole thing.

"By the time I finished with Etta," Cheryl said, "the fire had started and Kelley had brought Jenny out. If she hadn't, I'd have gone back after her myself."

"Sure you would," Kelley said, not believing it. Not if it would have singed a strand of the woman's bleached hair to rescue the child.

With a baleful look toward Kelley, Cheryl went on. "Louis Paxler knew about the situation with Etta, but he made it clear that with Randall's stature as a cardiac surgeon, and his own need to protect the hospital's reputation, it would be better if someone else—Kelley—was blamed. She was already suspected of doing things wrong to treat those influenza patients." She looked up directly at Kelley. "He told you all about that tonight, didn't he?"

"No," Kelley said quietly.

Cheryl looked taken aback, as if she realized she would have been better off staying silent. Then she said, "I'm sorry." She stood. Instead of heading toward the room where Jenny was, she hurried toward the door.

"One more question, Cheryl," Shawn said. "Were you trying to protect Randall, or did *you* do something that might have led to Mr. Borand's postsurgical infection?"

Her eyes were stricken as she looked back at him, and then she fled from the room.

"I think we can take that for a 'yes,'" Shawn said wryly.

SHAWN WENT INTO THE playroom with Kelley to fetch Jenny. He had a question for the child, and now, after talking to Kelley, he was sure he knew the answer.

Jenny was seated at a table beside Stephanie, the child-care intern, who looked up as they entered. "We were putting together a puzzle," the intern said.

"I see," Shawn acknowledged as Kelley approached her daughter. Jenny was dressed in small, soft blue jeans and a blue top that went well with her light-colored hair.

"Time to leave, Jenny," Kelley said.

"In just a minute," Shawn said. When she looked at him quizzically, he added, "Bear with me."

He went into one of the cabinets where he had begun keeping the stacks of caricatures he hadn't handed out to the kids.

Stuck in the middle were a couple of the pictures Jenny had drawn on days she had been particularly unruly. They included the ones from yesterday with jagged red lines that he'd figured signified fire, along with straight lines that seemed fuzzy at the bottom. Shawn hadn't been able to figure the straight lines out—before.

"Don't, Shawn." Kelley sounded distraught behind him. No wonder, after all she had gone through that day. He didn't want to put her through any more, but this was to help Jenny.

"It's better," he said gently. "You'll see." As if he really were a child psychologist. Ha!

But he did think, now, that he had an idea how to relate to kids. And now, he particularly had to help Jenny.

He knelt beside the child at the table and put his arm around her shoulder as he laid the drawing down with his other hand. He wanted to hug her tight, protect her.

First, he had to question her. "Jenny, are the red lines fire?"

Her brown eyes huge, she nodded solemnly.

"And I'll bet I can guess what this other line is."

She stood up fast, but he steadied her.

"It's okay. There's nothing to be afraid of anymore. Do you understand?"

She said nothing, but she didn't move, either.

"Is this line supposed to be a mop?"

Shawn heard Kelley inhale sharply but didn't turn toward her.

"Is it?" he asked gently when Jenny didn't answer.

"Yes," she finally whispered.

"Did you see Mr. Cortes, the janitor, set the fire?"

"Yes," she repeated, tears running down her face.

Shawn folded her into his arms. A chill nearly froze his heart. "Did he threaten you?"

When Jenny didn't answer, Kelley, who stooped beside them, said, "She might not understand what a threat is. But now that you've started this... Honey, did Mr. Cortes see you the night of the fire and say something bad to you, something that scared you?"

"No, Mommy," Jenny responded tearily.

That surprised Shawn. "Did he talk to you *after* the fire?" He pulled back to look at Jenny.

She shook her head.

"Never?"

"No, but I see'd him, and I was scared."

Shawn thought he was beginning to understand. "So you got upset when you saw him and sometimes even threw treats he brought and other food."

Jenny nodded. "And I drawed fire."

Shawn picked her up and kept her small, fragile body snugged against him, reveling in the feeling of the girl's head on his shoulder. "You know, that's possible," he told Kelley. "Cortes always brought the morning treat to KidClub early, before you two arrived. Their paths might not have crossed much."

"And, thank heavens, he probably didn't know Jenny saw him set the fire," Kelley said. "I didn't think anything about it before, but he and I talked about the fire. I'd told him, like everyone else, that Jenny was left behind in KidClub. In case she saw what happened, I didn't want the arsonist to know she had been wandering around."

"Good move." Shawn smiled at her and was rewarded by her relieved grin.

Jenny wriggled in his arms. "Is there going to be any more fire?" she asked softly.

"No, honey," he reassured her. "The police have Mr. Cortes, and he's not going to set fires, or scare you, ever again. I promise."

He melted as the child hugged him tight. "Thank you, Shawn," she said.

He loved it. Loved this child.

And her mother.

Could he let them go, now that this assignment was nearly over?

He'd never considered himself the family type. Hell, he hardly even knew what a family was.

And yet, with Kelley and Jenny, he felt…well, whole.

But he'd hurt Kelley. Accused her of arson and conspiring to let her patients die.

He'd just been doing his job. But he doubted she'd ever forgive him.

And he couldn't really blame her.

KELLEY MADE A BIG production of letting Jenny pick out doughnuts the next morning. They had sliced fruit at home. "We'll get the other kids to help from now on," she told her daughter once they'd reached the hospital, "or maybe we'll stop morning treats. All that sugar isn't good for you kids anyway."

"But I like doughnuts, Mommy," Jenny said, then added, "And oranges and apples, too." She took an end of the box to help carry it down the corridor, then stopped. "Mr. Cortes isn't going to bring more, is he?" Her small brow puckered in worry, and Kelley wanted to smooth away all her daughter's fears.

"No, sweetheart," she said. "I don't think you'll ever see Mr. Cortes again."

She might, though, if she had to testify against him in court.

Shawn wasn't at KidClub when Kelley signed Jenny in. She hadn't expected him to be. He'd seen them to her car last night, then said goodbye. He'd called later but had seemed distracted.

She'd missed him in her bed.

She missed him now.

But she would have to get used to it. She was no longer his suspect, his assignment.

At least, she hoped not. She wasn't sure she'd been totally cleared of suspicion in her treatment of the Silver Rapids epidemic. Still, it was getting around that she wasn't the arsonist. Maybe the day would come soon when she'd hear acknowledgment that she'd managed those patients just fine, within accepted medical standards—as she'd always known she had done.

She checked her calendar for the day at her office, then started on rounds. Outside her second patient's room, she ran into Madelyne Younger.

"Hey, kiddo," the older doctor said, "is everything I heard about yesterday true?"

"That depends what you heard," Kelley said with a small laugh. She felt a little embarrassed, for the crew at the nearby nurses' station was watching.

"All greatly exaggerated, I expect. Except that Marge Ralston swears she was in the room with you when Cheryl Marten confessed to some pretty nasty stuff."

"Well…yes," Kelley admitted.

"In any event, I owe you one big apology if I ever made it seem as if I doubted your competence."

"Thanks," Kelley said with a big smile. "I appreciate it."

"And I'm not the only one." She motioned over Kelley's shoulder. "Hey, Randall, get your butt over here."

Kelley wished she could just slip away. "Oh, Madelyne, don't—"

"No, you wait right here."

In moments, Randall was beside them. He scowled down his patrician nose at Kelley, but there was something uneasy in his gray eyes.

"Don't you have something to say to Dr. Stanton, Dr. Stanton? From Dr. Randall to Dr. Kelley, that is."

"I...er, Kelley, I want you to know I wasn't aware of what Cheryl was doing."

Hey, Kelley thought, *this is fun.* She'd never imagined she'd see the day when Randall was uncomfortable. She didn't help him. She remained quiet, regarding him with eyebrows raised expectantly.

"I'm sorry, Kelley," he finished.

She just nodded at him without accepting the apology. Maybe she could get him to grovel some more.

"You're not finished," Madelyne told him. "Tell Kelley exactly what you think of her doctoring skills."

He glared at Madelyne before turning back toward Kelley. "You've turned out to be a fine doctor," he said, wincing as if the words gave him gas. "I always knew you would, Kelley."

He hurried away while the nurses at the station behind them cheered. Madelyne gave a giggling Kelley a high five.

THAT TURNED OUT not to be Kelley's only major surprise of the day. She returned to her office to find that her long-missing friend Dr. Wilson Carpenter had finally returned her phone calls. She responded immediately to his message. His phone number was an 800 toll-free number, so she didn't know where he had called from.

"Where have you been?" she demanded, sitting at her desk with her fists clenched.

"On an all-expenses-paid sabbatical to Europe," he said. "Look, Kelley, about the influenza epidemic—"

She interrupted him. "I have a long story to tell you about that, but not now. Just tell me if you know its origins, and explain that Q fever reference you made when you called me.''

''I still can only guess,'' he said. ''And maybe I was foolish to accept the trip to that prestigious medical conference in Switzerland, but thought it was my only choice.''

''What are you talking about?''

While she stared unseeingly toward her office window, he explained that he'd been stewing about the epidemic for weeks before he'd called her. He'd run some tests of his own that had had odd results—including Q fever antibodies—but he'd kept his doubts to himself when he didn't hear of any diseases detected at Gilpin besides influenza. But eventually, as the suspicions ate at him, he'd needed to talk to someone and had decided to consult with Kelley.

But he supposed he'd been too vocal in his questions at the time of the epidemic. ''I think my phone line was tapped,'' he said. ''So when I called you, we were cut off, and I couldn't get through again. Then came the threats, followed by a call from a physician in Switzerland who invited me to an important international infectious disease conference, all expenses paid, but only if I came right away. I was suspicious, of course, but it made sense to take it and get out of here.''

When he'd gotten to Switzerland, he'd confirmed that his trip was subsidized by someone back home. Someone who didn't want him around for a long time. ''The conference was great, actually. But there were some elements there—well, they made it clear that my life was in danger if I tried to go home or to contact anyone. Maybe ever.''

''So why are you back?''

''I was tracked down—some people with connections to a supersecret undercover outfit, it seems, though I really don't know much about it. They promised me protection if

I come home right away, told me you were in trouble and that I was the cause. Is that true?"

Kelley laughed. But she found herself wondering why Wilson had been sent overseas rather than killed. People had died from the epidemic. If, as she suspected, the disease had been manufactured, whoever had done it could be accused of murder. To cover it up, why not just kill someone else?

But all she said to Wilson was, "Could be. I'll explain over drinks some day. But I'll need for you to back me about your suspicions about Q fever and the Silver Rapids epidemic. Okay?"

"You got it."

"YOU CAN GET ME immunity in exchange for my testimony, can't you? And into witness protection?" Paxler's voice was weak, and he looked like hell lying in his hospital bed, a large bandage covering the side of his head. Nearly a week had passed since he'd been shot by Cortes, and the gray roots were already beginning to show in the hair that was visible.

Shawn knew the police interrogators had gotten nothing from Paxler. Shawn hadn't been permitted to see the guy until now.

He replied to Paxler's question the only way he could. "No promises, Louis. But I'll put in a good word, and my agency will do all it can to ensure your security if you cooperate."

"Thank you." Paxler shrank back into his pillow, but Shawn wasn't about to let him get away that easy.

"So tell me what you know."

Paxler gave a beseeching look, but Shawn wasn't about

to back off. Even though the guy's head still obviously hurt like hell.

"All right," Paxler said. He told Shawn a fascinating tale that dovetailed right into every suspicion Colorado Confidential had about the origin of the epidemic.

Paxler had been roped into cooperating because he owed an enormous gambling debt to the Swansong casino in Silver Rapids. In exchange for not being forced to pay it all immediately, which he couldn't afford to do, he'd been coerced into hiring that reptile Juan Cortes—not his real name—as janitor when the first disease patients reached Gilpin Hospital. Cortes had actually substituted blood samples to prevent the true disease pathogen from being completely analyzed.

Cortes's employers had also wanted to make sure that, if the furor about the deaths of the Silver Rapids patients didn't blow over immediately, a doctor was blamed. The vulnerable Dr. Kelley Stanton had had the dubious distinction of being selected as sacrificial goat, particularly since she had asked a lot of questions and ordered too many tests that had to be squelched. She had to be discredited so that no one paid attention to her.

Kelley. Shawn wanted to throttle both miserable s.o.b.s for involving her. He missed her, damn it.

She'd been acting polite and friendly to him all week. But he *missed* her.

He forced himself to concentrate again on Paxler's story.

When things had finally seemed to calm down, Kelley's suspicions had been resurrected by a call from Dr. Wilson Carpenter, a Silver Rapids doctor with suspicions of his own. He'd been dealt with, but Cortes had set the fire to destroy records of the Silver Rapids patients, just in case.

Cortes's cover had been perfect, Shawn realized. No one

would notice a janitor cleaning up a lab where the blood samples were swapped or a file room that caught fire. Not even *he* had paid attention on the days Jenny had gotten upset—days when she had come in early and seen the ''janitor'' bringing treats to KidClub. Apparently, the guy who had no reluctance about setting fires or even attempting murder genuinely liked kids.

Cortes had followed Kelley, informed Paxler of anything she did, anywhere she went, that might help in discrediting her. He'd hung around for months, Paxler said, to make sure no trails led to the real cause of the flu epidemic.

''Which was?'' Shawn asked.

''I honestly don't know,'' Paxler said in a weak voice. ''But based on all this, my guess is that it was some kind of manufactured illness. Bioterrorism, if you will.''

''And the source?'' Shawn pressed.

''I don't know,'' Paxler replied wearily. ''But I'd check the casino, if I were you. Someone there knew about my debt and used it against me.''

Someone indeed, Shawn thought. He would let Colleen know the latest. Soon.

But he had somewhere to go first.

''Is EVERYTHING OKAY with Jenny?'' Kelley asked Marge Ralston, who stood by the sign-in desk at KidClub. She had received a message to get there as soon as she could.

''She's fine,'' Marge said. The child-care coordinator wore a huge, knowing grin that Kelley couldn't interpret. Was Cheryl there again spilling confessions? Why else would Marge look so smug? ''There's someone else here who wants to see you, though,'' Marge continued.

''Who—'' Kelley began, but knew immediately when Shawn strode through the door from one of the playrooms, a whole Pied Piper troupe of kids with him including Jenny, who held his hand.

What was he doing here? His undercover role was no longer necessary.

They'd spoken now and then over the past week. She'd told him how grateful she was for all he'd done. He'd apologized for doubting her and even for issuing her orders.

She'd told him she understood. She had been his assignment. And when he had told her what to do, it had sometimes been for her protection.

But did she really understand?

Maybe. It still hurt, though. For she had fallen in love with him.

And now, he was returning to his real life. To investigate some other woman, she supposed. To tell *her* what to do, even as he skillfully sought her secrets. Maybe get the new woman to fall for him, too.

Kelley sighed, even as she felt her pulse rate triple as she watched him. Now she knew why Marge was grinning. She couldn't help smiling herself.

"Hi, Dr. Stanton," he said in the voice she had come to know—and love—so well. There was a look in his gorgeous blue eyes that she didn't understand—but if she could bottle and sell it, she'd make a fortune from women all over the world. It was hot and fiery yet uncertain and… Well, she wasn't sure what all it contained. She only knew it made her want to rush toward him. Touch him. Embrace him.

It took all her willpower to stay still.

"Did you leave a message for me to come here?" Kelley asked, attempting to sound friendly yet remote, despite the way she trembled.

"Yeah," he admitted, an unfamiliar catch in his voice.

"I'm about to give a drawing lesson and want you to watch."

What was he up to? Kelley couldn't imagine. But she obediently settled herself uncomfortably into one of the tiny chairs around a miniature table and watched him whip a blank sheet of paper from a large pad. He took colored pencils from a large box and began to sketch.

Kelley drew in her breath the moment she realized what he was doing. "Oh," she whispered, feeling tears rush to her eyes as he continued.

He glanced at her, smiled uncertainly, then turned back to his page. All the while, the children crowding around them whispered. "It's a mommy and a daddy and a baby," said one.

"Yeah," said another. "A fam'ly."

"No," Jenny said. "See the dress. I see'd a dolly dressed like that in a store. It's a b'ide."

"A bride," Kelley corrected softly. There were three figures on the page—a woman wearing a wedding gown, a man in a tuxedo and a child in between them holding their hands.

Their caricature faces were easily identifiable: Kelley, Shawn and Jenny.

Shawn finished and handed the page to Kelley. "I— er..." He cleared his throat winsomely. "As you know, I've a good imagination, or I wouldn't be able to draw caricatures. But this time, I'm picturing something I really want." He slid off the low seat onto his knees. "You can say no, of course, in front of all these impressionable, optimistic kids, but you'll destroy them for life." He grinned with adorable smugness—yet she could see uncertainty in his expression. He'd undergone a lot of rejection in his early life, and had opened himself up to it now. For her.

Kelley knew what he was going to say, but she let him continue.

"Now, I know you probably don't forgive me for all the bad things I thought about you, but if you marry me, we'll have a lifetime for me to make it up to you. I could order you to marry me, but I know you don't like to take orders from men. So, I'll ask you instead. I love you, Kelley. Will you marry me? Pretty please with powdered sugar on it?"

Breathless, so full of love she felt she would explode, she looked away from his adored face toward Jenny. "What do you think, sweetheart? Should we give the guy a break?"

"Yes, Mommy," her little daughter said excitedly. "Are you gonna be a b'ide?"

Kelley stood, pulling Shawn to his feet, too. "Yes, honey," she whispered without looking at her daughter. "Mommy is going to be a br—" She didn't finish, and she was only vaguely aware of the cheering around them as Shawn's mouth stole the rest of the word.

Epilogue

"So you survived being a nanny." Colleen leaned back on her chair at the table in the secret meeting room beneath the ranch house at the Royal Flush.

"Sure did," Shawn acknowledged. Sitting across from her beside the grinning Fiona Clark, he was dressed for ranch work and he crossed his jean-clad legs nonchalantly. He looked smug. As well he might, since he'd done a good job—and not just as a child-care provider.

He'd wrapped up the arson case. Plus, he'd amassed a lot of evidence that tied the Silver Rapids flu to the Gettys's sheep ranch.

Despite all the questions that remained about how both might be connected to the missing Langworthy baby.

"You heard, didn't you, that your pal Juan Cortes isn't talking, at least not much."

"Anyone find out yet what his real name is?" Shawn asked.

"The one he used when he worked at the Swansong Casino," Colleen said drolly, "or his *real* real name?"

"He actually worked there?" Fiona asked, her attention obviously stoked. Colleen's attractive blond employee had returned from checking on another possible lead to the

Langworthy case and kept pressing Colleen for a further assignment.

"Not only that, but it was at the same time that Helen Gettys, Senator Gettys's former wife, worked there. Of course, she was Helen Kouros then."

"So they knew each other," Shawn said slowly, obviously mulling over the ramifications.

As had Colleen. *Ad infinitum.* Without, unfortunately, getting all the answers. Helen Gettys's powerful ex-husband, Senator Franklin Gettys, owned part of the Half Spur sheep ranch. Helen had worked at the casino in Silver Rapids at the same time as Cortes. Cortes had been ordered to confuse the situation at Gilpin Hospital regarding the Silver Rapids flu epidemic.

Too many connections to be coincidental. The experiments being run at the sheep ranch were probably connected with the Silver Rapids epidemic, but she didn't know how yet. Plus people who'd been at the casino and certain eating establishments on one particular day a few months ago had caught the disease—including Holly Langworthy, who had been pregnant with little Schyler, the kidnapped baby. Another connection. They had yet to find out who Gettys's partner in the ranch was. Perhaps that would shed some light.

"Yes, they knew each other," Colleen said aloud, "but your buddy Cortes claims he hasn't seen Helen in years, knows nothing about sheep and definitely had nothing to do with the Langworthy kidnapping."

"Helen Gettys now lives in Washington state, with her brother," Fiona said. "While they seem to have cut all ties to Senator Gettys, the brother does have a criminal record. He also was in Colorado when Baby Langworthy disappeared. Supposedly on a camping trip."

"Right," Colleen acknowledged. "We'll be following

up on that lead. Meanwhile all Cortes will say is that he knows nothing. No admissions about fudging blood tests, setting the fire, blackmailing Louis Paxler or setting up your fiancée.'' She smiled at Shawn. ''So how are Kelley and Jenny?''

''Fine. They're out watching the horses. Jenny's excited about living in my cabin on the ranch. She loves 'an'mals.'''

''So they're staying here?'' Fiona asked. ''What about Kelley's medical practice?''

''She's considering opening her own small one around here,'' Shawn said. ''She's determined to leave Gilpin Hospital behind—which is fine with me. She's also looking for a preschool for Jenny, since the kid'll turn four in a few months.''

''What? You haven't offered to stay on as her nanny?'' Fiona's tone was teasing.

''Only as her new daddy.'' Pride emanated from Shawn's voice.

Fiona sighed. ''How romantic. When's the wedding?''

''Soon.'' He looked at Colleen. ''I'll need time off, boss.''

''Give me a heads-up, and I'll arrange it. Let's just hope we get some better leads on little Schyler Langworthy's whereabouts first.''

Shawn's face clouded. ''Yeah. I can only imagine now how awful that family must feel.''

And that from a guy who'd wanted nothing to do with families or kids a few short weeks ago. Colleen was happy for him.

But Colorado Confidential still had a big case to solve. Fast.

''Did you get anything else from Kelley's friend Wilson

Carpenter?'' she asked. Not that Dr. Carpenter was likely to know anything about the missing baby's whereabouts.

"The disappearing doctor?" Shawn replied. "Not really. But I do have a theory as to why he was sent on what was to be a very long vacation rather than a permanent disappearance."

"And your theory is…?"

"Just that the death of yet another person connected to the flu would arouse too much additional speculation. The doctors in the practice next door would have squawked. That many people can't be silenced unnoticed." Shawn rose. "Anyway, I've got to run now. Dex is expecting me to go ride the range or something, and I've still got a cover to maintain here."

"You sure do," Colleen agreed. "Kelley knows about both your covers as a ranch hand and a private detective in Denver?"

He nodded. "She's aware of Colorado Confidential now but I'd bet my life on her keeping it secret."

Colleen, who'd been getting to know Kelley better, couldn't disagree.

The moment Shawn left, Fiona said, as Colleen had anticipated, "I need a new assignment. What's next?"

"Well, I've been thinking about that 'interview' you did when you went undercover as a reporter to talk to Todd Houghton."

"Right," Fiona said. "Our esteemed governor didn't say anything useful."

"He's taken the same position, though, as Senator Gettys," Colleen reminded her. "They both seem to think the Langworthys staged the kidnapping. If the public feels sorry enough for the family, it could help Joshua Langworthy in his gubernatorial campaign against Houghton. That's where you come in."

"How?" Fiona's brown eyes narrowed.

"You're going to investigate Joshua Langworthy. See if he knows anything about the kidnapping of his sister's baby. It would be a heck of a thing if he really was involved, simply for political gain."

"It certainly would," Fiona acknowledged grimly. "What's the plan?"

Colleen smiled, and told her.

Once Fiona left, Colleen went to the adjoining basement room—a secret surveillance room that was hidden, as was the meeting room, but that contained all sorts of useful equipment. She checked the far-ranging video monitors first, as always, to make sure nothing at the ICU office or on the ranch looked amiss, and found herself grinning as she watched Shawn talking to ranch foreman Dexter Jones.

Damn, but Dex was one handsome cowboy!

But she had to get her mind on business.

She had another assignment to make, and she knew just the man for it.

Colleen picked up the phone and called the ICU office. "Becky," she said when the office manager answered, "have Ryan Benton give me a call. I've a new assignment for him. I want him to investigate Helen Gettys and her brother further."

"The senator's wife?" Becky sounded surprised.

"His ex-wife. Is Ryan there?"

"No," Becky said, "but he's only a cell phone call away. I'll have him get in touch with you."

"Thanks," Colleen said. She headed for the door, then stopped herself. She needed to check her e-mail.

Good thing she had, she told herself a few minutes later. There was an important message from Wiley Longbottom, the Director of the Department of Public Safety, who'd established Colorado Confidential under the guise of ICU to help find the Langworthy baby. He'd sent her another lead—and a directive.

The e-mail said, "My conscience tells me that a look at Mills & Grommett might help your investigation."

Mills & Grommett? From what Colleen knew about the company, it was part of the Langworthy Centennial conglomerate, a pharmaceutical research and supply outfit. Interesting.

Not for the first time, Colleen wondered about this mysterious "conscience" of Wiley's. She suspected it was a person, one whose identity Wiley kept to himself.

It piqued her curiosity, but no matter.

She shut down her computer and headed out the secret exit—a broom closet. Her mind swirled about how best to approach an investigation of M&G.

Upstairs in the old, plush barroom, she almost didn't hear Dex's approach. "There you are," he said. He sounded grumpy.

He was definitely gorgeous when he scowled. There was something infinitely sexy about those hazel eyes of his.

"Yes," she said mildly, "here I am. Anything wrong?" She almost wished she'd put on a newer pair of jeans or a shirt dressier than the old plaid thing she wore, but nearly laughed ironically at herself. It didn't matter to Dex how she dressed. She was only his boss.

She sighed.

"You made any decisions yet about trying that new cattle feed I recommended?" he demanded.

"Yes. I've decided you should make the decision." She smiled at him. "As usual."

"Damn it, Colleen, this is *your* ranch. You're supposed to be in charge." He ran one rough hand through his salt-and-pepper hair in obvious agitation at their long-standing argument.

"I am in charge." She tried to keep her voice level. "And what I've decided is to rely on my very capable foreman." She decided to try to appease him, if only a little, and stepped behind the bar to the small refrigerator. "You look as if you need a cold drink." She pulled out a bottle of soda. "Ice?"

"Stop trying to change the subject!" he all but shouted at her. "Look, I'm not stupid. I know you could hire experienced hands instead of training these admittedly intelligent tenderfeet to run the Flush. Something else is going on here. For all I know, you're running an escort service."

Controlling her amusement and exasperation, Colleen glanced up at the portrait over the bar. Her ancestress Eudora Wellesley gazed out primly. Dora had seen worse than an escort service here, in this room, where ladies of the night had once met their men for the evening, then led them upstairs.

"For the ninetieth time," Colleen said, "I'm not running an escort service. Now do you want a drink or not?"

"If I did, I'd want something stronger than soda, damn it."

"Not in the middle of the day," she said.

"Is that an order?"

"Yes, that's an order."

They were standing toe-to-toe by then. She had slung her head back to look way up into his face. She was conscious of how muscular and sexy this man was. Though she frowned at him, she wanted nothing more than for him to bend down and kiss her. Deeply. Then lead her—

"Stop teasing me, damn it!" He pounded one fist against the wall behind them so hard that she wondered for a moment if she was hearing the bones in his knuckles break.

And then she realized it was a different thing she'd

heard, as something small and thick fell from behind the portrait of Dora Wellesley. They both turned to look.

"What's that?" asked Dex suspiciously.

"I don't know." But Colleen stooped to pick it up from the floor where it had fallen. It was dusty, but it appeared to be made of leather. A book of some kind. A very old book.

She opened it, very carefully, and gasped. "I think it's Dora's journal!"

"Really?" Dex leaned over her as she rose. She bumped into him. Her eyes met his, and she couldn't move. Couldn't breathe.

She wanted him to kiss her, damn it.

And it sure looked, from the desire glowing from his eyes, that he wanted to kiss her.

"Dex," she said softly. Trying to encourage him.

For a moment, he stood still, as if trying to work up the nerve to—what?

And then she heard a noise. Dex took a quick step away from her, and she turned, furious, toward the door.

Fiona stood there. She looked embarrassed and distressed. "Sorry, Colleen," she said. "There's something I need to talk to you about right away. Something important has come up."

Something, she didn't need to say, involving Colorado Confidential.

"Er—I'll take care of cleaning that journal up so you can read it," Dex said, as if that had been the only reason they had been so near one another.

"Thank you," she said formally, handing the little book to him. She was curious about its contents, eager to read it.

And very, very frustrated.

Damn it all! Colleen thought as she hurried out the door

behind Fiona. Some days she wished she *was* only a rancher. Being the head of an organization so covert that she couldn't even talk about it with the person she was interested in was hell.

On the front porch, as Fiona began animatedly but quietly to describe the latest Colorado Confidential dilemma, Colleen glanced left, toward the horse barn. Little Jenny Stanton stood on the bottom rung of the split rail fence, watching the horses inside. Wistfully, Colleen watched Shawn, who stood near his stepdaughter-to-be, take Kelley into his arms and kiss her, very tenderly.

Someday, Colleen thought wistfully, thinking of the moment with Dex that had been interrupted. *Someday...*

* * * * *

*Don't miss the next exciting installment in
the COLORADO CONFIDENTIAL series
COVERT COWBOY
by Harper Allen
Coming in November from
Harlequin Intrigue.*

*And be sure to pick up
the thrilling anthology
COLORADO CONFIDENTIAL
with USA TODAY bestselling author
Jasmine Cresswell
available in October.*

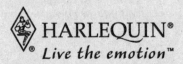

Your opinion is important to us! Please take a few moments to share your thoughts with us about your experiences with Harlequin and Silhouette books. Your comments will be very useful in ensuring that we deliver books you love to read. *Please take a few minutes to complete the questionnaire, then send it to us at the address below.*

Send your completed questionnaires to:
Harlequin/Silhouette Reader Survey, P.O. Box 9046, Buffalo, NY 14269-9046

1. As you may know, there are many different lines under the Harlequin and Silhouette brands. Each of the lines is listed below. Please check the box that most represents your reading habit for each line.

Line	Currently read this line	Do not read this line	Not sure if I read this line
Harlequin American Romance	❏	❏	❏
Harlequin Duets	❏	❏	❏
Harlequin Romance	❏	❏	❏
Harlequin Historicals	❏	❏	❏
Harlequin Superromance	❏	❏	❏
Harlequin Intrigue	❏	❏	❏
Harlequin Presents	❏	❏	❏
Harlequin Temptation	❏	❏	❏
Harlequin Blaze	❏	❏	❏
Silhouette Special Edition	❏	❏	❏
Silhouette Romance	❏	❏	❏
Silhouette Intimate Moments	❏	❏	❏
Silhouette Desire	❏	❏	❏

2. Which of the following best describes why you bought *this book*? One answer only, please.

the picture on the cover	❏	the title	❏
the author	❏	the line is one I read often	❏
part of a miniseries	❏	saw an ad in another book	❏
saw an ad in a magazine/newsletter	❏	a friend told me about it	❏
I borrowed/was given this book	❏	other: _____	❏

3. Where did you buy *this book*? One answer only, please.

at Barnes & Noble	❏	at a grocery store	❏
at Waldenbooks	❏	at a drugstore	❏
at Borders	❏	on eHarlequin.com Web site	❏
at another bookstore	❏	from another Web site	❏
at Wal-Mart	❏	Harlequin/Silhouette Reader	❏
at Target	❏	Service/through the mail	
at Kmart	❏	used books from anywhere	❏
at another department store or mass merchandiser	❏	I borrowed/was given this book	❏

4. On average, how many Harlequin and Silhouette books do you buy at one time?

I buy _____ books at one time	❏
I rarely buy a book	❏

MRQ403HI-1A

5. How many times per month do you shop for any *Harlequin and/or Silhouette* books?
One answer only, please.

1 or more times a week	❑	a few times per year	❑
1 to 3 times per month	❑	less often than once a year	❑
1 to 2 times every 3 months	❑	never	❑

6. When you think of your ideal heroine, which *one* statement describes her the best?
One answer only, please.

She's a woman who is strong-willed	❑	She's a desirable woman	❑
She's a woman who is needed by others	❑	She's a powerful woman	❑
She's a woman who is taken care of	❑	She's a passionate woman	❑
She's an adventurous woman	❑	She's a sensitive woman	❑

7. The following statements describe types or genres of books that you may be
interested in reading. Pick *up to 2 types* of books that you are most interested in.

I like to read about truly romantic relationships ❑
I like to read stories that are sexy romances ❑
I like to read romantic comedies ❑
I like to read a romantic mystery/suspense ❑
I like to read about romantic adventures ❑
I like to read romance stories that involve family ❑
I like to read about a romance in times or places that I have never seen ❑
Other: _____ ❑

*The following questions help us to group your answers with those readers who are
similar to you. Your answers will remain confidential.*

8. Please record your year of birth below.
19 ____

9. What is your marital status?
single ❑ married ❑ common-law ❑ widowed ❑
divorced/separated ❑

10. Do you have children 18 years of age or younger currently living at home?
yes ❑ no ❑

11. Which of the following best describes your employment status?
employed full-time or part-time ❑ homemaker ❑ student ❑
retired ❑ unemployed ❑

12. Do you have access to the Internet from either home or work?
yes ❑ no ❑

13. Have you ever visited eHarlequin.com?
yes ❑ no ❑

14. What state do you live in?
_____

15. Are you a member of Harlequin/Silhouette Reader Service?
yes ❑ Account # _____ no ❑ MRQ403HI-1B

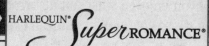
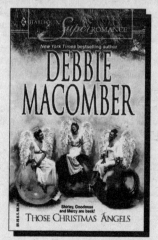

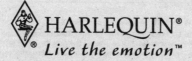

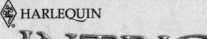

HARLEQUIN

INTRIGUE

COMING NEXT MONTH

#729 FAMILIAR DOUBLE by Caroline Burnes
Fear Familiar
When Familiar, the famous cat detective, signed on as a stunt double for a movie, he soon found himself up to his whiskers in another mystery! Nicole Paul had been framed and arrested for a theft she didn't commit. After her sexy boss, Jax McClure, bailed her out of jail, the two were swept into discovering who really stole the cursed diamond twenty years ago...*and* the secrets of their hearts.

#730 THE FIRSTBORN by Dani Sinclair
Heartskeep
When Hayley Thomas returned home to claim her inheritance, she found strange things happening around her—doors locked by themselves and objects disappeared before her eyes. The only thing she wasn't confused about was her powerful attraction to blacksmith Bram Myers...but did the brooding stranger have secrets of his own?

#731 RANDALL RENEGADE by Judy Christenberry
Brides for Brothers
Rancher Jim Randall never expected to hear from his college sweetheart again. So when Patience Anderson called him to help find her kidnapped nephew, Jim knew he had to help her...even if it meant facing the woman he'd never stopped loving. This Randall had encountered danger before, but the battle at hand could cost him more than his renegade status.

#732 KEEPING BABY SAFE by Debra Webb
Colby Agency
After Colby Agency investigator Pierce Maxwell and P.I. Olivia Jackson were exposed to a deadly biological weapon that they were sure would kill them, they gave in to their growing passion. But when they miraculously lived, they were left with a mystery to solve...and a little surprise on the way!

#733 UNDER HIS PROTECTION by Amy J. Fetzer
Bachelors at Large
When a wealthy businessman was murdered, detective Nash Couviyon's main suspect was Lisa Winfield, the man's wife and the woman Nash had once loved. Would he be able to put aside past feelings—and growing new ones—to prove Lisa was being framed?

#734 DR. BODYGUARD by Jessica Andersen
Someone wanted Dr. Eugenie "Genius" Watson dead, so her adversary, the very sexy Dr. Nick Wellington, designated himself her protector. But when painful memories of the night she was attacked began to resurface, Genie discovered some shocking clues regarding the culprit...and an undeniable attraction to her very own bodyguard.

Visit us at www.eHarlequin.com

HICNM0903